Nymphopervtress 2:

Degenerate

Rachelle Jarred

Nymphopervtress 2: Degenerate

Copyright and Disclaimer

DEDICATION

I dedicate this novel to all of my readers that have been riding along with me on this journey. Your love and support are greatly appreciated. This is my third novel and without you all sticking around, my words would still be unheard and stacked in piles of notebooks.

This book is also dedicated to my family and friends that supported me and believed in me when I said that I was gonna be an author someday. To my children and my significant other, you three are the best blessings that God has ever sent my way. Without you three, believing in me and helping me when I got hit with writer's block, my books would have never surfaced to the world.

Special Dedication

I would like to thank my new guardian angels my baby sister, Shyra and my niece, Jasmine for watching my back. I lost you both in one night to a tragic car accident and now April 18 2019 will always be remembered as the day I lost a piece of my soul. Y'all both were so young and left behind beautiful children and also woke me up to the realization that life is too short and tomorrow is never promised to anyone. I love and miss you two ladies so much and I want you all to continue to fly high.

Contents

Nymphopervtress 2:
Degenerate Prologue

Hey y'all!! It's your girl Desi, back again. Shit has been up and down, both good and bad for Mario and me. Well, when I left you guys, it was a few years ago. I had gotten married to Mario and had given birth to my beautiful baby girl, Zaniyah.

Fast forward five years later: Mario and I have been at each other's throats over anything and everything known to man. If I didn't check-in, I got cussed out by Mario. If he didn't pay a bill, I cussed him out. At first, my mother was like, *it's normal for newlyweds to have arguments*. But now, that's straight up bullshit! We have been married for six years as of today and it's driving me crazy. I don't know what to do.

Zaniyah, my little princess, is the only joy I have been getting nonstop this entire time. No matter what, I can always look to her and she flashes that smile and it changes my whole mood. My baby's birthday is coming up in two months, and I cannot wait. She will be turning seven years old! She has been doing well in school and all of her other activities. I love her to death; I don't think I can even imagine not having her in my life.

Dr. Nicholson is still around; I am seeing her for our weekly therapy sessions, as usual. She keeps telling me that Mario and I should consider marriage counseling with her. I told her I would ask him, but I never did. *Why should I? If he barely talks to me at home, except when we're having sex, what makes her think he will talk to me with her in the room?*

After all I have been through in the past six years; it's hard to even believe I don't have a head full of gray hair! Everything and everyone is getting on my goddamn nerves! They are driving me crazy. If it isn't my mother or my sister, it's Mario and his bullshit. If not him, it's my boss and my stupid job. This shit is driving me fucking insane! If I don't get some type of peace, I swear...

Chapter One
Happy Anniversary

I woke up to Zaniyah running into my room and jumping on the bed.

"Good morning, Mommy," she said, lifting up my eyelids.

I just stirred awake, laughing.

"Good morning, Niyah," I said, rubbing my eyes and stretching. I had been sleeping so peacefully before my human alarm clock woke me up. I turned and looked at the time. It was 9 o' clock. *Oh shit!*

"Where is your father, Zaniyah?" I asked her as I sat up.

"Daddy said he was going to the gym, Mommy."

"Why didn't he take you to school?"

"Because it's Saturday, Mommy," she said giggling at me. That's right, it was Saturday. Lucky for me, I was off today, because I would have been one cranky soul this morning for running behind schedule.

"Well, what you want to eat for breakfast?"

"I already made my own breakfast. I ate cereal."

"That's good, baby. Did your daddy help you?"

"Nope, I did it all by myself," she said proudly. My rambunctious little girl was growing by the day. I still looked at her as if she was my little seven pounds of joy. I could just imagine what my kitchen probably looked like right now. I got up and put on Mario's t-shirt that laid across the back of the chair. I grabbed Zaniyah's hand, and we headed downstairs. I was shocked to see what awaited me in the den.

"Happy anniversary, Desiree," Mario said, holding a single multi-colored rose out towards me. I walked into the den and I looked from left to right and saw all the beautiful roses and gift boxes surrounding the room.

"Oh my God, Mario. What is all this?" I asked, walking towards him with tears falling from my eyes and a smile on my face. He handed me the rose and lifted my chin. He kissed me deeply. When he freed me from the kiss, I stumbled back a little, but he caught me.

"This is all for you, Baby," he said. "Desi, I love you so much, boo. I want you to always know that. No matter what we may go through, or what problems we may have, I love you and only you."

"I love you too, Mario," I said, throwing my arms around his neck and trying to squeeze the life out of him.

"We got you good, Mommy," Zaniyah said, hugging the both of us.

"Good job, Stink," Mario said, picking her up into his arms. They slapped fives, and I just smiled at them. These two here; I loved them both with all my heart, and I swear I wouldn't give them up for anything in this world. I loved them more than life itself. Hell, they were my life.

"Put me down, Daddy. I have to give Mommy her gift from me first."

"You got Mommy a gift, Sweetie?" I said with a smile.

"Yep. Come on, Mommy. I'm gonna show you." She grabbed me by the hand and led me over to the sofa. She handed me a gift wrapped in paper. It was obvious she tried her best to wrap it herself.

"Did you wrap it yourself, Niyah?"

"Yes. You like it?"

"I love the paper."

"I hope you do because I like the butterflies, too," she said, giggling.

I tore the paper off the gift and my heart instantly melted. It was a picture frame. She had drawn a picture of me, her, and Mario. It was the most beautiful thing I had ever seen. I started to cry.

"What's wrong, Mommy? You don't like it?" she asked sadly.

"No, Baby, I love it," I said, wiping my tears from the corner of my eye. I grabbed her and hugged her tightly. "I love it so much. I love you so much, Niyah."

"I love you, too, Mommy. Now open the gifts from Daddy."

"Okay."

Mario walked over to me with a few gift bags and two boxes.

"Open one of the bags first."

I reached for the biggest bag. I took out all the tissue paper, with the help of Zaniyah, and pulled out a Gucci bag and a matching belt. My jaw dropped.

"Mario, what the hell?"

"What the hell nothing. You deserve it. There's more so open up the rest, Bae.

I opened the next bag: shoes. However, they weren't just any shoes. My baby had gotten me some red bottom Louboutins. "Well damn, Nigga," I said, laughing.

"There's more," he said, motioning me to open the last bag.

I grabbed the last bag and pulled out a box. I opened it and lifted up a sexy black mini dress. It had slits all over it, which barely left anything to hide. It was short as hell and a lot of people were going to definitely enjoy the peep show.

"Oh, wow, Mario. I love it. I love everything," I said.

He handed me a small box. I opened it and inside was a tennis bracelet and a pair of earrings to match. It was beautiful.

"I have one more gift for you, Desi."

"What could there possibly be left to give?" I asked, laughing.

He knelt down in front of me with his last box in hand. My eyes flew open wider. My heart started racing.

"Desiree Michelle Davis, these past six years have been wonderful. Even though we have been going through some really rough times, we got through it all and we're still here, sticking it out together. You have blessed me with a beautiful little munchkin that I love as much as I love you. We're a team. You, me, and Niyah are a family. I would be honored if you would marry me again," he said.

"Yes, I will marry you again, Mario," I said. The tears were now streaming down my face.

"Yay! Daddy is gonna marry me and Mommy again," Zaniyah said, bouncing happily on the couch.

We just laughed at our little girl and kissed her.

"Now can we have breakfast for real?" Zaniyah asked.

"Yes, we can, Baby," I said, picking her up and heading in the kitchen.

Chapter Two

Roleplay

I didn't know what to get Mario for our anniversary today honestly. There were only a few hours left in the day and I was still empty handed. I had called Jessica and Shannon on three-way to see if they had any ideas.

"Just get that nigga a Rolex and be done with it," Shannon said bluntly.

"Yeah, but what else?"

"What the hell else does he need?" Jessica asked, chiming in.

"I don't know. That's why I called you bitches for help. He bought me all this shit and I just want to make him feel special, too."

"Man, look, Desi. You like to write poetry, right?" Shannon asked.

"Yeah, so?"

"So, get him the damn watch and write him a poem."

"That's a good idea."

"I know it is," she said nonchalantly.

"Thanks, Shannon. Anyway, Jess, what is Niyah doing?"

"Girl, she's in here playing with that damn dog, Coco."

"She loves that dog," I said, laughing.

"I know, right? I'm about to put her in the bath, though, and get her ready for bed."

"Okay. Thank you so much for keeping her tonight for me."

"No biggie. You better enjoy your anniversary, girl. Maybe y'all will make another one tonight."

"Bitch, please," I said playfully, snapping at her. I heard Shannon in the background, laughing. I told them I would see them tomorrow and I got off the phone. I had to hurry up and beat Mario back home.

✳✳✳✳

I arrived at the house fifteen minutes later, and noticed that Mario still wasn't home, which was a good sign. I rushed into the house and ran upstairs to take a shower.

I was so busy in the shower that I almost didn't hear my phone ringing. I quickly turned off the shower water and grabbed my phone off the sink.

"Hello?" I said answering the call before it got sent to voicemail.

Nymphopervtress 2: Degenerate

"What are you doing, Baby?" the voice said through the phone.

I realized I never even looked at the caller ID. I pulled the phone away from my ear and looked at the phone. It was a familiar looking phone number, but for the life of me, I couldn't remember who it belonged to.

"Hello, are you there?" the male voice asked.

"Yeah, I'm here, umm," I said, hoping they would help me out.

"You don't know who this is, do you?"

"Not at all."

"It's Jay."

Oh my God, Jay. I hadn't heard his voice in years. How the fuck did he remember my number? He must have never deleted it. But, nonetheless, what the hell did he want? "Ohhh, hey, Jay."

"That's all I get: 'Hey, Jay'?" he asked, laughing a little.

"Uh, yeah. What kind of greeting did you think you were gonna get, Nigga?"

"I see you still haven't changed, Desi. You're still as feisty as ever."

"Is there something that I could help you with, Jay? I'm kind of in the middle of something," I said as I began rubbing baby oil all over my body. I put my Bluetooth headset on so I could finish getting ready for Mario.

"Yeah, as a matter of fact, there is. I'm in town for a couple weeks on business and wanted to know if you wanted to hook up, like old times."

"I don't think that's a good idea," I said quickly. Our old times consisted of me in some type of position and getting my back blown out by him. Just reminiscing started to make my body heat up. I ran back into the bathroom and wiped up the little bit of cream that I had released.

"Are you sure about that? I never thought that I would see the day that Desiree Logan turned down the bomb D from me," he said in a playful, shocking tone.

"Well, it's Desiree Davis now, Jay. I have to go before my husband gets back."

"Husband, huh? How long have y'all been married?" he asked seriously.

"Six years today. That's why I have to go. I'm getting ready for him to come home."

"Oh, I see. Are you gonna grab and lick on his balls like you used to mine? Or are you gonna squirt all over his face while he eats you out?"

"I don't think that's any of your business, Jay."

"Like hell it isn't. You were my girl first, or did you forget?"

"Look, Jay, that's the past. I'm married to Mario now. We have a daughter, I-"

"Do you love him?" he asked, cutting me off.

"Excuse me?"

"You heard what the fuck I said. Do you love that nigga?"

I hesitated for a second before responding to his question, "Yes, I do."

"No, you don't. You had to think about it."

"Look, Jay, I love Mario and he loves me. Now, I have to go."

"But, Desi, I really wanted to- "

Click.

I hung the phone up right in his ear; I had no time to deal with his bullshit. I had finished oiling up my body and was putting my lace bra and panty set on. I heard the front door open and close downstairs. I quickly threw on my sexy silk robe and my new red bottoms.

I fingered through my hair to make sure it looked good for my Boo. I grabbed the watch and lay across the bed, placing it in front of me. I heard the footsteps coming closer to the door. The door creaked open, and Mario's eyes grew large.

"Happy anniversary, Baby," I said, rubbing on my thigh to tantalize him. His jaw dropped. I looked at his crotch area and saw him getting an instant hard-on.

That's what I want, I said in my mind. I got up from the bed and strutted towards him.

"Happy anniversary to you, too, Baby," he said, wrapping his arms around my waist and kissing me.

"I got this for you," I said, handing him the box.

He opened the box and went off. "Aye, yo, kill. I love it, boo," he said, snatching it out the box and trying to slip it on his wrist, but I quickly took it out of his hand.

"Ah, ah," I said, waving a finger.

"What, Boo?"

"You got work to do, Honey. Come play with me."

"Oh, yeah? Can we play cops and robbers?" he asked, raising his brows.

"We sure can," I said, climbing up on the bed and resting on my knees. "Make sure you bring your nightstick."

"I never leave home without it," he said, grabbing his dick through his pants. He walked over to the dresser drawer and reached in to retrieve the stainless-steel handcuffs. He turned back around to me. He ripped off his shirt and took off his shoes and pants. He stood before me, all muscled and toned with the cuffs dangling from his hand in the air. "I'm sorry to inform you, Ma'am, but you're under arrest."

"Why, Officer? What did I do?" I said, playing the role.

"For being so damn sexy. Now assume the position," he said, walking around the bed.

"What position would you like me in, officer?"

"Face down ass up, Ma'am."

"Yes, officer," He handcuffed me and made sure my hands couldn't be freed before continuing.

"You have the right to remain silent. If you scream or make any noise, I will torture you."

"I will not be silent."

"Is that right?"

"Yes."

"Do you have any weapons on you, Ma'am?" he asked, fondling my ass and breasts.

"No, Officer."

"I think you're lying to me. I'm gonna have to give you a cavity check."

"How am I gonna hide anything, Officer? I barely have any clothes on."

"I think you're hiding something in your bra, Ma'am," he said. He turned me over onto my back. He released the snap on the front of my bra and my boobs fell freely. He squeezed and grabbed at them. He started kissing on my neck and my breasts.

"Is this standard procedure, officer?" I asked.

"Didn't I say be silent? Don't make me take out my nightstick."

I got quiet. He moved down to my thong and snatched them off, ripping them, and continued on with the foreplay. He stuck two fingers inside my vagina, going in and out, getting me hotter, and I started moaning.

"Ohhh. Oh, God," I said loudly.

"I'm gonna need for you to remain silent, Ma'am. I think you're hiding something inside your pussy," he said. His rhythm had gotten faster. "What's that I feel?" he asked.

"I don't know what you're talking about, Officer," I replied through heavy breathing.

I had arched my back and my juices released all over his fingers.

"Assaulting an officer, Ma'am? I think I need to take out my nightstick," he said.

"Oh, no, Officer. I will be a good girl."

"Nope, it's too late for that," he said, pulling his dick out of his boxers. It was rock hard and standing tall like the Statue of Liberty. He turned me back over onto my stomach. He put me back in the position I was in, but adjusted me a little. He rubbed the head of his penis against my clit and I moaned softly.

"Oh, Mr. Officer."

"What is it, Ma'am?"

"I think I want the nightstick."

"You sure about that?"

"Yes, Officer."

"You asked for it," he said, before pushing his manhood inside of me putting each inch in slowly. When it was all in, he just sat still and let it grow inside of me. For the life of me, I could swear it was in my stomach.

He paced himself a little and then he started to speed up.

"Ohhh, shit," I screamed at the top of my lungs. I couldn't even run away because I was still handcuffed behind my back. I just had to take it like a big girl.

"Oh, damn, this pussy feels so good," he said, panting. "I will stop if you promise not to break the law again."

"Oh, fuck. Shit. I will try not to, Officer."

"Good girl. Oh, fuck, I'm about to cum," he said. He held pushed down on my shoulders and fucked me harder. I felt him move his hands and grip my hips, pushing deeper inside me. He ejaculated right inside me and I just knew for a fact that I was gonna end up being pregnant, but I didn't care.

He turned me over onto my stomach and released my wrists from the handcuffs. He pulled me up onto his chest like he always did. He was tired and so was I. I laid there in total bliss as my body ached from the pleasure it had just received.

"I love you so much, Baby," I said into his chest.

"I love you, too, Wifey," he said, kissing my forehead.

He reached over to cut out the light on the stand. After he got situated again, I laid my head back on his sweaty chest. He stroked my hair until I fell asleep.

He fell asleep not too long afterward.

Chapter Three

Police Raid

I woke up the next morning with a smile on my face. I turned over to Mario's side of the bed and my smile quickly vanished when I saw that he was gone. In his spot there was a note that read:

'Sorry babe had to run some errands at work. Will be back later. Love you'

What the hell? I said to myself. His ass was always fucking working. I grabbed my phone and checked the time. It was 9 a.m. What the hell kind of errands could he possibly have to run working in construction?

I called his phone.

"Hello?" he said after answering.

"Where the hell are you, Mario?" I said, yelling into the phone.

"I'm at work, Desiree. You didn't get my note?"

"Yeah, I got it."

"Okay, then, you know where I am," he said, laughing.

I didn't see shit as funny. I was so tired of waking up some mornings or going to bed some nights and he wasn't lying next to me. "What time will you be back, Babe?" I asked, disregarding the noise. It was probably the loud ass guys at his site. Their asses are always loud.

"Not sure, Desiree. We're gonna probably work until seven today. And you know it's Sunday, so we might go to the bar after work and watch the game."

"That means you will be gone all fucking day!" I yelled into the phone.

"I know, but somebody has to pay the bills, right? Go and get Niyah and y'all have a girl's day on me. I left my credit card on the table in the kitchen."

"Whatever, Mario. I love you."

"Yeah, you too." *Click.*

What the fuck did he mean 'you too?" I called his damn phone right back and guess what? His freaking voicemail came on, so I hung up and hit redial again. Voicemail again. *Fuck it!* I said to myself. I called Jessica and told her to have Zaniyah ready for me in a few hours.

I got up and showered. It felt so good to have the scorching hot water and suds running down my skin, making me feel like I was in heaven. I got out of the shower twenty minutes later and wrapped my body in a towel before walking across the carpet with my wet feet.

I rummaged back and forth in my closet. I didn't know what in the hell I wanted to wear today, but it was supposed to be nice. The weather on my phone said around eighty-five degrees! I chose to wear a pair of skinny jeans and a simple t-shirt with my Vans. I decided that I was gonna take my baby out to get her nails and feet done then out to lunch and then the toy store. By the time we got back, Mario should be home.

After moisturizing my legs and everything, I packed a small bag for me and my baby girl that consisted of our sunglasses, our slides, her sandals, and an extra change of clothes for her. Even though she was about to be older, I never wanted to be caught unprepared. I did a once over and headed downstairs.

I reached the kitchen and saw that everything looked to be the same and nothing was out of place. That was a shocking surprise, because Mario always left a mess in the kitchen before he left. Guess he was in too much of a rush this morning. I decided to eat a bagel with cream cheese; didn't wanna put too much on my stomach.

I heated up the bagel and spread the cream cheese across it. I grabbed a napkin, two of Zaniyah's juice boxes, my keys, and Mario's credit card and left out. As I was locking the door, I could see the guy that delivers newspapers pull up. He parked the car and jumped out with my paper in hand and headed towards me.

My eyes were glued to his frame. He was roughly about five ten, two hundred and ten pounds of milk chocolate goodness. Boy would I love to make a banana split with him!

"Mrs. Davis?" he said.

"Huh? Yes?"

"I said here's your paper," he said. He was eyeballing me strangely. Probably because I got caught staring at him.

"Oh, yes, thanks, Malcolm. You running late today, aren't you?"

"Yeah a tad bit. I had a long night last night."

"It's okay, Malcolm." I said, heading to my car.

"Let me help you," he said. I handed him the paper and the bag. "You look nice today, Mrs. Davis," he said, looking me up and down. I knew he was looking at how my ass sat in my jeans but I didn't mind though.

"Thank you," I answered. I unlocked the car door and bent over a little bit inside acting like I was cleaning my seat off. I gave him a much better view of how nice my ass actually looked from this angle.

"Oh wow," he said in an almost whispered tone.

"Did you say something, Malcolm?" I said, standing back up.

"No, Ma'am."

"Ma'am? Call me Desiree, please."

"Okay, Desiree," he said, smiling. He even had a beautiful smile and looking at him longer was causing my panties to get wet. *Time to go,* I said to myself. I got in the car and closed the door. He walked around to the passenger side and put the bag and paper on the seat. He shut the door and walked back around to the driver side. "Is there anything else you need help with, Desiree?"

More than you know. Yeah, you can help me by pulling my jeans down and bending me over in the backseat and fuck me rough in the doggy style position while I cum all over you and my leather seats, I thought. "No thanks. I'm good, Malcolm. Thank you."

"Anytime."

He walked away and I just stared at his back. I waited until he got in his car and drove down the block. I backed down my driveway and drove in the same direction. I watched as he slung papers out of his car window on the next street. For some reason he turned me on every time I saw him. Shit was crazy.

I drove past him and honked the horn. I pushed him to the back of my mind as soon as I hit the corner of the street and started to focus my mind elsewhere. My baby girl was waiting to spend the day with me and I was looking forward to it as well. I couldn't wait it' been a while.

Nymphopervtress 2: Degenerate

We had been walking through the mall for two hours, going in and out of various stores. Everything Zaniyah saw she wanted. Shoes, toys, clothes, even some smell good lotions and whatnot from Bath & Body Works. I was carrying four bags and only one belonged to me. This was ridiculous. My little girl was a shopaholic! My feet were starting to hurt and I was ready to get pampered.

"Hey, let's go to the nail salon, Boo," I said, grabbing her hand tighter and leading her to the other end of the mall.

"Really, Mommy? Can I get any color I want?" she asked, ecstatically.

"Yes, just nothing too bright or too grown."

"Cool beans."

Did my daughter really just say 'cool beans' to me? I burst out laughing. She was too much and I swear whenever I look at her, all I see is me. From her long beautiful hair to her little toes, she was my twin through and through, but I just hope and pray she doesn't end up like me. I wouldn't know how to take the news of finding out that my own child was a nympho. It would be so saddening.

We headed into the nail salon and the receptionist told us to head to the foot spas and she would be right with us. I practically ran to the chair. I put our bags down and we slipped off our shoes. We got up in the chairs and I adjusted the back massager. I put hers on low and put mine on high. I was so stressed and I could feel the knots loosening in my back.

Two nail techs approached us and started. The massage was feeling so good it was sending chills up my spine. I couldn't even remember the last time I had a foot rub or any rubdown for that matter. I looked over at my daughter who was squirming and laughing in her seat and it made me laugh.

"Are you okay, Niyah?"

"It tickles, Mommy."

"I know, but it's almost over," I assured her. They weren't gonna do her foot massage that long anyway because she was so young. After they cleaned our feet and everything, we were able to choose what color we wanted and what design. We picked it and watched them work. After they finished, we went over to get our nails done and that took all of twenty minutes for me and only about ten minutes for hers. We sat there alone afterward to let our nails dry.

"I'm having fun, Mommy," Zaniyah said to me as she bounced in her seat.

"I'm glad you're having fun, Baby. I'm having fun, too. What you wanna do when we leave here?"

"I wanna go home and take a nap," she said yawning.

"I thought we were going on a lunch date, Sweetie?"

"How about dinner?"

"That's fine. Where you wanna go?"

"Nowhere."

"Nowhere?"

"Nope! I just want us to order pizza and watch movies and eat popcorn."

"You know what? That sounds fun."

We finished up at the salon and walked around to a couple more stores before heading home.

We arrived at the house and it was going on six. Still no sign of Mario's ass. *Un-fucking-believable,* I thought to myself. *Oh well.* Niyah and I went into the house and put our bags down. Then we headed upstairs to my bedroom and took our shoes off and climbed up on the bed. It was cold in the house, because of the damn air running, so we got under the cover and quickly fell asleep.

✳✳✳✳

I woke up to the sound of Bugs Bunny and Michael Jordan. Niyah was sitting up next to me, wearing pajamas, watching Space Jam.

"When did you change clothes, Sweetie?" I asked her, rubbing my eyes.

"Forty-five hours ago, Mommy," she said proudly.

I laughed. It didn't matter what kind of mood I was in, she always found a way to make her Mommy smile. I loved my little stink for that. "Did you at least wash up, Niyah?"

"Mmhmm," she said, nodding her head.

"Okay, good. Well, let me go shower really quickly and put on my pjs, too."

"Okay, Mommy."

I quickly jumped in the shower and washed off my skin from today. I was looking forward to spending some more time with her. I got out and put on my emoji pajamas that matched hers because she loved it when we dressed like twins. I left out the bathroom and noticed her on my phone having a full blown conversation.

"Who are you talking to, Zaniyah?" I asked her quizzically.

"I'm talking to Auntie Shannon."

I didn't even hear my phone ring. I guess my mind was elsewhere when I was showering. I took the phone from her. "Hey, girl, what's up?"

"Nothing much. I was just calling to see what y'all were up to."

"Oh, nothing much. We just sitting here about to watch movies and junk."

"Sounds fun. Well don't let me interrupt. Go ahead and spend time with my niece. Hit me up later, Boo."

"Later," I said hanging up. I opened the Domino's app on my phone and ordered what we usually got; a medium pepperoni pan pizza and cinnastix. We loved that combo for some reason. I checked my phone. No sign of Mario. No calls. No texts. Nothing.

What the fuck is this nigga's deal? I put my phone down and got up on the bed with Niyah. My favorite part was coming up when Jordan got sucked down in the golf hole.

I was so lost in the movie and Zaniyah that I didn't even notice someone ringing the doorbell. I checked my phone and the app said our food was out for delivery. I guess that was the pizza guy. But why didn't his ass just call? Dumbass. "I'll be right back, Stink," I said to Zaniyah.

I grabbed the cash and tip off the nightstand and headed downstairs. I didn't even look through the peephole before opening the door but boy I wish I had.

Instead of it being the pizza guy, a group of police officers swarmed into our house and spread out. *What the hell?*

"Um, what the fuck is going on?" I asked, yelling over all of the commotion.

"Ma'am is this your house?" a black cop asked me.

"What the hell do you think? What the fuck are y'all doing in my house? And do y'all have a warrant?"

"Yes, Ma'am, we do," he said presenting the warrant to me. "We're looking for a Mr. Mario Davis. Are you related to him?"

Mario? Why the hell was the police looking for Mario? "Related to him? That's my damn husband. What the hell do you want with him?"

"Mommy?" I heard Niyah calling from upstairs.

"Just go in my room and close the door, Niyah. Stay in there until I come up there." I looked back to the officers. "Can you tell your flunkies to get the hell from upstairs in my house, please? They're scaring my daughter."

Just then a cop that led the small group that bum rushed me came down the stairs. "We're all clear, Lieutenant. There is nobody upstairs but the little girl."

"No shit, Sherlock," I said sarcastically and rolled my eyes. I put my focus back on the cop in front of me. "I'm still waiting to hear what the fuck you're looking for Mario for."

"Ma'am, your husband has a warrant out for his arrest."

"What the hell for?" I asked again with clenched teeth. I was getting beyond annoyed.

He took a deep breath. "Drug possession and other drug related charges, amongst a few other offenses."

"You got to be fucking kidding me," I said with a little laughter in my voice.

"Look, when you see him, tell him he needs to turn himself in or we will be back. Here's my card," he said, handing me a business card. He gathered his men and left. I watched as they pulled off and slammed my front door shut. I texted Mario a 911 text and waited for him to respond.

Knock. Knock. Knock.

What is it now? I snatched the door open. "What the fuck- "

It was the pizza guy.

"Oh shit. I'm so sorry. Here you go," I said, handing him the money and he handed me the pizza and told me to have a good night. I closed and locked the door back and headed upstairs, joining Zaniyah in my room.

"What's going on, Mommy? Why were the police here looking for my Daddy?'

"I don't know, Baby. But, hey, our food is here. Let's start our movie over."

"Okay, Mommy," she said reluctantly.

We went back to the movie and ate pizza and I kept calling and texting Mario, but still no response. This shit was blowing my life. *Fuck that nigga,* I thought. I wasn't gonna let his ass ruin my night with my child.

We finished eating our food and watching the movie and we were getting tired. I looked at the time and it was going on eleven. There was still no sign of Mario. Zaniyah and I brushed our teeth and took our trash down to the kitchen.

We got back in the room and laid down. Not long after, Zaniyah had drifted off to sleep and I watched her as she slept. I wish I could sleep peaceful like that right now but I couldn't. I had too much on my mind. But the biggest question on my mind was where the fuck was Mario at?

It grew later and later into the night and many hours had gone by and I was still wide awake. This shit was ridiculous. I looked at my phone and the time on the clock read 3:08 a.m. *What the fuck?!* I decided to take a gigantic sleeping pill. I got out of the bed and went into the bathroom and took the pill bottle out the medicine cabinet. I threw the pill in my mouth and put some water in the drinking cup. I looked at myself in the mirror.

"What the hell is going on, Desiree?" I said to my reflection. "You got to get your marriage back on track, Bitch." That felt good to say, but will I really be able to fix it? I can start by finding my husband.

I went back into the room and still nothing. I texted Mario a goodnight and an I hate you text before settling next to my little princess. I held her close to me and laid on the same pillow with her. All I could think about were those cops running through my house with their guns drawn. I couldn't even imagine how scared Zaniyah must have been.

Mario, where are you? I thought. That was my last thought before falling asleep a little after 4 a.m.

Chapter Four

Unexpected

It has been days since I had heard anything from Mario. I was just ready to give up and call it quits, because this didn't make any sense. This wasn't like Mario at all. Maybe he found somebody else. I got sad just thinking that. That's what it is. Maybe I wasn't good enough for him anymore. Or maybe the police had him. No. He would have called me, wouldn't he? I decided to try calling him again. Still no answer. An idea popped in my head. I haven't tried his best friend Tyrone's number! I scrolled through my phonebook until I found his name. I called him and he answered on the fourth ring.

"Hey, what's up, Desi?"

"Maybe you could tell me. Have you heard from Mario?"

His line went silent.

"Hello? Tyrone?"

"Yeah, he, uh. He had to make a run."

"A run, huh? Where, Ty?" I asked. He was lying.

"Look, Shorty, where you at?"

"Home."

"I will be there shortly. I have something to tell you in person."

'Okay," I said softly. I hung up the phone and panicked. Something was wrong. I could just feel it and I started to cry. Lucky for me, Zaniyah was at school, so she wouldn't see me. I hated when my baby saw me upset.

It seemed like an eternity waiting for Tyrone to get here. I heard someone fidgeting with the lock as I stood in the kitchen, drinking my coffee. I reached for a knife and headed towards the door. The door flew open and it was Mario! But he wasn't alone. He had a bitch with him!

"Mario, where the fuck have you been? Who the fuck is this bitch?" I yelled with my knife pointing at the girl.

"Mario, who the fuck is she?" she asked.

I grabbed that bitch by the throat and slammed her against the wall. "Bitch, I'm his wife. Like I said who the fuck are you?" I repeated, all up in her grill with the kitchen knife on her throat.

"I'm Ashley," she responded with the little breath I spared her.

"How do you know my husband?"

"He has been with me all week. We've been cooped up in my house smoking, drinking, and sexing. I didn't even know he was married. I just met him last week."

I looked into her eyes and I could tell she was scared, but she didn't look like she was lying, so I let the bitch drop to the floor and headed straight towards Mario.

"Is this why you haven't been returning my calls and shit Mario?" I yelled as I pushed him. He was slumped over standing up.

"Don't trip, Desi, Baby," he said, standing up straight. "I brought her for the both of us. We can share her just like we used to do back in the day." His words were slurring. He was drunk or high. Shit, it was probably both.

"Mario, what the fuck?! I don't do that shit anymore."

"Come on, now," he said, heading towards me. "You know you ain't gonna ever change, Desiree. Them hoe ways are just waiting to be released."

"I'm not like that anymore," I repeated at the top of my lungs as I backed up. He fell on top of me and I fell back onto the floor. He started pulling at my clothes and ripping at them.

"Take this shit off, Bitch," he said angrily. "Me and Ashley want some of your pussy."

"Mario, stop," I cried, but my cries fell upon deaf ears. I looked over to Ashley and she was just standing there, looking jittery and scratching her skin at the track marks. Her hair was disheveled and all, and Mario didn't look any better. His hair was all over the place, clothes were dirty, and he reeked. This stranger was not my husband. This wasn't the guy I made love to every night. This definitely was not the guy I had made a beautiful creation and everlasting memories with. This man that was lying on top of me and crushing my body atop the hardwood floor was a monster.

"Come on, Ashley," he yelled at the girl. "I got her panties off."

Ashley rushed over and examined my nakedness. She started fidgeting and running her hands through her hair. I saw her licking her lips like she was about to eat something she had been craving forever and a day for. Mario moved over top of my head and held my hands down. *When did he take his pants off in this last couple of minutes?* I wondered. I looked back to Ashley who was getting down on the floor leaning between my legs to eat my kitty. And you know what I did? I kneed that hoe right in the fucking nose. She looked up to my face and I saw the blood gushing from her nose. She slapped me in the face and wiped the blood on my mouth. I spit right in that bitch face and she slapped me again, and then went back down. She locked my legs in her arms and started eating my pussy.

She was biting me and pulling on my clit with her teeth as if it was a tough piece of meat. Mario shoved his dick into my screaming mouth so he could muffle my screams. I squirmed, but I couldn't be freed from the two and I was gagging from Mario shoving his manhood deep into my throat. My front door flew open and it was Tyrone coming in with a gun pointed.

"Get the fuck up off her, Mario," he yelled.

Mario stood up and I turned over and threw up. I managed to kick Ashley in the face and she flew back on the floor. I looked at Mario and he just stared at me with a blank stare. I attacked him. "What the fuck is wrong with you, Mario? What the fuck?"

He just laughed and kept trying to get out of my reach, blocking my punches. Tyrone grabbed me around the waist and held me back. "Get the fuck out, Mario," he yelled.

"I ain't going no motherfucking where until I get what I came for," he said, looking at me.

"And what is that?"

"I need money, Desiree. Give it to me," he yelled.

I jumped at the sound of his deep voice and I ran up the stairs to our bedroom. I wasn't going to get any money though. I was calling the detective that was here looking for him the other night and he answered fairly quickly.

"This is Detective Warren."

"Hi, this is Desiree Davis," I said through tears. "Mario is here and he and some woman just attacked me. Hurry please."
He hung up the phone and I went into my closet and got my gun and headed back downstairs.

"Where's the money, Desiree?" Mario yelled at me.

"What you need money for, Mario?" I asked, pointing my gun at him and he put his hands up in the air.

"I need drugs, Baby."

Nymphopervtress 2: Degenerate

"Drugs? How long have you been on drugs, Mario?" I asked with tears continuing to fall from my eyes.

"A while now. That's why I am gone so much. You thought I was really going to work for all those hours?" he said laughing loud and obnoxiously.

The tears were really flowing now. "How could you do that to us, Mario?"

"To us? It's your fault, Desiree. I should have never married your hoe ass."

"Stop calling me that. I'm not a hoe, Mario. I'm your wife."

"Hey, I just call it like I see it," he replied.

"I'm not like that anymore," I yelled again. "I'm getting help so I won't have to go back down that road. And what about Zaniyah?"

"What about her? She's probably not even mine, anyway. You know she's gonna end up being just like you, right?" he said with a sly grin on his face.

"Don't say that. She will not."

"She will. Every time I look at her I see you. It's destiny for her to end up like a thot. Like mother like daughter."

I cocked my gun and put one in the chamber. "Stop saying that."

He dropped his arms and rushed me. I shot my gun and he flew back: I had shot him in his right shoulder. I heard sirens approaching. Tyrone took my gun out of my hands and ran upstairs.

"Don't let the police know I'm here, Desiree," he yelled.

For the third time today, my door flew open from being kicked in.

"Where is he, Mrs. Davis?"

"Over there," I said through painful tears.

He ran over to Mario, who was lying on the floor in a fit of laughter. He threw the cuffs on him, and Ashley ran towards Detective Warren. I intervened and caught her ass with a clothesline; she hit the floor with a hard thud.

Detective Warren threw handcuffs on her too. I just stood there in astonishment; I had never seen shit like this before. Mario never stopped laughing, so I knew he was really high off of something. He picked up both Ashley and Mario and walked them towards the door. I looked at the blood that Mario's wound had left behind and I grew angrier.

"Will you be okay?" he asked as he saw that I was half naked, wearing only a t-shirt and I was bruised a little, my face smeared with blood.

"I'll be fine, Detective," I said, wiping my tears away again.

"Give me a call if you need anything, Mrs. Davis, and thanks for contacting me. We have been trying to catch your husband for two years now. I will be in touch. Get some rest."

With that, he left my house. I watched from the porch Mario and Ashley being placed in the back of the police car. I zoomed in on Mario who had finally stopped laughing and had borne a stone-cold killer face. He mouthed the words *I'll be back* as Detective Warren pulled off down the street. Mario looked at me until he turned the corner.

I closed the front door and Tyrone was coming down the stairs. I forgot that nigga was here.

"Coast clear?" he asked.

"Yeah," I said, heading back upstairs to my room.

I could feel his eyes on me as I walked up the stairs. "Need any help, Shorty?"

"Naw, I think I'm good. I just need to get some rest. Zaniyah's not here right now, so I think I'm gonna take advantage of this. It's a lot to take in, you know?"

"Yeah I do. Hey, call me if you need me though. I'm only a call away," he said.

"Got you. Lock the door behind you, please?"

He did, and I went into my bedroom to get to the shower.

I turned the water on scorching hot and closed the bathroom door as I looked for a night shirt to put on afterward. I hopped in the shower and let the scalding hot water rain over my body.

I could do nothing but cry. All this shit happening at once was really painful. My marriage was falling apart; my husband was going to jail, and then Jay popping back in the picture. Jay?

I don't even know why I was even thinking about him or vice versa. Our relationship was bad and ended badly. He was such an asshole, and an abuser; he was the only reason I was glad we had moved.

I got out the shower and oiled up my body before putting on deodorant and my night shirt. I grabbed my phone and checked the time. It was only 10:00 in the morning. Lucky for me, Zaniyah wasn't due home until around 4. I got back in the bed and set my alarm for 3:30. I took a sleeping pill and was out with quickness.

✳✳✳✳

Instead of my alarm waking me up, I was startled by the ringing of my phone. I looked at the caller ID and it was Jay's number.

"Hello," I said groggily.

"Eww, what the hell?" he said jokingly.

"Shut up, Jay. What the hell do you want?"

"Damn, I see you still got that dirty mouth."

"And I'm gonna die with it, too," I shot back.

"I bet. What are you doing?"

"Lying down."

"I know you said you were married but, how about we catch up later over dinner?"

I thought about it for a second. Since Mario wasn't here, I guess it couldn't hurt. "What time should I be ready and where am I meeting you?"

"I can come and get you if you like."

"Doesn't matter. I will text you my address."

"Be ready by six please."

"Whatever," I hung up on him and my phone started buzzing. *Time to get Zaniyah's after school stuff ready for her*, I thought.

I went into her room and grabbed her two books to read, her writing pad to practice her handwriting, and took it downstairs to the living room. I went to the kitchen grabbed a pizza lunchable and a juice box and sat it next to everything else. As I was turning on her cartoons, the doorbell rang. Like clockwork.

"Mommy," she said, excitedly jumping into my arms. I caught her and held her tight in my arms. "You're squishing me," she said, trying to break free.

"Sorry, Niyah. Did you have a good day at school?"

"Yep. Where's Daddy?" she asked, running up the stairs.

"Daddy's not home, sweetie," I said once I reached my room.

"Daddy's never coming home, is he?" she asked, turning around and pouting.

I walked over to her and picked her up. "Daddy will be home. He got into some trouble and he has to be gone for a while."

"Oh, so he in jail?" she asked.

"Yeah."

"I guess. Will you be okay, Mommy?"

I looked into her beautiful brown eyes and hesitated. I wanted to say no, but I didn't, because I knew I had to be strong for her. "Yeah, I will be fine. How about you?"

"As long as I got you, I will be okay."

She gave me a hug and a kiss on the cheek. We went upstairs so she could put her backpack in her room and we went back down the stairs. She sat down on the carpeted stairs and slid all the way to the bottom. By the time I reached the bottom of the stairs, she was already into her daily activities. I wasn't gonna bother her. I texted my mother to tell her what happened and to ask if she could watch Niyah tonight. She gave her input about Mario as usual and agreed to watch Zaniyah until 11:30. That was cool with me, because I would be home in bed by then. Thankfully, she had her own key to get in because my lazy ass did not like hiking those stairs all the time.

✳✳✳✳

The time had come and Jay would be here any minute and I was still putting on the finishing touches. I looked myself over in the mirror on the back of my bedroom door. I decided to wear my short green dress with my new Louboutins. I looked great! I looked down at my wedding ring and I could feel the tears in the making. I held them back and continued. I wasn't gonna let Mario's stupidity interfere with me catching up with Jay. I was still unsure of what he wanted to catch up on, exactly. Guess I had to wait and see.

My doorbell rang and I tiptoed downstairs to the front door. I opened it and it was Jay, and damn was he looking good, looking like a whole snack. I stood there looking so dumbfounded that I swear I felt myself drooling.

"Nice to see you, too, Desiree," he said, laughing and pushing his way inside.

"Hey, Jay," I said in a seductive tone. I don't know where that came from.

"Nice place you got here. Is hubby here?" he asked.

My entire mood instantly changed. "No," I said softly and held my head down. I walked into the living room and took a seat.

"Is everything okay, Desi?" he asked as he sat down next to me.

"Desi?" I repeated laughing. "I can't believe you remembered my nickname."

"I remember everything about you," he said with a straight face.

I could smell the scent of his Hugo Boss cologne. It was so intoxicating.

"You look a little stressed, Babe," he said. "I might have something for that."

"I thought we were going to dinner?"

"I mean we can. I really just wanted to spend some alone time with you. You still look as good as ever," he said as he rubbed my knee with his fingertips and licked his lips. I didn't even budge.

"What do you have for my stress, Jay?" I asked as I pushed his hand away. He reached into his jacket pocket and pulled out a rolled up blunt. "Oh okay," I said smiling. I hadn't smoked in a while. If I didn't smoke with Jess and Shannon, I didn't smoke at all. Mario smoked reggie and I didn't want any parts in that bullshit. I took the blunt from him and grabbed a lighter off the stand and I sat back down and lit it. I inhaled the herb deeply, held it for a few seconds, and then exhaled. I took several pulls of the weed and let it slowly free me from my burdens.

"Damn, I would like a taste," Jay said. I forgot he was even there. I passed him the rest of the blunt, which was only half now.

I laughed as he started smoking. "Sorry, dude. My bad."

"If you really stressed out, I got something else for you?"

"What?" I asked inquisitively.

He reached in his pocket and pulled out a little baggie. I examined the bag closely. It was a white powder mixture. *Was that crack?* I thought as my eyes bulged out of my head.

"Oh no," I said, scooting away. "I don't like nor do that shit."

"Have you ever tried it?"

"Fuck no! Are you crazy?"

"Well how you know you're not gonna like it?"

"Fuck that. You outta your fucking mind if you think I'm gonna try that shit."

"I think you should lower your tone, Desiree," he said with a stern tone as he looked at me. I shut my mouth quickly. I couldn't believe he still had this type of hold on me. I scooted back over next to him. "Just try it. For me," he said. I looked back at him and nodded my head in agreement.

I watched attentively as he laid the powder on my coffee table in three lines. He swished it around a little with his pinky nail before pulling out a rolled-up dollar bill. My eyes grew wide as I watched him suck that stuff up in his nose like a damn hoover vacuum.

He dumped three more lines on the table and looked at me. "Your turn," he said, smiling.

"I can't snort that like you just did."

"I don't expect you to either. Go slow but not too slow."

I took the bill from his hand and stuck it up my nose. I hesitated before putting my face close to the table. I took one deep sniff and my nose started burning and I started sneezing. I could feel my eyes growing. Probably damn near jumping outta my head! I sneezed a couple of times, but I was good. I continued the other two lines without stopping.

I sat back on the chair and let the drug work its magic. My body felt like it was heating up. Like it was coming to life for the very first time in my life. I felt exhilarated and full of energy all of sudden. I could feel my stress decreasing dramatically and a tingling sensation taking up the inside of my body.

"How you feel?" Jay asked me.

"I feel great."

"That's good to know. What you wanna do now?"

"We can head out to dinner," I said, getting up.

"How about something else?" he said, grabbing my wrist and pulling me back onto the sofa.

He pulled my legs around towards him spreading my legs apart and pushing my thong to the side. He looked down at my freshly shaved pussy and placed his head between my legs. He made circles and sucked on my clit and nibbled on it, just like he did back in the day.

"Ohhh," I moaned softly. "What about dinner?"

"I'm already eating dinner," he replied as he continued without stopping. He started doing the alphabet with his tongue. By the time he got to 'R' I was coming all over his lips. He pulled his head up from between my thighs and stood up.

He took off his jacket and threw it onto the other sofa. He pulled off his shirt and I examined his torso and I saw that it had more tattoos and muscle than it did years ago. He removed his shoes and pants and put them in a pile. He pulled off his boxers and his dick was already standing at attention.

He got on top of me and inserted the tip of his penis. My pussy instantly welcomed him without hesitation as he slowly put each inch in until I arched my back and couldn't take anymore. He held me in place as he fucked me so good. He was pressing on my clit with his thumb and getting me hotter, but I wasn't ready to come yet. I pushed him back on the sofa and straddled him. I kicked my heels off, not even caring about them getting scuffed, or, not at the moment.

I made sure he was as deep as I wanted him to be before I rode him. I gyrated my hips into his, and started to bounce up and down on his shaft as I held tightly onto the back of the sofa. He grabbed my hips tight and slammed me up and down repeatedly on top of him. As soon as we were both about to cum, I heard my front door slam and a loud gasp. I turned to look to see who it was.

"What the fuck is going on here?" my mother yelled.

Chapter Five

Caught in the Act

I looked at my mother and she looked at me, neither one of us broke our stares until Niyah came around from behind my mom.

With innocence in her eyes, she asked, "Mommy, why are you on top of that man naked? That's not Daddy."

I couldn't even answer her. I just held my head down in shame. Jay just sat there quietly. My mother grabbed Niyah by her hand and led her back out the front door.

"Mom, wait," I yelled, getting up. I raced to the door to stop her and she turned back around and looked at me with tearful eyes.

"I cannot believe you, Desiree. After all you've been through, and then you lied? I will take my granddaughter with me, because I see you're still acting like a damn teenager."

"I'm not acting like a teenager, Mom," I said.

"Pssh. Could've fooled me!" She went down the stairs and never looked back as I called her name. She put Zaniyah in the back seat and got in on the driver's side. She still didn't look at me as she drove away with my baby.

I felt Jay's warm breath on my neck before he lightly kissed it. "You ready for another round, Baby?"

I turned and looked at him with disgust. "I think you should go, Jay. "

"What? Why? I thought we were having fun?"

"Fun? Nigga, my mother and daughter just caught me in here fucking you while my husband is in jail."

"That's not my fault."

"Doesn't matter; just get the fuck out of my house and my life. Don't come the fuck back!"

"Come on, Baby."

I guess this nigga didn't get the message. I started pushing him out the door, still butt naked. I slammed the door and went to retrieve his stuff from the living room. I opened the door again and threw his stuff out to him on the front lawn. I slammed the door back and locked it. I slid down to the floor and cried loudly as I curled up into a fetal position behind the door. My high was wearing off and I was starting to feel pain again. I cried and cried, until I thought I had run completely out of tears.

✳✳✳✳

I awakened the next day still naked, laying behind the front door in the same fetal position. My phone kept ringing but I didn't budge. *What was the point?* I was miserable. My husband had gotten taken away in handcuffs yesterday and my daughter caught me riding another nigga's dick last night. My phone started ringing again nonstop, so I just built up some energy to remove myself from the floor and go over to it.

I snatched my phone up from the table and answered it without looking at the caller ID.

"Hello?" I said in an agitated tone.

"I see you finally decided to answer the phone," my mother said.

"Yeah, I've been sleeping."

"Yeah, I bet. God knows how long you were riding that man for after I left yesterday."

"Really, Ma?"

"Don't you 'really, Ma' me."

"He left right after y'all left."

"I hear you."

"I'm telling you the truth, Ma!" I yelled into the phone.

"I don't know what the truth is anymore."

I became silent on my end of the phone. I didn't even know what was true about me anymore. This shit with Mario was taking a toll on me far too quickly. I didn't even give him time to be missed before I hopped on another nigga.

"Desiree, I'm so disappointed in you and your behavior," my mother blurted out.

"I know," I responded sadly.

She took a deep breath and continued. "I think it will be a good idea if I just keep Zaniyah with me."

Nymphopervtress 2: Degenerate

"Wait, what? What do you mean 'keep her'? You can't do that."

"I do what the hell I please," she yelled at me. "You will not have my granddaughter around you and your nonsense."

"You can't keep my fucking child!" I yelled again.

"If you don't like it, do something about it. I'll see you in court," she said before hanging up in my ear.

I couldn't believe my ears. How could my mother try to take Zaniyah from me? She was my pride and joy and she was all I had left in this world; the only person that really loved me no matter what the circumstance.

If my mother wanted a custody battle for my child then I was gonna give it to her. I'm not letting anybody come between me and my daughter. I wish I would sit back and just watch them snatch my baby away from me. I'm going down to the courthouse first thing in the morning and talk to somebody, because nothing or nobody was gonna get in my way of having my daughter back with me.

✳✳✳✳

"I'm sorry, Mrs. Davis, but your mom does have a solid case against you."

"How the fuck is that possible?" I asked, raising my voice.

"Please lower your voice, Mrs. Davis. It's all a matter of he say she say."

Nymphopervtress 2: Degenerate

"He say she say, huh? Well I say fuck you, this court system, and whoever else is against me," I said, standing to my feet.

"Nobody is against you, Mrs. Davis. In cases like this, they look into everything. I don't know what your mother may have up her sleeve, so be prepared. Cases like this do tend to get ugly."

I looked at her. "How ugly are you talking?"

"To the point where neither party gets the child and he or she becomes a foster child until the age of 18."

"Are you freaking serious?" I asked as I sat back down and held my head on the table. I didn't want this lady see me cry.

She walked around her desk and placed a hand on my shoulder and handed me some tissues. "Look, I cannot promise you anything, but I will try my best and you need to be truthful about everything that your mother may throw out in court."

"Everything?"

"Everything, Mrs. Davis."

"Well let's go back to when my husband and I started having problems."

"That's a good start," She walked back around her desk to her chair. She had a seat and put on her listening ears.

I talked and answered her questions as she wrote down everything like she was a therapist or something. We were probably there for about three hours. She gave me a court date after she confirmed it with a judge and told me to be ready two weeks from today.

****

I didn't even wanna go into my house, but I did anyway. Only because I had held my pee for about forty-five minutes as I sat in the car. I ran into the house and used the downstairs bathroom. After I finished, I went upstairs to my bedroom. I walked by Zaniyah's room first and looked in there.

My baby would probably be drawing, or reading a book, on her princess bed right now. I started to tear up as I walked into her room. I could smell the scent of her kiddie perfume that Mario had bought her for her birthday. I looked on her desk and papers were everywhere. I flipped through her pictures and came across a family picture. It was me, her, Mario, a turtle and a dog. I laughed so hard through the tears. She had wanted a pet forever. Maybe I'll get her one when she comes back home.

I walked over to her bed and noticed that it was left the same as always. She had one side of the cover thrown to the side and her nightgown was at the foot of her bed. I picked up her pillow and inhaled the sweet scent of her Mixed Chicks shampoo and conditioner.

I balled up on her bed and cried some more. My phone was ringing off the hook and I just let it while I held my baby's pillow closer to my face and tighter in my arms as I cried myself to sleep.

Chapter Six

A Night Out

I had been so miserable these past couple of weeks that I hadn't even shown up for work for three days straight, so they fired me. I was lying down in my bed just wondering how in an instant my entire life had spiraled out of control. Tomorrow I had to be in court to try and get Zaniyah back and I haven't even been out of my bed in a week. I haven't even taken a proper shower. My therapist, Dr. Nicholson, had reached out to me and left a couple of messages telling me to come in for an appointment, but I disregarded them because I didn't wanna be bothered by her and her mind games. Jay had been calling me nonstop, Mario had called me multiple times from jail, and my friends have been blowing me up like bill collectors. I wish I could just run away from all of my problems and never look back. I want my old life back. I want to live in happiness again. Where did my joy disappear to?

My phone started ringing and someone started knocking on my door simultaneously. I ignored them both. I heard my front door open and slam and I still didn't move. I heard voices and footsteps coming up the steps and I reached for my gun in my

Nymphopervtress 2: Degenerate

nightstand drawer. I aimed it at the door and cocked it. I saw a shadow closing in and I shot at it. I heard low gasps and murmurs. I sat up straight on the bed and watched as Jessica and Shannon walked into my bedroom.

"What the fuck, Desiree?" Jessica yelled at me as she walked over to the bed.

"What?" I asked as I put the gun back in the drawer.

"You almost fucking shot us," Shannon said.

"Almost doesn't count," I said. "Who the fuck just breaks into somebody's house anyway?"

"Bitch, we didn't break in. We have keys remember?" Jessica said, holding up her key ring. I smacked them out of my face and they landed on my bed.

"Why the hell is it so dark in here?" Shannon asked.

"Because I like it dark."

"Well it's freaking depressing," she said, walking over to the windows. She pulled the curtains back and let the bright sun rays shine through the blinds. I quickly buried my face under the comforter from the light.

"Oh no, Desiree. You need to get up right now," Shannon said, pulling the entire blanket off my bed and tossing it to the floor.

"Leave me alone, man. Let me be miserable."

"What kind of friends would we be if we did that?" Jessica asked as they both pulled me up off the bed by my arms.

"Good ones," I replied sarcastically.

"Don't think so, Desi," Shannon said.

They drug me into the bathroom and ran me a hot bubble bath. After the tub was half full, they lowered my body into the steaming hot water. It actually felt amazing. The hot water was not only cleansing my body but also taking away a little stress. Shannon and Jess sat in the bathroom as I sat in the tub and drilled me.

"So, what the heck is going on?" Jess asked.

"Everything is going wrong. Mario got locked up. My mother took Zaniyah from me-"

"Hold on. You said she took Zaniyah? Why the fuck did she do that?" Jess asked.

"Well she kind of caught me and Jay downstairs having sex on the couch."

"Jay?" they both said in unison.

"Yeah."

"The same Jay that you were dating as a teenager?" Shannon asked.

"The same one that you told us used to fuck you up?" Jessica added.

"Yep. The one and only," I said, nodding my head.

"Goddamnit, Desi. What were you thinking?" Jessica asked.

"I wasn't thinking at all. I was too damn high to think rationally."

"Ain't no fucking way," Shannon said. "There is no weed in this world that would have you doing some shit like that, man."

"Well it wasn't weed. It was coke."

"So now you a damn cokehead, Desi? Is that what we're doing now?" Shannon asked.

"I said I wasn't thinking straight, goddammit!" I yelled at them. I was so tired of their asses already.

"Don't you yell at me," Shannon said, storming out the bathroom.

"Don't mind her," Jess said. "I know you're going through a lot of shit right now, Sis, but drugs are not the answer, and messing around with Jay definitely isn't good either. You understand?"

I nodded my head in agreement, even though it went right in one ear and out the other.

"So, what now? What are we gonna do about Zaniyah?"

I looked up at her. "We?"

"Yeah, Bitch. That's my damn niece and she needs to be here with her mama."

"I have a court date tomorrow at eleven."

"We're going with you," she said.

"Thank you," I said. She leaned down into the tub and hugged my wet body.

"Now wash your funky ass and get some clothes on," Shannon said, popping her head into the bathroom.

"Why?"

"Dr. Nicholson just called and said she will be here in an hour."

"Thanks," I responded. Even though I was really mad on the inside about Shannon answering my phone and inviting Dr. Nicholson over here, I knew she was just looking out for my best interest. So, I pushed my anger and stubbornness to the side for the moment.

They stepped out the bathroom and I turned on the shower. I washed my body in my vanilla scented body wash that Mario had given me for Valentine's Day. I shed a few tears thinking about him. I closed my eyes as I reminisced about the last time we showered together.

I could feel his strong hands all over my body as he washed me with my green pouf. I could feel his lips on the back of my neck and his tongue tracing the tattoo of his name on my shoulder blade. My eyes flew open and my head whipped around. He wasn't there. I missed him.

I got out the shower and moisturized my body with my baby oil. I brushed my teeth and brushed and combed my disheveled hair. I walked out the bathroom and Shannon and Jessica had already gotten me some loungewear out of my drawer. I got dressed in front of them as they watched TV.

"Feel better?" Jessica asked.

"Much better," I said smiling.

"You damn sure look better," Shannon added.

"Thanks, y'all," I said, pulling them into a group hug. I could really feel the love from them as they held me. I knew if nobody else had my back, they definitely did. They were the kind of people I needed in my circle. They've been down for me since day one.

"Enough of all this funny shit, y'all," Shannon said, pulling away.

We bust out laughing as we separated from one another.

"Girl, chill out," I said, still laughing. It felt good to laugh for a change. God knows I needed it.

"We about to bounce," Jessica said.

"What y'all heifers doing today?" I asked.

"Not sure. We about to go take our cars to the car wash first. We might hit a bar tonight."

I walked them down the stairs to the front door.

"You should come," Shannon said.

"Maybe. I'll think about it."

"Call us if you need us," Jessica added. They both gave me a hug and a kiss on my cheek before heading down the front steps.

"I will," I said, waving goodbye to them. I closed the door and walked into the living room. It wasn't that bad, but it needed to be straightened up a little.

I started by sweeping up the little bit of dirt I saw on the floor. Once I threw that in the garbage, I moved my heels and dress from the middle of the floor. I ran them upstairs and came back down. I went to the coffee table and noticed that it was still a little bit of coke left in the bag and I froze for a minute.

I quickly ran over to the front door to make sure it was locked. Once I confirmed it was, I ran back to the couch and quickly dumped the contents of the bag onto a magazine. I swished it around with my pinky nail like I saw Jay do and picked up the rolled-up dollar bill. I snorted the coke up fast and sat back on the chair. I let the drug take over my body and numb my pain.

Jessica and Shannon didn't know what they were talking about. This shit was like any other medicine for pain, it just wasn't prescribed by a doctor. It was okay for me to take. Shit, I was depressed and this was good to deal with depression. I've heard many stories about people becoming addicted to cocaine, but I wasn't gonna be like that. I was not gonna become a drug addict. I wasn't.

✳✳✳✳

I heard a hard knock at the door and I jumped off the couch. I peeped through the blinds and saw Dr. Nicholson standing on the porch. Oh shit. "One second," I yelled through the door.

I ran into the kitchen and got a dish rag and wiped the cocaine residue off the coffee table. I checked my appearance in the mirror by the door. I wiped away a little powder that was left behind before opening the door.

"Hey, Dr. Nicholson," I said in a fake cheery tone.

"Hey, Desiree," she said as she walked through the door and headed straight for the living room. "Sorry I'm late."

"It's cool. I was taking a nap anyway."

"How are you, Desiree?" she asked as soon as I sat down.

"I could be better," I responded honestly. She pulled out her tape recorder and that signaled the start of our session.

"What's going on with you? I haven't heard from you in weeks."

"I know. I have just been going through a lot. That's all."

"Where's Mario and Zaniyah?" she asked, looking around.

"Well Mario is locked up and I guess Zaniyah is at my mother's house."

"Wait, what? When did Mario get locked up?"

"Almost three weeks ago. Drug possession, weapons, and assault."

"Assault? On whom?"

"Me," I said, holding my head down.

"I'm so sorry to hear that. Zaniyah is with your mother, why?"

"Something went down and my mother took her. Now she's taking me to court and she's trying to get custody of her and take her from me," I said. The tears that I had been trying to hold back escaped and poured themselves down my face. Dr. Nicholson pulled me into a tight embrace and I fell into her chest.

"Oh, Jesus. I'm so sorry, Desiree. Why would she do such a thing?"

"She caught me having sex with my ex."

She pushed me away and stared at me. "You went back?"

"Yes. I feel so bad," I said, crying more.

"Don't be. It's completely normal, Desiree," she said, handing me some tissues from the box on the end table. I wiped my face with it and continued. "When a person with your condition becomes too overwhelmed, they tend to turn to the escape that works for them."

"We have a court date for tomorrow," I said, speeding past what she had just said.

"Would you like for me to come? I can speak on your behalf if that's okay with you."

"That would be great, if you could."

"Just let me clear my schedule and I will be there." She picked up her phone and made a call to somebody, whom I guessed was her assistant. She cleared her entire schedule within minutes. Just like that. She did it for me and I realized I had another loyal person on my team.

"Thank you so much, Dr. Nicholson."

"No problem. I want nothing more than to help you get through this ordeal. It's a shame when people try to come in and take your child. It's sad," she said, shaking her head.

"But it's my entire fault."

"No, it's not. It's not you at all. It's your addiction trying to take over your vulnerability. You're running to the only thing that has ever given you an escape from pain. Don't worry; we will get through this together. Just like before."

"There's something else," I said, standing up and turning my back to her.

"What is it?" she said, standing up as well.

"I, um, I've kind of been doing cocaine, too."

"Oh my," she said. "Do you need to go to a class for it? Is it serious? How long?" she said, throwing questions at me one right after the other.

"No, it's not," I said aloud. In my head I was just praying I was telling the truth. Hopefully it didn't become too serious.

"If you need counseling let me know. As a matter of fact, I have a list of counselors that can help you for free. And they are anonymous," she said. She reached into her bag and ruffled through some papers. She pulled out two stapled papers and handed them to me.

"Thank you," I said as I took it and sat it on the coffee table.

"No problem. Anything else?"

"Well, I lost my job."

"We offer employment services, Desiree. Just email me your resume and I can send it out for you."

"Cool."

We wrapped up our session and we parted ways. I had promised her that I would be in touch and that I would see her in court tomorrow morning. She gave me a tight hug and then left.

I was left alone again in this quiet ass house.

It was around nine when Shannon, Jessica, and I headed to the bar. We arrived there about 9:30 and it was already lit. People were dancing to a mix of 90s hip-hop and today's hip-hop music and drinking and just having plain old fun. These were the people that didn't really have a care in the world.

I kept catching glances of the guy behind the bar. Every time he looked my way, I caught him staring and vice versa. Jessica saw it and put me on the spot. She had walked over to him and whispered in his ear. I knew they were talking about me because he looked my way. When she came back, she handed me a napkin with his name on it.

"You're welcome," she said and sat back down on her bar stool.

I smiled on the inside and out. I didn't even feel bad for talking to another guy anymore. I have been unhappy for a long while and I deserved to smile. To hell with Mario. I looked at the napkin. The bartender's name was Sean.

Mr. Sean was looking mighty good. Caramel skin, a goatee, long locs, and a muscled body. He knew exactly what he was doing wearing a damn tank top to work and showing off his tats and muscles. I was thirsty and I wanted to drink his water.

We stayed there and partied until it was almost closing time. I told Mr. Sean that I would be calling him soon, and then we left. We didn't have to worry about food because we had already eaten at the bar. So, we just headed to my house.

We hit a jay during the thirty-minute ride to my house and discussed what I should say and how to act at court in a few hours. I was honestly not gonna be prepared, no matter how much I rehearsed. I was trying to be strong through this situation, but for the life of me, I couldn't. I didn't wanna be strong. I wanted to be miserable, but being miserable wasn't gonna get my baby back. I needed her more than life itself.

I reached my house and left my girls. They said they would be picking me up at ten tomorrow morning. I went into the house and headed upstairs to my bedroom. I kicked off my sneakers and stripped out of my clothes. I hopped in the bed wearing nothing but my bra and panties.

I grabbed the napkin from the night stand and called Sean.

"Hello?" he said, answering the phone.

"Hey, Sean," I said playfully.

"Who is this?" he asked.

"This is Desiree. I was at the bar earlier with my friends. My friend came over and-."

"I remember," he said, cutting me off. "What's up with you?"

"Nothing really. Just a little lonely. Was wondering if you would like to be my company tonight."

"That's cool. Um, I'm still at work cleaning up. I might not get there for about an hour. Is that cool?"

I rolled my eyes. "Yeah that's fine," I said.

"Cool. Send me the address and I will see you in a little bit."

"Okay," I said, hanging the phone up. I checked the time on my phone and it read 2 a.m. I needed his fine ass here before some damn 3.

I took a picture of my sexy toned body in my panty set and sent it to him. Not even two minutes had passed before I received a text back from him. I read it and he said he would be there in twenty minutes.

I laughed out loud. It was amazing how quick guys came running for some pussy, and as bad as I was wanting for some dick, I was hoping this booty call was worth it.

Almost twenty minutes later, I heard a knock at my door. I ran down the stairs and peeped through the peephole. I could see Sean standing there, looking delicious. I opened the door and let him in.

As soon as I closed the door, I jumped in his arms and wrapped my legs around his waist and kissed him. He kissed me back and he carried me up the stairs in his arms. I showed him where the bedroom was and he entered into it.

He quickly removed his clothes and my two-piece set. He slid a condom on over his big dick and positioned himself between my thighs. He licked my clit a few times, just to let it moisten a little. He got on top of me and gave my pussy a good, and well needed pounding.

We went for a few hours. I kicked him outta my house around five in the morning. He told me he would hit me up later on today. I closed the door and headed back upstairs. I tossed and turned for about thirty minutes. I couldn't sleep. I had an idea.

I looked through my phone until I found Tyrone's number.

The phone rang four times before he answered. "Yo?" he said groggily.

"Hey, Ty, this, Desiree. Can you make a sale right now?"

I could hear him shuffling around on the other end. "How much weed you need?"

"Weed? No, I need the other stuff, Ty."

"Seriously, Shorty? Mario would kill me."

"Man, forget Mario. Are you gonna bring me some or not?"

"I got you, Shorty. I will drop it through the mail slot. You can pay me later."

"Cool. I'm good for it."

"I know."

He hung up the phone.

About ten minutes later, I heard a light knock and my metal mail slot close. I ran down the steps to retrieve my package. I could see his car through the glass window driving away from the house as I snatched up the bag and ran back to my room.

I was grinning from ear to ear like a kid getting their first piece of candy on Halloween. I went into the bathroom and sat down on the toilet. I dumped the powder onto a magazine and got it ready for my nostril.

I pushed down on one side of my nose as I placed my nose close to the magazine. I sucked up two lines like a boss. By the time I got to the third line, I was starting to feel the effects. I cleaned up my face and tucked the book under the bathroom sink with the cleaning products and I hid the rest of the bag under the sink as well. It was just a precaution since both of my best friends and my mom had keys to my house and I didn't need them seeing that shit.

I went back to bed and was feeling sleepy now. My mind was free and I was a lot more at ease. Now I will be able to fall asleep with no problem.

Chapter Seven

Court Hearing #1

Oh fuck! It was almost fifteen minutes to 10 and my ass was just getting up. I rushed into the bathroom to quickly wash my ass. I ran back out and threw on a clean pair of underwear and a bra before putting on deodorant.

I rummaged through my closet and a drawer trying to find something presentable to wear and it was pretty hard considering I wore jeans and stuff to work. I managed to find a pair of black slacks and a blouse hanging up in the back of my closet. I threw on some flats and put my jewelry on. By the time I was finished brushing my teeth, my phone was ringing and it was Shannon telling me they were outside. I grabbed my purse with my ID and stuff in it and ran downstairs. I locked the door behind me and ran to the car. I slid into the backseat and we pulled off.

"You look like hell," Shannon said, looking at me through the rearview.

"I know," I said as I rummaged through my purse for my hair brush so I could quickly fix my hair. "How about now?"

"Still look like hell," she said, laughing.

"Fuck you, Shannon."

"Not anymore, Desiree."

"I bet you wouldn't mind it."

"Touché."

"Anyway," Jessica chimed in. "Here's a coffee for you," she said, handing me a Starbucks cup and as I drank the hot liquid, I could swear I had died and gone to Heaven.

"Thanks, Jess I needed that."

"I bet you did. Long night?"

"Yeah, Sean came by."

"How was it?" they both asked at the same time.

"It was bomb as fuck," I said, smiling from ear to ear.

"Well at least somebody got laid last night," Jessica said.

"What your man didn't come through?" I asked.

"Nope. Forget Gucci."

"You always say that," Shannon said.

"Forget you, too, Shannon."

"You know what? Fuck both of y'all. We need to be worried about Zaniyah. Chick, are you ready to get your baby back?"

"You damn right I am."

"Well good. Let's go get this over with."

We drove and arrived at the courthouse twenty minutes later, finding parking at the Showplace Arena and we had to walk back over the bridge to the court building. We walked into the building and went to through the metal detectors.

We walked down the hall and looked on the screen for my courtroom and once we spotted it, we headed upstairs. We stood outside the door and did something we didn't do too often, we prayed. I had forgotten how good it felt to pray and right now, I needed all the prayer I could get. We walked into the courtroom. I saw my mother sitting in the back and she saw me.

She rolled her eyes at me and made a disgusting face at me. I spotted Dr. Nicholson a few rows up and we sat next to her and we talked for a few moments before the judge started the cases.

✱

The bailiff had finally called my case around 11:30 a.m. and I was sitting here thinking the bastards had forgotten about me, but I guess not. But, in my defense, I did forget I was in Upper Marlboro. Every important building in Maryland always did shit so slowly and I'm not sure why I was even surprised by the time they called our case. My mother practically ran through the little doors to get to her table. I rolled my eyes and sat down at my table.

"We will now begin the case of Logan vs. Davis. Opening statements please."

My mother's lawyer stood up. "Well, your Honor, Ms. Logan here is requesting full custody of her granddaughter, Zaniyah Davis. She believes that it would be in the best interest that the child is in her care from now on."

"And why is that?" the judge intervened.

Nymphopervtress 2: Degenerate

"Well, your Honor, she says that her daughter, the defendant, is neglectful and she believes that the child is at harm living with her mother, Mrs. Davis."

The judge wrote down notes, I'm guessing, about what he had said. I looked over to my mother with disgust. In turn, she looked at me with a sly grin on her face.

"Where is your lawyer, Mrs. Davis?" he asked, looking at me.

"I, um, I wish to represent myself. I couldn't afford a lawyer."

"I don't recommend that, but if you insist."

I stood to my feet. "Your Honor, my child is not in any harm at home with me and I do not neglect my child. I love her with all my heart. I need my baby back home with me. She's all I have."

"Are you working, Mrs. Davis?"

"I was. I recently lost my job due to the recent events in my life."

"Other than this, what other events have occurred?"

"Well, um, my husband went to jail, and I lost my job."

"Is that all?"

"Yes."

"And she's sleeping with a lot of men and doing drugs with her daughter in the house, your Honor," my mother stood up and blurted out. Everyone, even me, gasped and looked her way. "And I dare you say I'm lying," she said, looking at me. I stood there in shock and I could hear people around the courtroom talking and murmuring about what my mom had just said.

"Order in the courtroom," the judge said, slamming his gavel. "Is this information valid, Mrs. Davis?"

I held my head down in shame. "Yes, your Honor, some of it is but not all of it. My mother is referring to events in my past life. I'm not like that anymore."

"Well explain the nigga whose dick you were riding when Zaniyah and I walked in and caught you in the living room. How about that? Or the drugs that were all over your table and fucking nose."

"Ms. Logan!" the judge yelled at her. "I will not tolerate that type of language or behavior in my courtroom. One more outburst like that and you will be dismissed from the courtroom. Do you understand?"

"Yes, your Honor."

"Good. Now take a seat before I have you arrested for disrupting my courtroom."

She sat back down and I began to cry into my hands. I looked up momentarily and the judge and I exchanged glances at one another. I was hoping that he would have a little sympathy for me.

"We will take a one hour recess and court will resume at 1," he said before banging his gavel again.

We all exited to the hallway outside the courtroom and as soon as I saw my friends, I collapsed in their arms and cried.

"I can't believe she said all of that stuff about me in court," I screamed.

"I told you she was gonna fight dirty, Desiree," Dr. Nicholson said, joining us. "It's not looking good, Honey, but you need to pull yourself together."

"You better listen to her, Desiree," my mother said, walking over to us. Dr. Nicholson moved and stood next to me and my girls. "Nice to see you all are here to support this trash."

"You are such an evil bitch," I said through clenched teeth.

"You better watch your mouth, you little tramp, and remember that I am still your mother."

"What kind of mother are you, trying to take a child from their mother? You're gonna rot in hell for this!"

She laughed in my face. "That's perfectly fine with me. I'm trying to save that child and I'll be damned if she grows up to be a whore like your black ass," she said, then turned on her heels and walked away.

"You bitch!" I yelled and went after her. I managed to grab her by the throat and I had a tight grip, too. Jessica and Shannon were grabbing me around the waist trying to pull me away from her while Dr. Nicholson was trying to free my grip from my mother's throat.

"Cut this foolishness out!" one of the big burly officers bellowed running over to us. It took five minutes for the two officers and everybody else to get me off of my mother.

"You are such an evil child, Desiree," my mother yelled at me through tears.

I was shedding tears of my own. "I got it from you," I yelled back at her.

"Everybody calm down," the other officer said.

"Don't have me lock all of y'all up in here. Has she calmed down?" the first officer asked.

"Yeah we got her," Jessica said. They all surrounded me and we walked a little way down the hall.

"You cannot act like that, Desiree," Dr. Nicholson said. "Don't let her get to you. You want Zaniyah back, right?"

"Yes," I said, wiping away my tears.

"Ok then, but this is not how you need to go about it."

"She's right, Desi," Shannon said in agreement.

"We all need to take a deep breath calm down," Jessica added.

We all stood in the hallway for another twenty minutes, just lingering about before we decided to walk to the cafeteria to grab a quick snack then head back upstairs at a quarter to one. I stopped in the bathroom to clean up my face and fix my makeup before I went back inside. We made our way back into the courtroom and I sat back down at my table. The courtroom had brought in four more guards, whom I guessed were there for me.

"Welcome back everybody," the judge said as he entered and sat back down and so did everyone else in the courtroom.

My mother and I exchanged dirty looks at one another again before giving the judge our undivided attention.

"Now it was brought to my attention about the incident that occurred during the recess. I will say this one last time I will not tolerate behavior like this inside or outside of my courtroom. Is that clear Ms. Logan and Mrs. Davis?" he yelled at us as if we were children.

"Yes, your Honor," we said in unison.

"Good and now that we got that covered; the jury has come up with their verdict." The bailiff passed the paper to the judge. "The final verdict is that the child in question, Zaniyah Davis, will remain in custody with the grandmother, Ms. Logan. Mrs. Davis, your parental rights are temporarily revoked as of today. You will have one day a week of supervised visitation with your daughter and that will go on until we meet back in court in ninety days. Court is adjourned." He banged his mallet for the last time.

I lost control of myself in the courtroom. I went after my mother again, who was smiling as hard as a pageant queen but this time I couldn't get to her. The judge threatened me with jail time and I calmed down. As we were all walking out of the courtroom, I fainted.

As I was passing out, the only thing on my mind was how I had just acted. *Did my actions just cost me my child?*

Chapter Eight

Emmitt

I had been crying all day and all night since the court hearing. The only upside was that I would see my baby in a couple of days. Sean had called me several times but I didn't bother to answer. My phone was ringing again. I looked at the caller ID; it was an unknown number. Mario. I connected the call and he came on the line.

"Hey, Mario," I said through sniffles.

"Where's Zaniyah?" he asked with a temper.

"She's at my mother house for the night," I said, lying.

"You're a goddamn lie, Desiree."

"What are you talking about?"

"I already heard that she had gotten taken from your dumbass and I'm telling you right now, you better get her back."

"I'm trying."

"Slim, I didn't say try. You better get my fucking daughter back and bring her to see me next week."

"Okay, Mario. Is that all you called for?"

"No. I called to tell your ass to keep them niggas out my house, you know how you are. If you wanna be a hoe, go be a hoe somewhere else. Take your shit out my house and take the keys to my mama, Slim." He hung up the phone in my ear.

Was he fucking serious right now? How the fuck he knows about Zaniyah? Matter of fact, how in the hell did he know about anybody coming over here? Tyrone lil' blockhead ass probably said something. But my thing is why was he spying on me? Did Mario really not trust me at all? If that's the case, why would he waste time marrying me? And now I'm wondering if he told Mario that I came to him for some cocaine.

My mind was racing a mile a minute and I needed some relief. I picked up my phone. It was 1 o'clock in the morning and I was hoping his ass was awake.

"Hello?" he said, answering the phone with music playing in the background.

"Hey, Jay are you busy?"

"Never too busy for you, even though you kicked me out your house," he said sarcastically.

I rolled my eyes up to the ceiling and laughed. "I hear you, but you know I was just playing, boo. You think you can maybe swing by?" I said, cutting straight to the chase.

"Look, Desiree, I'm not one of these hoe ass niggas that you got wrapped around your finger and call whenever you feel like being bothered. Understand?"

I had been taken aback a little. *Damn, was I doing him like that?* "Um, well, I'm sorry if you think that, but-"

"Aha, sike, I'm just fucking with you, Desi," he said, laughing into the phone.

"I can't fucking stand your ass, Jay, but for real can you slide through?"

"As long as I can slide through you."

"Duh, why you think I was calling, Nigga?"

"I'll be around there in about fifteen or twenty minutes."

"Aight, cool. Jay?" I yelled into the phone, trying to catch him before he had hung up the phone.

"Yeah?"

"Don't forget the good medicine."

He got quiet for a second. "Uh, sure. No problem."

"Thanks."

He hung up the phone and I started smiling. I couldn't wait for Jay to get here. But, mostly, I couldn't wait to get some more cocaine.

✶✶✶✶

I woke up the next morning with a sore body from all the screwing Jay and I had done in the previous hours. I looked over at him and he was sleeping so peacefully. He didn't even look like the type of nigga that beats up pussy to the point where it shed a little blood, but he was.

I went into the bathroom to pee and clean myself up. I turned on the shower water and it ran as I looked over my body in the mirror. I had bruises and hickeys all over my body and marks on my wrists from when Jay had me handcuffed to the bed railing

Nymphopervtress 2: Degenerate

in the last round of sex. My hair was all over the place. I turned around and checked out the back side of my body.

I had marks on my back from when he was digging his fingers in my back. I had scratches all over and my ass had slap marks on it as well. I smiled just thinking about last night and how wild it had been. As soon as he had gotten here, I snatched the bag out of his hand and went to work. He just sat back and watched as I did six lines straight, like a pro. One thing had led to another and before I knew it, Jay was on top of me and my legs were up to the ceiling.

I checked the water to make sure it was good for me to get in and once I confirmed that it was, I hopped in to wash the sex from my skin. I lathered up my pouf and catered to my body with my peaches n' cream body wash. I washed and rinsed my body three times before I turned the shower water off to get out. I pulled back the shower curtain and Jay was standing there.

"What the hell?" I yelled.

"What's wrong, Baby Girl?"

"How long have you been in here?"

"What does it matter? It ain't like I never seen that little pussy before anyway."

I rolled my eyes and got out the shower. I went into the room, grabbed my baby oil gel, and lathered up my brown skin.

"I got somebody I want you to meet," Jay said when he came back into the room. This nigga didn't have on anything. Just butterball ass naked walking around like this was his house. His dick was just swinging around like a damn snake.

"Who?"

"Just a friend of mine. Don't worry; I think it's about time that you two have met."

"Sure, I guess so."

"What you got going on today?" he asked as he began to get dressed.

"Well, I do need to start looking for a job."

"Real talk. Well I'm about to head to work for a few hours. Let me know later on this evening what time you wanna meet my homie."

"Okay," I said. He kissed me on the head and left out. I heard the door slam moments later. I watched from the upstairs window as he drove off in his Cadillac.

I threw on some yoga pants, my new balance shoes, and a t-shirt. I ran downstairs to make a cup of coffee and some breakfast. I looked in the fridge and I didn't have much of anything.

"I hate going to the grocery store," I said out loud. After my coffee had finished brewing, I poured it in my hot and cold coffee cup that Zaniyah had gotten me and decorated herself with permanent markers. I grabbed my hot java and car keys and headed to the grocery store.

I had driven for about fifteen minutes to the store, listening to the radio. They were tripping on WKYS radio station this morning. The topic of today was about how many sexual partners were too many for men and women. I wanted to call in but I chose against it. Instead I just listened in, like all the rest of DMV.

"Good morning, KYS," I heard the one of the radio hosts say when she had picked up the call.

"Good morning. I was calling about the topic of the day."

"Who is this?"

"My name is Shay."

"Tell us what's on your mind, Shay," I heard the guy say.

"Well, in my opinion, I just think more than five partners in somebody's life is beyond ridiculous. I mean, that's not how I roll, but you never know with somebody else."

"Yeah, that is true in most cases," the female host said in agreement.

"If you don't mind me asking, how many partners have you had in your life?" the male host asked.

"Only three. My two kids' fathers and my fiancé."

"Well at least somebody putting a ring on it now," he replied.

"You know it."

"Aight have a good day, Mama," the female said again before hanging up. "If you have anything to say about this topic, call into the station now." I was pulling in the parking lot of Shoppers when they cut to a commercial break.

Was this chick talking about me? I had more than five partners. Shit, I lost track of my body count, honestly, but I didn't bother to think about it as I got out of the car and walked across the parking lot. I grabbed a shopping cart and headed into the store. I walked slowly through the produce aisle to see if I wanted anything from that section. I looked through the bags of grapes until I found the most decent looking one. I grabbed some lettuce, tomatoes, celery, and a bag of potatoes. I headed towards the canned food aisles now. I was scanning the shelves looking to see what was on sale that I could get. Out of nowhere, somebody bumped my cart and it hit me in my side. I stood up straight and looked to see who it was.

"Excuse you," the girl said.

"No, Trick, excuse you. What the fuck?" I said, standing in a defensive manner. She walked past me, pushing her cart with another girl as they walked to the opposite side of the aisle. I went back to what I was doing and started throwing canned goods into my cart.

When I stood back up to grab my cart and go to another aisle, I bumped into the same two bitches again.

"Can I help you broads?" I asked bluntly.

"I think I know you. Isn't your name Desiree?"

"Yeah but you don't know me, Bitch," I said, bumping through them and walking down the aisle.

"Oh, that's right," she yelled. "You don't know me but I know your nigga, though."

I stopped in my tracks and swiftly walked back towards the two, leaving my cart. "So the fuck what? You know my nigga, and?"

"I heard he got locked up and I just wanted to know when he was getting out."

"Why does it matter to you?"

"I just miss that sweet chocolate dick of his."

I stared into her eyes as she smiled back. "I think you got the wrong person," I said and turned back around and walked away.

"Hmm, maybe. Mario Davis, roughly about six foot one maybe, chocolate. Oh, and that dick. You remember that dick, Shante?" she asked her friend.

"Girl you know I do. How could I forget? And that tongue? Oh God," she said, fanning herself and giggling with her friend. I just stood at my cart as I contemplated my next move.

"I can't wait for him to come home so he can bring me back to y'all house and fuck me all over the furniture."

"Don't forget the little girl's room, too. He had me in there bent over her little princess bed."

"I do remember that night and it was great. I think you were out with your daughter that day, Desiree."

I had had enough of these two lowlife cunts. I slowly picked up a can of spaghetti and meatballs. I quickly turned and launched the can at the first girl and it hit her dead in the nose. Blood started gushing out and flying all over the place. Her friend was so busy that she didn't see the can coming her way.

The can hit her in the side of her head and she dropped to the floor in agonizing pain. I watched as a knot was quickly forming at her temple. I walked over and stepped on her head, pressing it into the cold floor and I grabbed the other girl by her hair and gave her two blows to her already possibly broken nose. I dropped her on the floor next to her friend and squatted down close enough so they both could hear me.

"I better not ever see you two bitches again, and if I do, I will kill y'all, and I put that on my daughter. Think it's a game? Try me."

I kicked both of them one more time and walked off. I looked at the end of the aisle and it was a crowd of people with their phones out recording what just happened. I looked behind me and the same was happening on the other end.

I kept walking until they opened a space for me to get through then they all bum rushed the aisle to get pictures and videos of the chicks and I just laughed. I continued my shopping, and then made my way to checkout. Nobody said anything, but just kept staring at me. I got my change and bags and headed out to my car. After I finished putting the bags in the trunk, I got in the car and drove down the street a few blocks. I pulled into a vacant lot and burst into tears.

I yelled and screamed at the top of my lungs. I was so fucking upset and even madder at Mario. I calmed down and thought maybe I should go visit him. I was gonna give his ass a piece of my mind, and maybe a two piece as well before the guards got ahold of me. I wiped my face of the tears and touched up my makeup. I called the jail to see when visiting days were. Once that got confirmed, I headed home feeling a little better.

✳✳✳✳

I had been nervous this entire ride with Jay. I was going with him to meet some guy named Emmitt that he said lived past Baltimore in some unheard-of ass city. I just rode in silence as he rapped to music on the radio.

After almost an hour of driving, we pulled into a parking lot of a building that looked like a little vacant warehouse.

"Now be cool when we go in here, Desiree," Jay said to me once he put the car in park.

"Why wouldn't I be?"

"Just do as he asks and we won't have any problems."

I looked at him oddly and he had that menacing look on his face that I remembered all too well. I swallowed a lump that had formed in my throat and nodded.

"Good girl," he said as he kissed me on my cheek and patted me on the head like I was a dog or something. I rolled my eyes as he got out before me. I opened my side of the car and got out. I stood there straightening out my tight-fitting dress that he made me put on. It had a long plunging neckline and the entire back was out and I had on some gold heels and gold accessories to match.

We walked into the warehouse and went through a security check and the damn guard was feeling all inside my dress and under my dress talking about he was making sure I wasn't hiding any weapons. I looked at him and shot him a "really nigga" look. Once we got through security, we were led up some metal stairs to two doors. The doors opened and all I could see were hundreds of people. Music was blaring through the speakers, strippers were on the pole doing tricks for cash, and people were at the bar while others sat at tables. I could smell a mixture of sex, sweat, weed, and cheap perfume as we walked through the crowd. I was getting felt up on by both females and males, and it felt good. My body was getting hot and I wanted to keep feeling hands all over my body but now wasn't the time. Jay wanted me to meet Emmitt and I was looking forward to it a little. I hope I would have time to enjoy myself afterward though.

"Yo, Emmitt," Jay said as he dapped up some dude that was sitting at the back of the club. From left to right, he was surrounded by beautiful women of all shades and nationalities.

"What's up, Dawg? Who is this fine woman you have with you?" he said, looking me up and down.

"Oh yeah, this is, Desiree," he said, pushing me in front of him.

"Hi," I said, throwing a seductive wave his way.

"Damn you look good enough to eat," he said, licking his lips.

I walked over and leaned in next to his ear and spoke loud enough for him to hear me over the music. "You might enjoy it if you do," I said, and then I playfully flicked my tongue across his ear. I stood back up and went back over to Jay.

"Jay how about you, um, find something to do," Emmitt said, standing to his feet. "And you can come with me, beautiful," he said, grabbing my hand.

"I thought we was all gonna kick it?" Jay said, looking dumbfounded.

"You heard what I said, Nigga. Just be in my office in twenty minutes. Got me?"

"Yeah I got you," Jay replied.

Emmitt took me by the hand and led me from the busy room into his office. It was huge. It had a chocolate leather sofa with a matching recliner and his desk was made up of cherry wood and it was adorned by different photos. I scanned the photos and they were mostly of children that favored Emmitt. I counted at least nine of them.

"So, did you come in here to look at pictures or did you wanna come see what I wanted to show you?" he asked, stepping close behind me.

I breathed in deeply and poked my ass into his groin. I slowly winded against him until I could feel his manhood come to life. "Is that what you wanted to show me?" I asked in a low voice.

"I don't think you're ready for that just yet," he replied. He stepped from behind me and went over to a large cabinet. He opened it and it revealed a safe. He pressed his finger on the scan pad and it popped open. He reached inside and pulled out a box. He closed it back and walked back over to where I was and placed the box on the desk. "You ready?" he asked.

I was so filled with anticipation that I couldn't even respond, so I just nodded my head yes. He opened the box and my mouth dropped open.

Chapter Nine
Making Me High

My eyes were bulging out of my head. I could feel the saliva wet my tongue and drip from my lips. Staring back at me was a cinder block size of pure white cocaine. I was in heaven.

Moments seemed like hours passing as I watched him remove the package from the box and began to pull back the clear wrapping, unwrapping this beautiful temptation.

"Would you like to do the honors?" he asked, handing me a metal scalpel to cut at the giant brick.

My throat had gone dry but I managed to say "yes," as I took the metal tool into my shaking hand. I tried to steady myself as I placed the knife onto the product. My eyes grew larger upon realizing that this wasn't all a dream and I was really standing in front of this beautiful white mountain of sin.

I first sliced a piece of the corner carefully retrieving it then popping it into my mouth and swallowing it. I managed to cut off enough to make three lines. It dropped onto the table and I shifted the powder around until the little lumps were completely out. Emmitt handed me a rolled-up bill and I smiled, smiled harder than

I probably ever have in my entire life. I snorted up two lines; one directly after the other.

I could feel the little beads of sweat quickly forming on my forehead. My skin was becoming wet with perspiration and it felt as if something was crawling on my skin. My mouth had suddenly become dry as well. The drug had given me an instant rush. I had never experienced the effects this goddamn fast. I was a little afraid as my heart began beating faster and I began to panic as the room spun around me and the walls and ceiling began to close in on me.

"Are you okay?" I could hear Emmitt ask me. I just giggled and snickered and watched as he cut out a chunk and chewed it before swallowing. He grabbed a brown paper bag and cut half of the block of cocaine and dropped it in. He folded the bag and handed it to me.

"What's this for?" I asked as my eyes damn near popped out my head.

"For you," he replied.

"Oh, no, no, no. I can't afford that Emmitt."

"It's okay, Desiree. I'm sharing with you. That is what friends do, and you are my friend, right?"

"Of course," I said, snatching the bag from his hands before he changed his mind.

"That's good," he said as he fed me a little more coke as well as himself.

I'm not sure how long this had gone on for, but the effects had subsided and everything was good again.

"To answer your question, before I forget, yes I am okay."

"Okay good. I thought I had lost you there for a moment. I should have warned you that this shit was different than that other shit you be getting. You should've taken it slow."

"I said I was good," I responded. "Besides, I don't like taking anything slow," I said as I pinched off a piece of the cocaine and stuck it in my mouth. I flicked my tongue around my finger to get the excess powder off. Emmitt just looked on in amazement. I pinched off some more and put it up to his mouth. He sucked on my finger until all the powder was gone.

"Mmm. That tastes good," he replied.

"Oh yeah? You know what else tastes good?"

"What's that?"

I sat on top of his desk and cut some more of the cocaine from the brick. I placed the drug on my thigh and motioned for him to come closer.

He came closer to me as instructed. He knelt down in front of me and started at my ankle as he kissed and licked up my leg to my thigh. He snorted up the powder and I put some more on there. I told him to use his mouth to get that portion up.

He slowly licked my thigh and my pussy began twitching. After he licked all the cocaine from my thigh, he kept going making his way to my panty less pussy. He flicked his tongue back and forth across my clit, awakening my pussy even more. I grabbed the back of his head and pushed his head in deeper.

He stood up and grabbed my hand and pulled me over toward the sofa. I pulled back and pinched some more powder off the brick before following in tow. We both sat on the couch and I laid my head back as my breathing had increased and the room began spinning again.

I could feel his hand rubbing my knee, before his fingertips began tiptoeing up my thigh until they reached my sweet spot. I wanted him to stop but then I thought about how good his tongue had felt moments ago. On top of that, I was thinking about the bag he had just given me. I didn't want him to take it back so I obliged. He leaned in to kiss me and I welcomed him.

Our tongues began wrestling as he held me and laid me back on the chair and got on top of me. I parted my legs again so he could reach my pussy without a problem. I could feel his fingers penetrating my vagina and making my juices start to flow. He inserted a third finger and my back arched, resulting in him shoving his fingers in deeper; faster.

He kissed and sucked on my breasts as he made his way down between my legs, removing his fingers and replacing them with his tongue. It was warm and the wetness of my pussy and his tongue intensified my high. He flicked his tongue back and forth over my clit. My juices flowed more and he slurped up my sweet goodness.

He stood up and removed his clothes and pushed my dress up over my hips and got back on top of me. He slipped a rubber on before pushing his dick inside me. He started out with slow strokes, then his pace quickened. I was enjoying the long deep strokes. We heard the door open and close. He stopped in mid stroke and we both looked. It was Jay.

"Damn y'all couldn't wait for me, Emmitt?" Jay said, coming into the office. He was holding onto an attractive female that had gray eyes. They both walked over to where we were.

"My bad, Bro. I tried to wait, but you were taking too damn long," Emmitt said when he came up for air. "It was just calling my name."

"I know what you mean," Jay replied, rubbing my shoulders how I liked. "Well, I'm here now." He walked over to the table and sliced a piece of the brick and devoured the white substance. He walked back over to us and dropped his pants to his ankles. I tilted my head back and he shoved his manhood in my mouth. I slurped and sucked it to life. He shoved his dick in and out; all the while the head of his penis was hitting the back of my throat.

Somehow, at some point, we had made our way back over to Emmitt's desk. I'm not even sure how long I was a human shish kabob, or how long I was getting my back blown out, before a sexy girl walked in and locked the door behind her. She walked seductively over to the sofa.

"Can I join in, too?" the sexy female said, rubbing her hand across my face. She leaned in to kiss me and I met her halfway with my lips. We kissed deeply as if we were longtime lovers. She grabbed the back of my head as she leaned me more across the desk.

My body was laid across the desk, with my head halfway hanging off, and Jay had come and stood over me. He pulled my dress off over my head and now I was just completely naked with nothing but my heels on. The girl grabbed my titties and caressed them as she sucked on my nipples.

"Ahhh," I moaned softly. Jay had finally removed his pants and other clothing and was now feeding his dick to me while my head lay upside down. Emmitt had gone up behind the girl and parted her legs. He knelt down and began eating her pussy like he had done mine.

A little time had passed and now everybody was getting fucked. We had made our way over to the sofa again. The girl was sitting on Jay's lap, with her back facing him, as he fucked her. Emmitt had me kneeling on the carpeted floor in front of the girl. He fucked me as I ate her out. We went on like this until both me and the other girl started spraying our juices everywhere. My face was covered in her sweet juices. She leaned up and kissed me again before licking all her nectar from my face. We changed positions again.

The girl had gotten up and walked across the room. I took this opportunity to have both Jay and Emmitt to myself. I sucked her juices off of Jay's dick as Emmitt continued to bang my back out. I watched her across the room as she took a couple lines to the head before strapping on a dildo.

"Bring that coke over her, NeNe," Emmitt instructed her. She brought it over to us and we all took turns cutting some off the block and placing it in our palms. We quickly snorted up a couple of times before getting back to our session.

I was not sure how long we had gone for, but it was well worth my time. I could see the time on the clock. It was 3:45am. I wanted to go home. I called an Uber and waited patiently. As soon as they pulled up, I dashed out the club with my heels in hand and hopped in the vehicle.

I settled in the back seat and smiled. I was high, exhausted, and completely filled up with cum from both dudes. Not sure what made me feel better, between the guys or the drugs that I had resting in my lap. Either way, I was happy, no doubt.

Chapter Ten
Visitation Day

I woke up in my own bed the next morning and there were no signs of Jay or Emmitt and I wondered how I had gotten here. I hopped out the bed and ran into the bathroom. I dropped to my knees in front of the toilet and vomited, just barely making it. I guess I was nauseous from the drugs last night. After I finished, I ran around the house looking for the bag Emmitt had given me. I didn't even find the damn thing until I went downstairs in the kitchen. *What kind of idiot would have put that in the kitchen? I* thought to myself.

I was getting ready to get my morning fix but my phone began ringing. "Shit," I said loudly. I closed the bag and headed back upstairs to my bedroom. I snatched the phone up and answered it before it went to voicemail.

"Hello?" I said, answering the phone out of breath.

"Girl, what the hell is wrong with you?" Shannon yelled through the phone.

I laughed. "What's up, Bihhh?" I screamed.

"Nothing, Desi. What you doing?"

"Girl, shit. Just getting up. I was throwing up this morning."

"Oh, shit. Let me find out you pregnant," she replied, laughing obnoxiously.

"Girl not even. Don't even wish that on me, please."

"Anyway, what are you up to today?"

I looked at the bag and thought *I just wanna get high, Bitch,* but instead I simply replied, "I don't know yet."

"Well Jessica and I are supposed to be going to the mall. Wanna go?"

"That sounds fun. I will call you when I'm ready."

"Cool," she said and hung up.

I threw the phone on the bed and hurried to the bathroom. I pulled out my magazine and a fresh box of razors. I dumped the contents out and began prepping my meds. I hit one line. Then another. Then two more. I was feeling great.

My body felt as if I was being lifted to the skies. I was lying on the cold bathroom tile looking up at the lights on the ceiling. The drug was lifting my spirits and getting rid of all my worries. After all the shit I had gone through this past month, hell, I deserved it.

I let the drug settle a little more before getting off the floor. I went downstairs, thinking about making breakfast. As soon as I walked in the kitchen, somebody began knocking on my door and ringing the bell simultaneously. "Seriously?" I said aloud. I walked to the door and looked through the peephole. My frown quickly turned upside down as I opened the door.

"Hey, Stink," I squealed as my baby ran into my arms.

"Mommy!" she yelled. "I missed you, Mommy," she said, holding on to me tighter.

"I missed you, too, Niyah." I picked her up into my arms and walked back to the kitchen, leaving my mother at the door. I heard the door close and footsteps coming towards the kitchen.

"I guess you didn't see me, Desiree," my mother said, sucking her teeth and folding her arms.

"Denise," I said, looking her way then rolling my eyes. "You want some breakfast, Zaniyah?" I asked.

"Pancakes," she said, jumping up and down.

"Pancakes coming right up," I said excitedly. I pulled the pancake mold of Frozen out the cabinet and prepped the batter.

"I would love some pancakes as well," my mother said, sitting on one of the barstools at the island.

"Better go catch McDonald's before breakfast is over," I shot back at her. I caught her glaring at me through the slits in her eyes.

She looked at Zaniyah. "Hey, Boo Boo, can you go to your room, please? Grandma had to talk to Mommy."

"Okay, Mama," she said, running out the kitchen and up the stairs.

My mother walked over to me as I turned on the stove to heat up the skillet. She grabbed me by the arm and spun me around. "I am so sick of you and your smart ass mouth, you little whore," she said through clenched teeth.

I snatched my arm from her grasp. "Fuck you, Ma. You make me fucking sick. Other than you bringing my daughter here, you have no other reason to be here."

"I am still your mother, Desiree."

"That sounds good from the outside looking in, doesn't it?"

"I love you, Desiree, and want nothing but the best for you."

"Bullshit," I said, turning back to the stove and pouring batter into the mold for Zaniyah's pancakes. She had become silent, but I could feel her staring at me. She was blowing the fuck out of me.

"Look, Desiree. I need some money," she said as she sat back down at the island.

"What the fuck that gotta do with me?" I asked her as I flipped the pancake.

"Well, I have your daughter. She needs clothes and stuff at my house. And- "

"That's your problem," I said, cutting her off. "You should've thought that through, genius." She sucked her teeth at me again.

I continued to cook more pancakes as she remained silent. It was so awkward. You could literally cut the tension in the kitchen with a knife, it was so thick. After the pancakes were finished, I made some turkey bacon and some scrambled eggs with cheese, just the way Zaniyah liked. Once everything was done, I called her back down. We had said grace and we all ate.

"What are your plans for today?" my mother asked. She just wouldn't give up.

"If you must know, Shannon, Jessica, and I are going to the mall."

"That sounds fun," she said, drinking her orange juice.

"Yeah. I hope it will be fun," I replied, hoping she would shut up so I could enjoy my meal.

"Can I go to, Mommy?"

"No, you can't, Sweetheart," my mother chimed in.

"And why the hell not? It's my visiting day anyway," I said, remembering what today was.

"That is true but it's also a supervised visit, and I don't feel like going to the mall."

"Nobody gives a shit, Ma, so I hope you brought your walking shoes."

Once again, she rolled her eyes and sucked her teeth. I didn't want her ass to come anyway. My patience with her was quickly wearing thin.

✳✳✳✳

We had been up and down the halls of several malls today. My mother was beyond pissed and I was glad. It served her right.

Nymphopervtress 2: Degenerate

"Can we go now, Desiree?" my mother asked, dragging her feet behind us.

"No," I blatantly said and continued on. I wasn't about to let her ruin my day out with my daughter and my girls.

"Why are you being so mean?" Jessica asked, walking closer to me.

"Whose side are you on?" Shannon asked.

"Right," I said in agreement. "She put herself in this predicament, not the other way around."

"I guess so," Jessica replied.

"Ooh, Mommy, let's go in there," Zaniyah said excitedly as she pulled me into the nail salon.

"I guess we're about to get manis and pedis, ladies," I said. They sat all of us next to one another and turned our foot baths on. Watching the colors change was illuminating. The hot water was working wonders right now. Other than my mother, my day was going great. I hadn't even thought about snorting all day.

After we finished up in the nail salon, we decided to grab a bite to eat before Shannon dropped us back off. Zaniyah and I got food from Chik-Fil-A while everybody else went to either McDonald's or Panda Express. She dropped me, Zaniyah, and my mother off at my house and we walked in.

I waved at her and Jess from the front porch as I opened the door. They drove off and we walked inside. My mother slammed the door behind her while Zaniyah and I sat down in the living room.

"Have you lost your fucking mind, Desiree?" my mother yelled at me.

I looked up at her from the couch. "I don't appreciate you talking like that in front of my child."

"Oh, you're worried about the way I talk in front of Niyah but you weren't worried about fucking another nigga in front of her? So it's not okay for your daughter to hear a little bad language, but she can learn how to be a whore like you? Is that what you mean?"

I was fuming now. I hopped up from the sofa and got in my mother's face. "You got some motherfucking nerve, Bitch. You lucky my daughter is sitting right here, because I would fucking kill you."

I felt a stinging situation on the left side of my face. I lifted my head up realizing my mother had just slapped me. Nothing could hold me back as I grabbed my mother around her throat and pushed her across the floor to the wall behind the door.

"I told you to stop playing with me, ma. I will fucking kill you, and I won't regret it either."

I watched as my mother's eyes bulged out of her head and she was trying to loosen my grip so she could breathe. The only reason I stopped was because when I looked up, Zaniyah was standing there looking at me with tears in her eyes. I dropped my mother on the steps and ran over to my baby.

"Mommy, why did you do that to Mama?" she asked, crying into my chest.

"I'm so sorry you had to see that, Zaniyah. Mommy and grandma got upset, but it will never happen again. Right, mother?" I said, looking her way.

She was walking towards us rubbing her neck. "You're right, Desiree. Come on, Zaniyah, honey. We should be getting home."

She held onto me tighter and cried more. She didn't wanna go. I didn't want her to leave, but she had to go. I gave her a kiss and I squeezed her and I told her I would see her in a few days.

It hurt me to watch her leave, but I think it hurt me more that she had seen me act the way I did. I couldn't believe I allowed my mother to take me there. I grabbed my phone and texted Dr. Nicholson and told her I needed an appointment. I needed one urgently, but until I saw her, I knew what would help me right now. I called Jay and told him to hurry and get here.

Not even fifteen minutes had gone by before I heard hard pounding at my door. I looked out the peephole and it was Jay. I opened the door and quickly pulled him inside and slammed the door back shut.

We kissed and tore at each other's clothing as we made our way upstairs. There was nonstop kissing, hugging, biting, everything. You name it, we did it. We were so entwined with one another. It reminded me of sex with Mario. Only thing different was the fact that Jay and I were high off of cocaine, intensifying our sexual desire for one another.

We fucked and snorted until we saw the sun peeking through the window. I couldn't move. My body was numb from the drug and sore from the sex. My mind was heavy from all my stress and my heart was empty without Zaniyah and Mario.

I quietly cried as I lay next to Jay's sleeping body. I wanted my life back. I wanted my husband. I wanted my daughter. I needed Dr. Nicholson. I needed help.

Chapter Eleven

Busting At Burlington

The next day couldn't have come faster than it did. I was anxious to say the least to be sitting in Dr. Nicholson's office. I had to wait ten minutes until she finished up in a meeting, though. I took this opportunity to check my Tagged page.

I checked my inbox and it had over twenty messages. I quickly opened the messages and closed several of them. One in particular caught my eye. I scrolled through the messages and pictures that he had sent me, and I got stuck on stupid.

Staring back at me was the most chocolate man I had ever seen in my life. He had the whitest teeth and the sexiest smile. I scrolled through the rest of his messages. I came up on several dick pictures that he took at different angles.

My body heated up and my heartbeat started racing. I could feel my pussy waking up and getting warm. I could feel my juices trickling into my panties and I started squirming in my seat. I got up and looked out the door, but Dr. Nicholson wasn't in sight.

I decided to take care of myself right quick. I rushed back over to the chaise and laid back. I slipped my hand in my jeans and put two fingers inside my pussy. I began a slow motion and created moisture in my panties. I looked at the pictures and my pace quickened. I could feel my explosion coming. It was right there, and right there in an instant, Dr. Nicholson walked in and caught me red handed. I froze. I could feel myself turning red from embarrassment.

"Um, hi, Dr. Nicholson," I said, easing my hand from out of my jeans.

"Hello, Desiree. Um, would you like to finish?" she asked with a light chuckle.

"No, not at all. I'm just gonna go and run to your bathroom," I said as I rose up from the chaise and went to her private bathroom.

I closed the bathroom door quickly and pulled my pants down. I turned on the water and unbuttoned my pants. It took me only two minutes to finish what I had briefly started. I grabbed some paper towels and wet them as I cleaned up my pussy juices. I washed my hands thoroughly with soap and water. I dried them off and doused my hands in hand sanitizer before heading back into session.

"Now I'm ready," I said as I sat back down on the chaise.

"Great," she said, opening up her notepad and clicking her ink pen. "So, what was so urgent that you needed to see me today?"

"Well I think I have an addiction," I said bluntly.

"Well we already found that out years ago, Desiree. Have you been taking your meds?"

"It is far worse than that I'm afraid."

"Oh?" she said, removing her glasses and staring back up from her notepad.

"Yes. I think I'm a drug addict, too."

"What kind of drugs have you been taking? Percocet? Xanax? What?"

"Crack."

She paused briefly before writing down what I had just said. She scribbled in her notes before continuing.

"What makes you feel as though you have an addiction to crack, Desiree?" she asked exasperatedly.

"Well," I began. "Ever since Mario had gotten locked up, my life has spiraled out of control. My mother has taken my daughter and that drove me more out of my mind. So, Jay came back around and he helped me cope, but now I need it to cope with everyday life not just for the pain."

"I must say I am taken back a little, but I also must say that doing crack like that does not help with the pain at all."

"Yes, it does," I argued.

"Sorry to tell you, Desiree, but it doesn't. It may numb your senses for a while but the pain and hurt will still be there."

"This is bullshit," I said, standing to my feet. "This is why I shouldn't have said anything about it. I came here for advice and that's all."

"Desiree, I am giving you advice. I'm here to help you. I want to help you beat all of these addictions and get you through all of this pain and heartache. Everything will be fine. Sit back down, please," she said calmly.

I contemplated but I obliged. I sat there and talked to her a little more, but I couldn't stay any longer. My skin started itching. It was time for a fix. I needed to get out of here.

"Are you okay, Desiree? Is it that time?"

"What time?"

"You need a fix?"

"Oh, no, no, no," I lied. "It's just my skin. I forgot to put lotion on this morning and it's just dry."

"Um, okay," she said.

"I think I'm gonna just go now," I said, standing up.

"But we aren't finished with our session."

"We can finish next week," I said, scratching more and scanning the room for my purse.

"Desiree, I know what it is and I wanna help," she said, standing up as well and placing a caring hand on my shoulder.

"You don't know what you're talking about," I said, snatching away from her. I ran out of her office and took the stairs. I could hear her calling after me but I kept going.

I hit the stairs and frantically ran down them to get to my car quicker. Once I got in there, I searched inside my junky purse for one of the baggies I packed this morning.

I reluctantly found one and smiled as hard as I did when I first met Mario. I drove down a couple of blocks and found an abandoned building. I pulled around the back to handle my business.

I quickly sniffed the coke up my nose. As soon as it hit my bloodstream, all my pain had subsided and I felt as if I was walking on cloud nine. Nothing in this world could be more satisfying than this right now. Hold on, I'm definitely lying. Sex. Sex would be satisfying right now, too. I put my car in gear and I drove away from the building. I was on a dick hunt.

I drove in and out of traffic for a few miles. I was getting exhausted and was just about ready to give up. I needed dick and I needed it bad. I could've settled for Jay's, but I was growing tired of him. I needed some fresh meat. I pulled up to a stoplight and pulled out my phone. I searched through my contacts of guys I used to sleep with. If I couldn't find somebody new, I guess I had to settle for some familiar dick.

The light had changed just as a sexy redbone pulled up next to me. We locked eyes and he smiled at me before pulling off. Without hesitation, I followed him. He was the chosen one.

He dipped in and out of traffic and I did the same as I trailed behind him. After about ten minutes of following him, I managed to get beside him. I got his attention by blowing my horn and motioning for him to roll his window down.

"What's up?" he yelled out the window while simultaneously looking back and forth between me and the road.

"Follow me," I yelled back.

"Why?"

"Just do as I say," I yelled again. *Shit. Why niggas always gotta ask questions? Just do it, damn.* I took the lead in front of him and he followed, like I requested. I pulled into the Burlington Coat Factory parking lot at Iverson Mall. I parked my car and I watched as he parked a few spaces over. When he got out, I walked over and grabbed his hand.

"Yo what gives?" he said as I pulled him.

"Just come on," I said sternly.

We got inside the store and I tried to act as normal as possible as we rode the elevator upstairs. I walked through the aisles pretending to be browsing as we made a beeline for the family restroom. As soon as we got inside, I locked the door and started easing out of my jeans.

"What are you doing?" the guy asked me.

"I want some dick nigga. What you think?"

"Shawty, I don't even know you like that."

"I don't give a fuck. I want your dick and you're gonna give it to me," I said as I struggled to get his belt and pants undone. Once I managed to, I dropped his jeans and boxers around his waist. "Lift me up and put your dick inside me," I demanded.

"I don't even have a condom," he said.

"Oh, for Christ sake," I said ad I pulled a condom from my purse. I ripped the packaging and snatched the condom from the wrapper. I quickly massaged his manhood before placing the condom on him.

Once it was on, I pushed him down on the toilet seat and I straddled him. I gyrated my hips into his groin. He held onto my waist as he cooperated with me. He pushed my shirt up over my titties and began sucking on them. That shit made me hotter. I grabbed him by the head and kissed him. Surprisingly, he kissed me back.

He stood up, holding me and never letting his penis fall out. He pinned me up against the wall and continued to beat my guts up. I was in ecstasy. He slammed me down on his dick and I could feel it grow thicker inside my pussy. I wrapped my arms around him and started fucking him back. It was time for me to come. He went faster and so did I. Within moments, we both had come.

He sat me down on my feet and I watched as my juices flowed down my inner thighs. We both cleaned up before exiting the bathroom. I thanked him and we exchanged numbers. He told me to call him anytime I wanted to do that again. I smiled as I walked away. *I might be calling your fine red ass tonight,* I thought to myself.

✳✳✳✳

I was sitting in a steaming hot bubble bath as I recollected my day. It was full of some extravagant activities, especially of the light skinned cutie whose name, I found out, was Leonard. He told me to call him Leo, though, because he was the king of the jungle. *Whatever the fuck that was supposed to mean.*

I finished up in the bath then I washed my body. I got out and towel dried before covering my body in Bath & Body Works sweet pea lotion. I went into my room butt naked and lay across my bed. It felt lovely to be able to do this without Jay's ass being here. I wish Mario was here. He would probably be sucking on my clit right about now. I was getting aroused just thinking about him. Before I could get deep into my thoughts, or touch on myself, my phone rang.

I grabbed it off the nightstand and looked at it the caller ID. It was Jessica.

"Hello?" I said once I answered.

"Hey, girl, what you doing? You in the house?"

"Yeah I am. What's wrong?"

"Bitch I will tell you when I get there. I already told Shannon to meet me over your house and bring some weed. I'm bringing a bottle of Ciroc."

"Cool. I will see y'all in a bit."

"Okay, babes."

I hung up the phone with Jessica and decided to put on clothes. Guess my personal time had to wait until later on. My girl needed me right now. I reached into my drawer and pulled out a pair of my PINK sweatpants and a t-shirt. I threw on some ankle socks and grabbed my phone and headed downstairs. I decided to just sit in the living room, since it was closer to the door.

I checked the time and it was nearing 9:30. I guess the ladies would be here soon since Jessica said it was urgent. I turned on the TV and flicked through the channels until I found Hell's Kitchen with Gordon Ramsay. He always made me laugh, the way he talked to people. Reminded me of how I am sometimes with my sarcasm. This was definitely a show I could binge watch all day and night.

I managed to watch another entire episode of Hell's Kitchen before I heard a knock at me door. I checked the time on my phone and it read 11:15. *These bitches is tripping,* I thought as I got up and walked to the door. I peeped through the peephole to make sure it was them. I had told Jay I wasn't gonna be home and I hoped that he wouldn't pop up or anything.

"You bitches don't keep up with the time?" I asked as they barged through the front door.

"Shut the hell up, Desi," Shannon said as she gave me a hug and kissed me on the cheek. Jessica did the same then we headed into the living room.

As we chatted about the TV show, we each rolled up a jay. After we rolled up, we poured liquor and took a couple shots to get the edge off a little.

"So, what's going on, Babes?" I asked Jessica.

"I'm just gonna cut straight to the point. That motherfucker Bryan cheating on me!" she yelled before taking another shot.

"Whoa, whoa, whoa, wait a minute. Are you serious, Jess?" I asked.

"Bitch! I caught the nigga in bed with the hoe."

"Exactly," Shannon said laughing as she hit the first jay and passed it to me.

"That's fucked up, man."

"Tell me about it," Jessica said.

"So, what are you gonna do?" I asked.

"I don't know."

"I say you get revenge on his ass," Shannon chimed in.

"And do what exactly?" Jess asked with raised eyebrows.

Shannon placed her hand on the back of Jessica's head and pushed her face closer to hers. She kissed her. But it wasn't one of those quick kisses. This was way more passionate. Just watching was making me hot. I watched a few seconds more before I joined in.

I grabbed a hold of Jess's titty and put the nipple in my mouth. I sucked on it and gently bit down on it. Shannon broke her kiss with Jess and started kissing me the same way. My panties instantly became wet. I leaned back against the chair and Jess removed my sweatpants from my body, exposing my naked flesh.

She put her face down between my thighs and started placing soft kisses to my pussy. I could feel my temperature rising as she began using the tip of her tongue to play with my clit. Shannon snatched my t-shirt off from over my head and began devouring my breasts. I grabbed the back of both of their heads, trying to push their heads deeper into my body.

"Let's go upstairs," I said in a soft tone. Flashbacks of my mother catching me and Jay filled my mind. And Lord knows I don't need that right now. We grabbed the liquor and headed upstairs to my bedroom to continue our rendezvous.

I bent Jess over on the bed and started licking her ass and fingering her hole. She moaned loudly and Shannon shut her up by putting two fingers in her mouth. Shannon leaned over Jessica and pushed my head deeper in her ass. I felt as if I was giving her a colonoscopy, my tongue was so far in.

"You still have your strap on, Desi?" Shannon asked me in a heavy breathing tone.

"Yeah. It's in that blue shoe box on the top shelf of my closet," I said, finally coming up for air.

She got up from the bed and went into the closet. She found the box and brought it over to the bed.

"You got two now?" she asked laughing.

"Yeah. The other one was on sale and I just had to get it."

"True shit."

She strapped on one and I strapped on the other. She stood in front of Jessica and shoved her dildo in her mouth. Jessica held that thing tight in her grasp and sucked it and licked it like it was the real deal. I got behind her and entered her pussy with mine as I simultaneously stuck my thumb in her asshole again She stiffened a little then relaxed again. I could hear her moaning on Shannon's dildo as I fucked her. Her juices were flowing and covering my toy.

I pulled out and lapped up her juices with my tongue. She came again and it dripped down my chin. This reminded me of the good old days when we would do this. I was so caught up in my thoughts, I didn't notice that Shannon wanted to rotate. We switched positions and continued taking care of Jess.

The night grew later and later as we took care of each other's sexual needs. The last thing I remembered was Jessica thanking us for helping her relieve some stress and getting back at Bryan for cheating. Afterward, I got under the covers with my besties and fell into a deep sleep.

I might have been looking peaceful as I slept, but in actuality my mind was racing a mile a minute. *I wondered what was in store for me tomorrow* I thought.

Chapter Twelve

Caught in the Act

The next morning had come and I felt rejuvenated and some more. As I stretched in the bed, I accidentally hit Shannon in the back of her head. *Damn, I forgot they were here.*

"There was an easier way to get my attention, Desi, damn," she said, turning over with her phone in her hand.

"My bad, Babes."

"Can y'all bitches be quiet? I'm trying to sleep," Jessica said turning towards us with her eyes closed.

We laughed and talked louder until she got up with us. I handed them both a long shirt to put on and we went downstairs to make breakfast. We agreed on making eggs, bacon, sausage, grits, and biscuits.

We were having fun cooking breakfast. We had the radio playing on WPGC 95.5 and we danced around. This how we used to be when we were in high school. I miss being a teenager. I was much freer and didn't have any responsibility. *Where was a time machine when you needed it?*

Our fun had been distracted by the sound of the doorbell.

"I'll be right back," I said to my friends and went to the door. I didn't even bother looking through the peephole. I just opened the door.

"Hello, are you Desiree Logan?" the sheriff asked me.

I started to say no because I didn't know what he was here for. However, I uttered "yes."

"You have been served," he said, handing me a big envelope and walking back down the stairs.

"What the fuck?" I said aloud once I closed the door and headed back into the kitchen.

"What's wrong?" my friends asked in unison.

"Where the hell is my phone?" I said looking around on the kitchen island and on the table under the mail. "I think I left it upstairs," I said as I ran up the stairs.

"What is wrong?" Shannon asked, running behind me. Jessica turned off the food and followed in tow. By the time she got upstairs, I was on the phone.

"Are you fucking kidding me right now, Ma? Seriously?" I yelled into the phone.

"Seriously what, Desiree?"

"You went and got a restraining order on me to stay away from my own motherfucking child?"

"I did, didn't I?" she said. Then she had the nerve to be laughing in my ear.

"You will not win and take my daughter from me you evil bitch," I said through clenched teeth. "You will regret everything you are doing."

"You were my biggest regret, Desiree."

I froze.

Did she really just say that? Tears started to fill my eyes and my phone dropped from my hands. I could hear the smashing sound of the glass break on my iPhone.

I ran to the bathroom and threw up my stomach. My friends quickly came to my aid. They held my hair back and they hugged me tight in their arms. They told me everything was gonna be okay, But it wasn't and it seemed like shit was getting worse by the day. I need to smoke. I need a nigga right now. Hell, I will even take a drink. Whatever could numb my pain, I wanted it.

****

After Shannon and Jessica left, I was moping around the house. They managed to force feed me before they left, because they knew I wasn't going to eat anything. I went upstairs to my room to figure out my thoughts.

As I sat on the edge of my bed, I caught a glimpse of myself in the mirror. I was looking raggedy as fuck. My hair was all over the place. My face looked as though I haven't slept in days. There was no life in my eyes as I stared at my reflection. I was empty. I decided to try this prayer thing again. Everybody keeps

Nymphopervtress 2: Degenerate

telling me God works miracles, but I don't believe them. Right now, I had no love for God.

What kind of God would put me through this kind of hell? What kind of God would rip a child from their mother's arms?

"What the fuck, God? Why are you doing this to me? Why? Why? Why?" I screamed at the top of my lungs, but, of course, nobody responded.

As my tears ran down my face, I got down beside my bed and cried up to heaven. "Lord, I need my baby back. I need my husband back, but I can't shake these addictions. I want to have my cake and eat it too. Dear God, what do I do?" I laid down on my bed in a fetal position. I held my pillow between my legs and I held it tight as I cried myself to sleep.

I had awakened in the middle of the night. I looked at the clock and it was nearing 2 in the morning. I grabbed my phone and checked it. I had one missed call from Jay and I was in a group text with Jessica and Shannon. There were 30 unread messages. *What the fuck were these bitches yapping about?* I thought. I read through all the messages and never responded. They weren't even talking about nothing important as usual.

I got up from the bed and went to the bathroom. I washed my hands and then went downstairs to get something to drink. My mouth was as dry as cotton. I made it to the kitchen and grabbed me an orange soda from the fridge. I popped the top and it was damn near gone with one gulp.

I tossed the can into the trash and was heading back upstairs when I heard someone jiggling my door knob. My heart jumped into my throat and then dropped to my stomach. I panicked, because my gun was upstairs. I hurried to the front door and grabbed the baseball bat from behind the door. I slowly crept back into the kitchen and the person was still there. Unbeknownst who it could be, I decided to open the door. I stepped closer to the back door. I took a couple of quick deep breaths then snatched the door open and swung.

"Ah, fuck. What the hell?" I heard the hooded figure yell. Whoever it was got hit a few more times with my aluminum bat until I saw that they could barely move. I grabbed them by the back of their hoodie and turned them over.

"Are you fucking kidding me?" I said as I stood over top of them.

✳✳✳✳

I threw an ice pack at Jay's head and it fell into his lap.

"What the hell you do that for, Desiree?" he asked, grabbing his head.

"Because you're a fucking asshole. Jay. Why the fuck were you trying to break in my fucking house?"

"I didn't think you were home and I was gonna sneak in and be waiting upstairs for you."

118   Nymphopervtress 2: Degenerate

"Nigga, are you fucking insane? That would have got you shot. Indefinitely. You should've just called with your dumbass."

"Whatever, man."

He continued to hold the cold compress on his head as I made me a quick sandwich. After I finished eating, I pulled my shirt over my head and dropped it to the floor. I walked over to him and he watched me as my titties bounced up and down. I stood in front of him and took his hand into mine. I placed it between my legs so he could feel the wetness that was forming. I sucked my juices from his fingertips and walked away.

He got up off the stool and followed behind me. I didn't even make it up the stairs good before he picked me up and laid me down on the steps. He pulled his dick out through the hole in his jeans and stuck it inside me. It was feeling good and bad at the same time. Those steps were killing my fucking back but I let it slide because I needed that meat right now. After he came, I quickly pushed him off top of me and got up. I walked the rest of the way to my bedroom and got in the bed. Moments later he joined me. I looked at the time and it was nearing four in the morning. I closed my eyes and within seconds I was asleep.

The sound of an alarm going off startled me. I jumped up out my sleep. I turned and saw Jay. I shook him awake.

"What's wrong, baby?" he asked as he stretched and threw his arms across my legs.

"Your phone is going off, nigga. Turn it off."

He turned around and turned it off. "That's just the alarm I set when I come over here."

"What the hell you talking 'bout?" I asked.

"I rather show you than tell you," he replied. He pushed me back onto the bed and positioned himself in front of me. He went down on me and began licking and sucking on my pussy. I grabbed his head and arched my back. I was trying to push his head inside my body. I was so caught up that I didn't even hear somebody come in the room until it was too late.

✳✳✳✳✳

"What the fuck is going on in here?" Mario screamed at the top of his lungs. Jay and I froze. My eyes grew large, as if a ghost had just appeared before me. In a blink of an eye, Mario came rushing toward us. Jay tried his best to get off top of me, but he wasn't quick enough.

Mario grabbed him by his throat and snatched him off the bed. He punched him three times in the face, and then dropped him to the floor. He kicked him in the stomach several times before placing his foot on his head and stepping on it. I sat there motionless for a while before trying to jump to Jay's aide. Bad move. I jumped off the bed and ran over and tried pushing Mario off Jay.

"Oh, you taking up for this nigga, Desiree?" Mario yelled at me. He grabbed my throat with one hand and pressed his foot harder on Jay's head. I was trying my best to remove his grip from my neck. My vision was becoming blurry and I couldn't breathe. My knees were getting weak and my life began to flash before my eyes.

"Bitch you ain't getting off that easily," he said, tossing me across the room. He picked me up and held me in the air by my throat before slinging me across the room like a fucking rag doll. I screamed the entire way. My body hit the dresser and the TV fell and hit the floor. Before I even fell to the floor good, Mario was on my ass. He came over there and pummeled me. Punches were going to my head, my face, my back and my stomach as I screamed more. Then he continued with kicks. I looked over to Jay and he wasn't moving. I didn't move anymore. My screams were falling on deaf ears. I'm not even sure how long he was beating on me, because after a while I completely blacked out.

✳✳✳✳

I could hear low beeps surrounding me. I struggled to open my eyes but they wouldn't open wide like they did normally. The beeps became louder as my hearing adjusted. Through the slits of my eyes, I saw two figures standing around me. I tried to talk but no words would form and come out. I tried to move my hand to signal them, but it was also a failed attempt. I let out a small sigh and all eyes turned to me.

"She's awake," I heard somebody say.

"How you feeling, Hun?" I knew that was Jessica. She's the only person that called people that, so that means the other person was Shannon.

I moved my fingers again to show them that I was okay. My vision became clearer but I still couldn't open my eyes. I watched as they both came to each side of the bed and held my hands. I gave them a tight squeeze and a tear fell from my eye. It caused pain as it ran down my cheek.

"Don't cry, Desi," Shannon said. "Everything gonna be okay. I'm gonna go and get the nurse," she said before leaving out the room.

"You're gonna be fine, Sis," Jessica reassured me. "We almost lost you, but God was watching over you. Do you remember what happened to you?"

I thought back to the last event that I remembered. That last thing I remembered was Mario stomping a mud hole in my ass. I saw as Shannon came back in the room followed by a nurse.

"Good evening, Mrs. Davis. How are you doing? I'm your nurse, Candace. Let me just check your vitals," she said. She placed two fingers on my wrist and looked at her watch as she checked my pulse. She took her stethoscope from around her neck and placed the ear tips in her ears. She pressed the cold diaphragm onto my chest and the cool sensation caused slight pain. "Well the good thing is her vitals are good. Better than when we she first got here," she said to Jessica and Shannon.

"Can you tell us what happened to her?" I heard Shannon say.

Nymphopervtress 2: Degenerate

"Sorry but I can only discuss that with her family."

"Bitch we are her damn family," Jessica said, coming around to the other side of the bed. The nurse backed up a couple steps and cleared her throat.

"Well, um, like I said she will be fine. We are not really sure what happened. Someone had called an ambulance when they found her on the sidewalk. She was thrown in a trash heap completely naked and covered in blood and bruises."

"Oh my God," I could hear Jessica cry out. I could see Shannon hold Jess as she cried.

"Is that all?" Shannon asked.

"Um, there was another person. A man. He was also in the heap of trash next to her naked and covered in blood and bruises. The paramedics couldn't revive him, though, and he was pronounced dead at the scene. That's all I have right now," she said as she retreated toward the door.

"Thank you," Shannon said. "We're gonna go to the cafeteria, Babes. We'll be right back," she said to me. I tried my best to nod in agreement. I watched as they left the room.

Oh, my goodness. Jay was dead and it was all my fault. I started to cry. The tears were burning my skin, but at this moment it didn't matter. Because of me, somebody was dead. He didn't deserve that, but right now, I couldn't do anything. I was starting to feel dizzy. It was probably from the meds. Maybe from the guilt. I was not sure, but I wanted to escape. I closed my eyes back and dozed back off.

Chapter Thirteen

The Spot

Three weeks had gone by before I was released from the hospital. The nurse came into the room with my discharge papers and some crutches. She told me I would have this cast and crutches for at least another month. This was gonna be bullshit; I could already tell.

Once I was in the car with Shannon and Jessica. They took me by my house. They were against it the entire ride, but I needed clothes. We pulled up and I didn't see Mario's car outside. *Maybe that's a good thing,* I thought to myself as I thought back on the last time I saw him. I grabbed my crutches and my girls helped me out the car. They walked on each side of me as I made my way to the front door.

I handed my keys to Jessica. She tried the house key but it wasn't working. That was odd. Maybe she put it in wrong. I took the keys from her and tried to open it myself. It still wouldn't budge.

"This motherfucker done changed the locks," Jessica yelled.

Nymphopervtress 2: Degenerate

"It's okay, Jess. It's fine," I said, trying to calm her down.

"Like hell it is," Shannon said. "We going in here to get your shit like we said and we are taking you to Jessica's house."

"How we gonna get in genius?" Jessica asked.

"The same way I get in my mama house. Through the motherfucking window, Bitches," she replied, walking to the back of the house.

I couldn't go, so I told them I would wait in the car. I told them to grab my gun in my spot in the kitchen too if they could. I watched as they both went through the gate towards to side window. They remembered I always kept that window unlocked in case of emergencies.

I could feel myself getting dazed from the meds. I tried my best to keep my eyes open, but my medication was winning this battle. I snapped out if the daze quickly when I heard I car door slam shut. I peered through the back window only to see Mario and some bitch getting out. I started fuming. I watched as he walked up to the car and looked through the windows. Lucky for me the windows were pitch black tint and he couldn't see anything at all. If I had my gun, I probably would have killed them both.

They made their way up the stairs and into the house. I started panicking and praying that he wouldn't see my girls in there. Only God knows what he would do to them. Would he really kill them like he did Jay? Or would he beat them near death like he did me? While I was pondering my thoughts, I hadn't even noticed Shannon and Jessica creeping from the side of the house with my belongings. They got closer and I popped the locks. They quickly got in without being noticed and we sped off. I breathed a sigh of relief as we hit the corner. They filled me in on how intense it had gotten when they heard him pull up and they had to rush the process. We all laughed at the situation, but I was grateful they didn't get hurt. I don't know how I would have reacted.

✳✳✳✳

We arrived at Jessica's house and they helped me to the guest room. It was a little weird being in here because I have only slept in here once; and I was intoxicated at the time, but no worries.

"So, like I said, you can stay here as long as you need to. Once you heal up, we can help you find a job and an apartment for you and Zaniyah," Jessica said.

"My mother will never give her back to me," I said with a cracked-up voice.

"Yes, she will," Shannon said, sitting on the bed. "You just gotta have faith and God will show you the way."

Jessica and I made eye contact with one another then at Shannon. "Oh, my gosh, you never talk about God, Shannon," Jessica replied. I started laughing at the way she was talking.

"You know what? I can say something positive every now and then. Fuck you bitches," she said, v storming out the room. We fell out laughing.

We all chilled and watched movies for a while until Jessica's new boyfriend, Jeremy, had gotten there. I could feel negative energy as soon as he walked in and smoke to Shannon. She told us she had to go. She gave us both a kiss on the cheek then jetted. I wasn't sure what that was about at all. It was my first time meeting him and I thought he was cool.

Later that night, I was tossing and turning. I couldn't sleep for the life of me. I tried sleeping a variety of ways, but nothing worked for me. I decided to get up and get some water to take one of my muscle relaxants. I didn't feel like being bothered with the crutches, so I just limped out the room to the kitchen. I decided to use the wall to balance myself the way to the kitchen. Once I got there, I saw Jeremy walking around the kitchen. He was talking on the phone in a hushed tone. I leaned on the opposite wall and listened closely.

"Yeah, man. I told you she would never expect anything. Bro, I know. Trip I know what the fuck you said do. No, I haven't slept with her yet. I will let you know when the time is right to break in. Her home girl here. I don't know why, and then she got a son. I don't want anything to happen to him or her. I'm not fucking playing. I'm gonna hit you up tomorrow." I couldn't believe my ears. He was trying to set up Jessica to get robbed. I had to tell her, but I didn't know when. I knew for damn sure I had to tell her soon though. As I was about to make an appearance in the kitchen, I bumped into him.

"Oh hey, Desiree, right?" he asked.

"Yeah that's right," I snapped.

"What's wrong with you?" he asked, laughing.

"I heard you on the phone, Jeremy. Who the fuck is Trip? Why they trying to break in here?"

"Yo, you are tripping. Maybe you need to take your meds."

"I know what the fuck I heard, nigga. I'm telling Jessica what the hell is going on right now," I said as I tried to limp away. He grabbed me by my arm and pulled me back. A crucial pain ran through my leg as it hit the cabinet.

"You ain't gonna tell her a motherfucking thing. You hear me? She ain't gonna believe you anyway," he said, smiling.

"I'm her best friend. She will believe me."

"Go ahead and see. When bitches get dick, their thinking process gets screwed up. So, go ahead and tell her. It's my word against yours. Think about it." Those were his last words before he released my arm and walked away.

I was now left with my thoughts. He was right though. Females did act crazy when dick was involved in the equation. I grabbed a bottle of water and limped back to the guest room. I sat on the bed, sulking as I took my medicine. I laid down and thought out how I would tell Jessica. I knew it was gonna break her, but I had to let her know. She would believe me. Wouldn't she?

The next morning at breakfast, I just sat at the table staring at Jeremy. If looks could kill, I swear that nigga would be as good as dead. I wanted to tell Jessica right now, but I didn't. I couldn't. Her son was there and he didn't need to hear or witness anything. Lucky for him, this wasn't the place or the time. Eventually he had to leave for work and I was reluctant. Jessica and I talked for a little bit before she had to step away to take her son outside to the bus stop. I took this opportunity to try and call Mario. I don't know why; I just wanted to call him. I called his cell phone and it went to voicemail as soon as it started ringing. I hung up and dialed again and the same thing happened. I waited a couple seconds and tried for a third time. This time, an automated voice told me that the person couldn't be reached. *This motherfucker blocked me?* I gave up and called the house number. He would have to answer it, because we didn't have a caller ID. Before I could dial the number, Jessica was coming back inside. I slammed the phone on the table as she approached me.

"Is everything okay, Desi?" she asked, staring at me with a worried look on her face.

"Yeah. Yeah, I'm fine, Jess," I replied, stammering over my words.

"Are you sure?"

"Yes. I'm just feeling a little woozy from those meds."

"Let me help you to your room."

"Okay."

I leaned on her as she helped me limp to the room. She sat me up on the bed and propped my leg up. She put a pillow behind my back then handed me the remote control. I wanted to blab right then and there, but I didn't. How do you even start out telling someone something like that? I would figure it out before it was too late, that's for sure. She left out the room and left to go to the store. She said that she'd be back in a couple of hours. We hugged and she was gone.

Once again, I was left alone. I grabbed my cell phone to see if Mario had called me or texted back. Both the message thread and call history were empty. I tried calling one more time, and yet again, I got connected to the automated message. *I still didn't try the house phone yet,* I remembered. Peeping through the blinds, I made sure Jessica's car was gone. Just in case he answered, I didn't want her to still be here and happen to hear us talking. I took a deep breath then dialed our house number. The phone rang six times. I was getting ready to hang up before the machine came on, but, surprisingly, someone picked up. I froze for a second as I listened to a female answer the phone saying, "hello?"

"Uh, yeah, who the fuck is this?" I snapped.

"Who the fuck is this?" she snapped back.

"Bitch don't worry about that. Who the fuck are you and why the fuck are you answering my phone? Better yet, what the fuck are you doing in my motherfucking house?"

"Your house? Bitch please. This is my nigga house."

"No, Bitch, you're sadly mistaken. That is me, my daughter, and my husband's house."

"Ohhh, this must be Desiree," she said in a silly tone. "Mario said that you would probably be calling and he told me to give you a message."

"What fucking message?" I yelled into the speaker.

"He told me to tell you to die."

"What?" I asked. I was taken back a little by what she said.

"You heard me. He said tell that hoe ass bitch to die."

"Look, Bitch. I'm gonna tell your ass one time to get the fuck out of my house before I drag your ass out."

"Oh, Boo, bye. I'm not scared of you. You lost your chance and now I'm the queen of this castle. And when he wins custody of y'all daughter, she's gonna be calling me 'Mommy," she said, laughing maniacally in my ear.

"Fuck you, hoe."

"Naw, I'm good, but your husband can damn sure fuck me whenever he wants."

"I'm gonna kill your ass."

"Good luck," she said before hanging up the phone on me.

I was fuming. I was beyond pissed right now. That bitch was gonna have to see me. I tried calming down moments later because my chest was starting to hurt. I needed a release. I needed to call Emmitt. He would take care of me and this pain. I had to escape, and I mean like now. I dialed his number and he picked up on the second ring.

Nymphopervtress 2: Degenerate

"Hey, baby girl," he said as soon as he answered.

"Hey, Emmitt. Where are you?"

"I'm at one of the houses right now. Why, what's up?"

"I need some of that good good."

"True. You mobile now?"

"No," I replied sadly.

"Well, if you can get one of those rideshare joints, you can go to my man, Jeff, over there on 49th."

"I don't know him, Emmitt."

"He cool, Desiree. He can get you right."

"Okay, if you say so," I replied like a spoiled brat. "Send me the address please."

"No doubt," he said before hanging up. He sent me the address within seconds. I ordered an Uber and saw that it was twenty minutes away. That was perfectly fine because it would take me at least ten minutes to get dressed and seven minutes to make it outside to the curb. Once I eventually made it outside, my Uber driver was pulling up. She helped me into the front seat and put my crutches into the trunk. I told her I didn't want to talk so she obliged. We listened to music the entire twenty-five-minute drive. After a while, I started fidgeting around in my seat and getting antsy. I was ready to get my fix. I looked at her phone and saw that we were ten minutes away. I beamed with excitement inside. I was so close to the destination that I could taste it.

Once we arrived, she looked around cautiously. I told her this was the right spot. She grabbed my crutches from the trunk and helped me out the car. We said our 'goodbyes' and she drove off. She was definitely getting five stars, plus a tip. I used my crutches as an aide as I entered inside the rundown building. I saw from a distance people being served and a couple people sitting on the side getting their fix. They were all looking zombified and I wanted to join them. I limped over towards who I guessed was Jeff. I walked up to him and he stepped back a little.

"Ay, yo, don't walk up on me like that."

"Like what?" I asked him.

"Shawty what'chu want?"

"Look, nigga, Emmitt sent me here for some blow. Now either give it to me or I'm leaving."

"Oh yeah. It's all good, ma. He told me you would be stopping by. How much you need?"

"I don't know. I need the pure stuff."

"Oh, you rocking like that? I got an eight ball for $300. It's pure quality. You want that?"

"$300?! Nigga, are you serious? That's high," I yelled.

"And your ass trying to get high. So, what you wanna do?"

"I want it, but I only got $200."

I watched as he looked me over. "You can pay the other $100 another way," he said licking his lips.

He was ugly as fuck. He looked like a cross between comedian Michael Blackson and Flavor Flav. I really needed that coke, though. I needed it badly. I nodded my head in agreement. Then this nigga started cheesing, looking like Eddie Murphy. All I

Nymphopervtress 2: Degenerate

could do was shake my head as he took me by the hand and led me out the door. He scooped me up in his arms and carried me over to the next abandoned building. There was a ratty old mattress lying in the middle of the floor. It looked like people had pissed and threw up all over it. I examined it a little more closely and noticed a dark, dried red stain. *Was that blood?* Oh fuck no. I was out of here.

"I changed my mind," I said hesitantly.

"What you mean you changed your mind?"

"Can I just give you the $200 for the cocaine? I really need it," I said pleading.

"Oh naw, Shawty, you gonna give me all of my money. Now you can either give it to me willing or I'm gonna take it," he said, grabbing my sweatpants and yanking them down.

I tried to fight him off, but because of my bummed leg, I managed to fall over onto the filthy mattress. Out the corner of my eye, I watched as he removed his shoes and jeans, exposing his Calvin Klein boxers. He didn't take those off as he came over to me. He flipped me onto my back and sat on my chest. He smacked his limp dick on my chin and rubbed it across my lips until it hardened. It was funky and smelly and smelled like salt and vinegar chips. I was moving my head back and forth so he couldn't stick it in my mouth. He pressed down on my forehead and held my head in place with one hand while he used the other hand to shove his dick in my mouth. *Yuck!* It tasted as bad as it smelled. The smell, mixed with the taste, almost made me throw up in my mouth. He

Nymphopervtress 2: Degenerate

was humping my face so fast. I could feel his dick touching the back of throat, triggering my gag reflexes. I counted the entire to time my attack just right. As soon as he pushed it deep down my throat, I bit down hard like I was a fucking pit bull. He screamed out and my lock got tighter. I was so caught up in the revenge that I didn't see the right blow coming at my face. The impact was so intense I let go of my hold and I swear I heard something in my face break.

"Oh, that's how you wanna play, you junkie bitch? I got something for your ass," he said. He stopped straddling my chest and got on top of me. He rammed his hard dick into my dry pussy. It felt like being a virgin all over again. I could feel the skin rip as he entered inside of me. He was rapidly pumping his dick in and out of me. I could feel my pussy start to get wet. I didn't want her to get wet. I didn't want this to be happening, but I couldn't stop my body's actions. It may have been feeling good to her but it was definitely not making me happy. After a while, the fucking stopped. This trifling motherfucker had the audacity to pull out and jerk his dick right in my face. I laid there as he busted his nut and assaulted my face with his cum. He smeared it all over my face with his dick and wiping the rest of the residue on my shirt. He stood up and put his stuff back. He reached down in his pocket and threw the drugs at me. He turned around to walk out the door. He turned back to me and said, "Can't wait to see you again." He left through the door opening and I could hear him on the laughing as he left out the house.

I could have killed him, but he did what he said. He let me give him the $200 and some pussy for the eight ball. I grabbed it and scrambled to sit on the bed. I sat comfortably in the middle of the lewd, nasty, stained mattress. I pulled out my dollar bill and a folded-up piece of paper. I straightened up the product and got ready to scratch this damn itch. I swiftly snorted up the first line. Then another. And another. Before I knew it, I was halfway through. I laughed to myself as I saw how much was gone just in that little amount of time. I laid back on the bed to rest my nerves. The drug was running all through my system right now. It felt as though an entire mountain of bricks had been lifted off my shoulders. I was at peace for now. I knew eventually I had to stop soaring on cloud nine and get back to reality. Before I did have to board the plane back to earth, I wanted to enjoy all the worry-free time that I could. My phone started ringing and I looked at the caller ID. It was Mario. I silenced it and put it back beside me. If I wasn't in this state of mind, I probably would have answered, but since I was high, fuck Mario and that little slut that he had. I was gonna kill both of those motherfuckers. My phone began ringing again. It was Shannon. I didn't wanna talk to her ass neither. I was tired of everybody always pretending to care; like they actually gave a shit about me and my baby's well-being. Why the fuck people can't just leave me alone? I thought about Zaniyah. She was so pretty. She reminded me of myself when I was a little girl. So innocent. So pure. She didn't deserve any of this, but it was my mother's fault. I think her and Mario were in cahoots. That's what

Nymphopervtress 2: Degenerate

it was. Those backstabbing motherfuckers were against me all this time. Just thinking about this caused tears to stream down my face. I just laid there thinking about how much my life has changed in these past six months.

Chapter Fourteen

Officer Dion

"She's still not answering the damn phone," Shannon said to Jessica.

"Oh my God. What the fuck?!" Jessica yelled. "We done called her ass fifteen times, and she knew it was us calling. Her ass kept sending us to voicemail. Where the fuck could she be?"

"You think she went back to Mario?"

"Hell no, Shannon. I think she done learned her lesson."

"You sure about that, Jess? You remember she went back to his ass that night he tried to run her ass over with her own motherfucking car."

"He was drunk, Shan."

"So that makes the shit okay? Are you kidding me?"

"I guess it doesn't hurt to check," Jessica said, grabbing her keys.

"Right," Shannon said in agreement as she checked her pockets to make sure her hunting knife was there.

"What's that for?"

"Protection."

"Girl, bye," Jessica said, rolling her eyes.

As they were headed out the door, Jeremy was walking in. "Hey, baby," he said to Jessica. "What's up, Shannon?"

"Fuck you, Nigga," she said, bumping him as she headed towards Jessica's car.

"What the fuck is that about?" he asked Jessica.

"Baby, I don't know, but look, an emergency came up, so I will be back," she said, kissing his lips and jogging to her car.

"What emergency?" he yelled from the door.

"I'll tell you later," she yelled back. She hopped in the car and they sped off down the street. They drove over the speed limit to make it Mario's house in a timely manner. When they pulled up, they saw Mario's car outside. They both hopped out the car and headed to the front porch. Instead of knocking on the door like civilized people, they were banging like they were the police. Instead of Mario answering the door, a pretty redbone answered. She wasn't wearing any clothes, but was wearing one of Desiree's negligees. They recognized because it was the one they had gotten her for a wedding gift.

"Can I help you, Bitches?" she said, snapping her neck.

"Bitch, who the fuck is you and where the fuck is Mario?" Shannon asked, jumping in the girl's face.

"Bitch if you don't back up out my face you gonna get your ass whooped," she said, pushing Shannon back a couple of inches on the porch. Without hesitation, Jessica punched the girl and the entered the house. She grabbed the girl by her throat and Shannon stood behind her in case she tried to run.

"Now we're gonna ask your ass again. Where is Mario?"

"He's upstairs," she said with the little air she could breathe. Jessica threw her across the floor and headed up the stairs. Shannon ripped the lingerie from the girl's body before kicking her in the face with her Timberland boots. She jogged up the steps so she could be in tow with Jessica as she hit the top step.

"Yo, Bianca, who was at the door?" Mario yelled. Jessica and Shannon kicked in the bedroom door and startled him. He threw his hands up in the air then dropped them when he saw who it was. "What y'all hoes want?" he asked as he laid back on the bed like he previously was. Jessica and Shannon walked more into the room and stood beside each other. "I guess y'all can't fucking hear clearly. What do y'all want?" he asked again.

"Where the fuck is Desiree?" Shannon yelled at the top of her lungs.

"Yo, I don't know who you think you raising your voice at, but you better chill, you little dyke bitch."

"I got your 'dyke bitch'," Shannon said before pulling out her hunting knife. She had it down at her side in a tight grasp. Mario let out a hearty laugh as he looked at her.

"What the hell you gonna do with that little knife, Bitch?" he asked, jumping off the bed. Both girls quickly took a couple steps back. Without a blink, Jessica pulled out a gun from behind her back.

"Where the hell did you get that?" Shannon asked her.

"I borrowed it from Desiree."

"Do you even know how to use that big boy, little girl?" Mario asked, taking an inch towards them. As he did so, they stepped an inch back.

"Look, Mario," Jessica began as she took the safety off the gun and pointed it at him. "We just wanna know where our friend is. We didn't come here for trouble."

"I don't know where that hoe is," he said, crossing his arms across his chest.

"Hoe? That hoe is your wife and the mother of your child," Shannon said, stepping in his face like she had an entire army standing behind her.

"So, what the fuck does that mean? She fucked around with another nigga and she had to learn the hard way."

"You're not anything but a wasteful piece of shit," Shannon said before spitting in Mario's face and walking away. Mario just laughed and wiped his face. Jessica still had the gun pointed at him as she backed out the room and caught up to Shannon. They were heading down the stairs when they heard Mario rummaging through some drawers. They jumped from the fourth step as a bullet zipped right past them. They jumped over Bianca as they ran out the door. They could hear Mario trailing behind them down the stairs. They made it to the car and locked the doors. Jessica was frantically panicking as she tried to find the right key to put in the ignition. They looked toward the house and saw Mario running out with his gun in the air.

"Hurry up, Jess," Shannon yelled at her.

"I'm trying. Stop fucking yelling at me," she said.

"He's about to shoot, Bitch!" Shannon yelled again. Just as Mario let a round out, the two women were able to duck down. In the midst, Jessica found the proper key and started the car. Not even picking her head up from her lap, she shifted the car into drive and floored that motherfucker. Several bullets ricocheted off her car as they sped down the block and out of sight. Once they got a good distance away from Mario's house, they pulled into a gas station to catch their breath.

"So, what the fuck do we do now, Shannon?" Jessica asked as she repeatedly hit the steering wheel.

"I don't know, Jess," Shannon replied. She went into a deep thought and then she had an idea. "Quick, get your phone out."

"Why?" she said.

"Just give me the damn phone," Shannon replied, snatching the phone from her hands. She tapped on the phone a couple times before yelling out, "Got it!"

"What? What you got?"

"Desiree's location. She over on 49th."

"49th?! There's nothing over there but a bunch of rundown houses. That's where all the pipe heads be staying at. What the fuck is she doing over there?"

"You just answered your own question," Shannon said sarcastically.

"Fuck you, Shan," Jessica said, putting the car in gear again.

"Maybe later. Right now, we gotta go find our girl."

They arrived outside the building about thirty minutes later. They gently closed the car doors. They held each other's hands as they ascended the stairs. They stayed so close to one another that one would have thought they were Siamese twins or something. They didn't wanna touch the walls or the people. One man walked up on Jessica and touched her and she freaked out. She screamed so loud that the other dope fiends were stirring awake. She punched the guy in the face and he fell into the moldy wall.

"We gotta hurry and get up out of here, Shannon," she said in a manic tone. They both went from room to room, looking for Desiree. They reached the last door at the end of the hall. It was closed and couldn't be pushed open. Shannon instructed Jessica to step out the way. She jogged to the middle of the hallway then ran full speed back to the door. She kicked the door in and it fell completely off the rusty hinges. "Desi," Jessica said as she ran over to her unconscious friend.

Shannon ran over to assist her. They both lightly slapped her face, trying to wake her up, but it worked to no avail. Shannon looked over Desiree and saw the semen that was stained between her legs. Her eyes went up to her arm and she saw a rubber band tied tightly around it with a needle hanging out. She snatched the needle out of her skin and tossed it across the room.

"Damn, Desi. What are you doing to yourself?" Jessica asked as she stroke Desiree's hair. Tears fell from her eyes and dropped onto Desiree's face.

Nymphopervtress 2: Degenerate

"Look, we don't have time for that, Jess. We have to get her out of here and cleaned up."

"You're right," she said in agreement. Both women grabbed each arm of their best friend and carried her out of the house. They got her out to the car and laid her down nicely in the backseat. They hopped in and they drove away.

✳✳✳✳

"What the fuck happened to her?" Jeremy yelled as he burst up in the bathroom.

"Can you lower your voice, Nigga?" Shan shot back.

"Right, Jeremy. Can you just chill, please?" Jessica said. He sucked his teeth and stormed out the bathroom like a spoiled child. Shannon and Jessica just exchanged looks and rolled their eyes.

They still hadn't been able to wake Desiree up fully. They had her in a warm bath right now washing the filth from her skin. They poured water over her head with a pitcher so they could wash the horrible odors from her hair. Shannon grabbed a bottle of Crème of Nature shampoo and doused Desiree's hair with it. She massaged it into her scalp and made sure not to miss a spot. They repeated this four times. Once they started washing her face with the warm rag, she jumped up.

"What's going on?" she said, splashing the water around.

"Calm down, Desi. It's just us," Jess said, reaching to grab her.

"Where am I?" I asked.

"You're in Jessica's bath tub," Shannon replied.

"How did I get here?"

"Hun, we found you in an abandoned building."

"Yeah. With a needle hanging out of your arm," Shannon added.

"Oh, wow. I'm sorry," I said.

"Is that all the fuck you can say, Desiree? Huh? I thought you were done with this shit? Why are you throwing your whole fucking life away on this stupid shit?" Shannon ranted.

"Calm down," Jess said in a soft tone.

"No, fuck that. I'm not gonna be calm. I'm not gonna sit here and watch my best friend kill herself with drugs. If you wanna be stupid, be stupid by your goddamn self." Shannon stormed out of the bathroom.

"Shan, come back," Jess yelled.

"I'm sorry," I said as I started to cry.

"Don't be sorry, Desi. You're under a lot of stress and people deal with their stress in many different ways, but I'm telling you this is not an acceptable choice."

"Do I have to leave?"

"No, crazy. I'm gonna help you get through this."

"Thank you," I said, reaching out to hug her. She threw her arms around my wet torso and squeezed me tight.

Nymphopervtress 2: Degenerate

"You know what?" Shannon said as she came back into the bathroom. "I'm glad your mother did take Zaniyah from your ass. You're fucking pitiful."

"Shannon!"

"Don't do that, Jess. Don't you do it. She needs to hear this. You are a disgrace of a human being and you should have never been able to have a child. That sweet child has a fucking abusive father and a drug addict mother. That's a Steve Wilkos show idea. Don't fucking call me when her ass does this again. I'm washing my hands of her ass." She exited the bathroom again. This time I knew she wasn't coming back. The way that front door slammed, I knew she was sticking to her decision and neither me nor Jessica was gonna be able to change her mind.

Jessica helped me out of the bath and helped me to the room. She took off my old cast and checked my leg for me. She said it was, in the majority, healed, and that I didn't need to keep the cast on. She wrapped my foot in some ace bandage and gave me my nighttime medications. We were talking for a while and I dozed off in the middle of the conversation. I felt as she pulled the covers up over my body and kissed a motherly on my forehead. I just hoped that tomorrow would bring a better day for me. God knows I need something positive to happen.

I woke up the next day feeling like I got hit by a truck. I immediately took three of the pain pills. I checked my phone and saw several messages from both Shannon and Mario. I scrolled through Shannon's messages first. She just talked about how much she hated me and wished I would just go back to therapy and get help. She even went as far as to send me numbers and addresses for some rehab centers. I rolled my eyes and backed out of her thread. I went to Mario's. He was threatening me and tell me he was gonna kill me and he hoped that I die before he got ahold of me. Something about sending my girls over there to beat up his girlfriend. *This nigga tripping hard,* I thought to myself, but I am kind of glad they went over there and beat that bitch ass. They were true and loyal friends. Well, Shannon *was.* She didn't want anything more to do with me. I had a missed call from an unsaved number. The number wasn't familiar, but they did leave a message. I hit the visual voicemail button and listened:

"Good morning, Mrs. Davis. This is Judge Meyer from The District Family Court. You were supposed to be attending court yesterday morning and you did not show up. I also have on record that you have not been attending your court ordered classes. If you have any intentions on getting your daughter, err, Zaniyah Davis back, it is critical that you give me a call back as soon as possible to reschedule your hearing. I can be reached at 301-246-0945 extension 215. Thank you and have a great day."

Well that was just great. I missed court and now I have to reschedule. All this is just pure bullshit. I refuse to go to those damn drug classes. That shit is for people that have a problem with them. I don't have a problem with drugs. They are to help me cope with all this mess. If they had never taken my baby from me, I

147 Nymphopervtress 2: Degenerate

wouldn't be going through this shit anyway. It was Mario's fault for cheating and my mother's fault for taking Zaniyah from me. They are the reasons why I am using drugs in the first place. Speaking about drugs, I could use some right now. I searched through my clothes I had on yesterday, but my pockets were empty. Knowing Jessica and Shannon, they probably left them on purpose. I tried calling Emmitt. Just like Mario's phone the other day, I wasn't getting anything but automated messages. *Fuck!* I guess I would just have to settle for a cigarette. I searched through my purse until I found my cigarettes and my lighter. I limped all the way to the back porch so I could smoke in peace. Plus, I didn't want Jess to know I was up already. I reached the porch and quickly smoked my cigarette. It was pouring down raining and it had my mind at ease. I checked my phone to see what time it was, and it was eleven. I went back in the house to my room and called the judge back. She didn't answer, so I left an urgent message with her assistant. I decided to call my mother next and ask how Zaniyah was doing. She answered on the fifth ring.

"What you want, Child?" she said.

I took a deep breath before I flipped out on her. "I was just calling to see how Zaniyah's doing."

"She's fine," she replied sternly. "She's at school."

"How is she doing in school?"

"Just fine, Desiree."

"Do you have a problem with me?" I asked bluntly.

"Yeah I do. Have you gotten yourself clean yet?"

"No, ma'am," I replied sadly. She didn't even reply back as she hung up the phone in my ear. I tried calling back twice, but she didn't answer. *Oh well,* I thought. I got back up and went into the kitchen. Nobody was here, but Jessica had left a note telling me that my plate was in the microwave. I walked over to the microwave and pressed the button for one minute. As soon as it finished, I snatched it out the microwave and flopped down in a chair. As I was stuffing my face with pancakes, my phone rang. It was the judge. I forcefully swallowed the food before answering.

"Good morning. May I please speak with Mrs. Desiree Davis, please?" the lady on the phone said.

"This is she," I responded, gulping down some orange juice.

"Yes, how are you doing? This is Judge Meyer. I left you a voicemail this morning. Did you happen to get it?"

"Yes, ma'am, I did."

"Great. Well like I said in the voicemail, we had to reschedule your hearing for a later date. So, it was rescheduled to the first of September, so that will be next week. Does that work for you?"

"Yes, it does," I responded quickly.

"Okay, great. I am writing that down right now. Is there a reason why you did not attend yesterday?"

I thought about it, but I didn't wanna tell her I couldn't make it because I had an overdose. I just simply told her I had got the days mixed up.

"I'm not sure if that's a legitimate excuse, but I will put that in your file."

After a few more moments of talking to her, and she gave me a number to call, I hung up the phone. As soon as I hung up, I dialed the number. When the guy picked up the phone, as soon as he said, "thank you for calling Addiction Anonymous. This is Maurice. How may I assist you today?" I ended the call. I did not have an addiction and I did not need to be calling their asses. I wasn't gonna be getting help for anything right now, but I was gonna help myself to a nap.

✳✳✳✳

I could tell I was lying on a bed right now. The soft quilt that was underneath me and the soft bamboo pillows where my head rested were a dead giveaway, but I could not see anything due to the fact of me being blindfolded. I used my hearing senses to listen to my surroundings. I heard a door close slowly, and the twist of the lock. I could hear someone breathing hard as they came closer. I could feel their eyes fixated on me, exploring my entire body. They started with a slight foot rub. They planted sweet kisses on my toes. They moved up to my ankle, then up my leg, then my thigh. Their strong hands massaged my inner thighs, as they used their tongue to leave a trail of their DNA. They reached my sweet center and teased my clit through my panties. I panted heavily and begged for them to pull off my underwear and French kiss my kitty cat. I felt as they pulled my panties to the side. They used the tip of their tongue to lick my clit. Whoever it was knew just how to treat a woman's pussy. They started slow then intensified their speed. My body got hot all over and my juices trickled down my thigh. I arched my back as two fingers were inserted into my wetness. I came again. They removed their fingers and traced them across my lips. I used my tongue to sop up the juices. They got on top of me and braced myself for entry. From what I could tell, they were in the perfect position for thrusting. They inserted their entire dick in one motion and I moaned out loud. It wasn't like a regular fuck session. It was more intimate than that. This person was making love not only to my body but to my soul. They ran their fingertips down my collarbone all the way to the center of my neck.

They grabbed my neck and gently squeezed. I could feel the cum oozing from my pussy again. They placed their other hand around my throat and used both hands to squeeze a little tighter. It was making my body have instant convulsions. I had never had sex this intensely before, not even with Mario. Something changed. Their grip was getting tighter and my breathing was becoming shallow. I grabbed at their hands, trying to pull their fingers from around my throat. It just got worse. They pressed their thumbs into my neck. I waved my arms, reaching for their face to claw their eyes out. Before I could even think, my brain felt as though it was getting ready to shut down, and my breathing was lessening. My heart felt as though it was shrinking. I tried screaming out for help,

Nymphopervtress 2: Degenerate

but when I opened my mouth no sounds or words came out but I did however, manage to rip the blindfold from my eyes. When I did, I found that I was in the room alone. I was panting heavily and was trying my best to get my breathing under control. I was having the hardest time slowing my heartbeat down as I looked around the dark bedroom. "That was crazy as shit," I said aloud. I looked at the time on my phone and it was midnight. It was time to take my meds again, so I popped the pills in my mouth and chased them with a few gulps of water. I unlocked my phone and saw I had a text from both Mario and my mother. Because I didn't want to be bothered with either one of them, I decided to not even respond right now. Maybe in a few hours.

I laid back down and turned the TV on. I knew I wasn't gonna be able to go back to sleep if I didn't hear any noise. It was weird but I have been like that my entire life. My environment right now was just too still; if that makes sense. I couldn't hear any footsteps moving around, no cars riding up and down the street, and surprisingly, there weren't even any damn stray cats purring outside the window as they searched trash cans for food. I wish I could just go home, but I no longer had a home. I didn't have a job. I didn't have a husband, but the thing that saddened me the most was the fact that I no longer had my child. When my mother took her away from me, she had taken my heart right with her. Zaniyah was my everything, and I fucked it up by fucking Jay. I knew I shouldn't have brought him to the house in the first place, but at the time my anger and frustration had got the best of me. In the process of trying to hurt Mario, I had actually only hurt myself and Zaniyah. Now I was lost, without everything. It felt like I had dropped into a mysterious black hole. I hopped up and grabbed my phone. I knew it was late but I still sent out two messages: one to Dr. Nicholson and the other to Shannon. I told Dr. Nicholson I was coming in for a session tomorrow around eleven if she had an opening and then I sent an extra-long paragraph to Shannon apologizing for my behavior lately. I placed the phone back on the nightstand and plugged the charger into it. I curled up into a fetal position under the cover and closed my eyes. As I was drifting back to dreamland, I prayed to God that my previous dream would not occur again.

✳✳✳✳

"Bitch, wake up," Jessica said as she ran into my room and shook me out of my sleep.

"Girl what the fuck is wrong?" I asked her, sitting up in the bed and rubbing my eyes.

"Girl, Mario is outside my house trying to break down my fucking door," she said pulling me by the arm. "He said if you don't come outside right now, he's gonna come in here and fuck everybody up, and my goddamn son in here!"

"Okay," I said, getting out the bed. I grabbed my phone and quickly called the police. I told them what was going on and they said they were sending somebody right away. "Where is Raheem, Jess?" I asked her, inquiring about her son.

"He's upstairs in his room," she said, damn near out of breath.

"Let's go," I said, grabbing her by the hand. I was running as fast and as best as I could with my healing leg. It was causing so much pain and discomfort but right now was not the time to be bitching about it. I would rather deal with this then what the fuck Mario would probably do to me. We got upstairs to Raheem's room and together we pushed the dresser up against the door.

"What do we do now?" she asked me.

'We wait until the police get here." I grabbed both of them by the hand and we hid in the closet. "Where the fuck is Jeremy?" I asked in a hushed tone.

"At work."

It seemed as though we were in that closet for eternity by the time we heard sirens coming near us. We scrambled to get out the closet and ran over to the window. Two police had just pulled up and hopped out in front of Jessica's house. We moved the dresser out the way and ran down the steps and as soon as we hit the bottom step, they were knocking on the door. I opened the door and standing before me was a fine light-skinned brother with a low cut. Even in a bad situation like this, my hormones were all over the place.

"Good morning, ladies. My name is Officer Dion Mitchell. We got a call about a break-in. Are there any items that were taken from the home?" he asked as he pulled out a pen and a notepad.

"Hi, Officer. Nothing was taken but he was trying to knock my door down," Jessica said, looking past the officer to make sure Mario was still by the other officer at the squad car.

"Do you all know this man?"

"Yeah, that's my husband," I said.

"And what is your name, Ma'am?"

"Desiree Davis," I said as I watched him scribble on his pad.

"Is this your residence?" he asked, looking at me.

"No, it's my best friend's place."

"Okay, and what's your name, Ma'am?" he asked Jessica.

"Jessica Daniels."

"Any idea why your husband was trying to break into her home, Mrs. Davis?"

"Not a clue."

"Because he's a fucking nut job," Jessica chimed in. I elbowed her to shut her up.

"Like I said, I have no clue. We have been separated for months." He wrote on his notepad again.

"Well, I have to get with my partner about the information she collected from your husband and I will have him removed from the property. If he comes back, give the police a call or give me a call," he said handing us a small business card, but before

Jessica could even reach her hand out, I snatched it out his hand and gripped it in mine. He said his goodbyes to us and retreated back down the stairs.

"Really, Desiree? You're thinking about sex during a time like this?"

"Sorry."

"Don't be," she said as we sat down on the couch in the living room. She turned on the TV and we just watched Jerry Springer while Raheem played in his room.

✳✳✳✳

Later that night, Jessica and Jeremy had gone out. She dropped Raheem off over his father's house and she told me she wasn't coming back until some time tomorrow. Now I was all alone. *What to do? What to do?* I thought to myself.

I went to take a nice, soothing bubble bath in Jessica's Jacuzzi tub. I turned on the jets and everything; my body needed this relaxation. I had my slow jams playing on my cell phone, enhancing my mood. R. Kelly's song "Sex Me" came on and I started touching on myself. It was something about his voice that sent a chill down my spine and electricity down to my sweet spot.

I reached between my legs and started fingering myself. I entered one finger and then another, as I used my thumb to flick my clit. It took me until the end of "Sex Me Part 2" to make myself cum. It was okay, I guess, but I needed more. I needed to climax and reach ecstasy. I thought about Officer Dion and wondered if he was off duty yet. I quickly washed my body and cleaned the Jacuzzi out. I rushed into my room and searched the pockets of my jeans I had on this morning. I found it and dialed his number.

"Officer Mitchell," he said upon answering the phone.

"Hey, uh, this is Desiree. Desiree Davis. Do you remember me? You met me this morning," I rambled.

"Oh, yeah, I remember you. Your husband was the nut job, right?" he said chuckling.

"Yeah that's him," I said, laughing along with him. "Hey are you still working?"

"I'm clocking out in about twenty."

"Got any plans for when you get off?"

"None that I know of."

"Would you like to play a game of the cop and the horny housewife?" I asked in a seductive tone.

He was silent for a moment. I was afraid he was gonna say no, but then he replied, "Yes."

I beamed from ear to ear. "Cool. Do you need the address?"

"I remember it. I'll see you shortly."

"Okay," I said. As soon as we hung up, I searched through my clothes looking for something sexy to wear for him. I came across a red lace negligee and decided to put that on with my black stiletto pumps. I sprayed on some Calvin Klein perfume and waited impatiently for him.

Time had gone by and I was getting worried. Before I had a chance to dial his number to see where he was, the bell rang throughout the house. I jumped up and almost busted my ass, forgetting that I had heels on. I was glad my leg and ankle were feeling a lot better now, so I could do my sexy walk for him. When I opened the door for him he was still in his cop uniform and had his handcuffs in his hand, swinging them. Showtime.

"Can I help you, Officer?"

"Yes, Ma'am, maybe you can. I got a call about a noise complaint. Do you know anything about that?"

"No, Sir," I said, staying in character.

"Well, the call was from one of your neighbors saying they heard a woman screaming."

"It wasn't here, Officer. Sorry."

"You're not lying to me, are you? I wouldn't have to run you in."

"I'm not lying."

"Do you mind if I look around?"

"Not at all," I said, stepping aside. He came into the house and I shut the door. "What are you looking for, Officer?"

"You're acting a little suspicious to me, and I think I'm gonna have to arrest you, Ma'am, while I do my search," he said, turning me around and slapping the cuffs gently on my wrists.

As soon as he locked my second wrist, I took off down the hall toward my room. I could hear him right behind me. I made it to the room, but he grabbed me by the arm and pushed me on the bed. With my face down in the bed, he took my heels off and searched me. He used his hands to grip my ass and to separate my cheeks. He slipped his tongue in and licked my crack up and down. He licked my body from my lower back up to my neck. He flipped me over and gripped a titty in each hand as he sucked and pinched my nipples and I let out soft moans. He took the lingerie piece off my body and kissed all over me.

He dropped to the floor between my legs and threw each one of my legs over his shoulders and dived into my pussy. He was sending chills up my spine as he licked and sucked on my clit. He even slapped my pussy a few times. He was doing it faster, and I was mad because I couldn't push him away because of the cuffs. I could feel my cum forming, but I wasn't ready to release. I was trying my best to hold it back, but he wasn't having it.

"You better fucking cum for me," he said, coming up for air.

"I'm not ready," I replied.

"You better or I'm not taking the cuffs off."

I threw my head back on the bed and still continued to hold back. Not even minutes later, I squirted all over the place. He sucked up all my juices like a Hoover vacuum cleaner. He turned me over and removed the cuffs off one wrist. He pushed me up on the bed and locked the open cuff to the bedpost. He undressed and slipped a condom over his big penis and I flinched at the sight of it. It was thick and wide; I was nervous. I was thinking, *what would happen if he splits me open? Am I gonna have to get vagina reconstructive surgery?* Before I could finish with the debate in my head, he stuck his dick inside me and went to work. As our session continued longer into the night, I took notice to his stroke game. It was so familiar. I got it. He fucks like the stranger in my dream. But how on earth was that even possible? I mean everything felt like my dream. I'm just hoping this wasn't another one right now. If it is, I don't wanna wake up. I threw my arms around his neck as I prepared to release more juices. I was at the point of reaching ecstasy.

Chapter Fifteen

Now Hiring

I hit the alarm on my phone so quick when it started going off at exactly eight in the morning. I stretched my arms up to the heavens and looked next to me. I was expecting to see Dion, but he was gone. I sat up in the bed and checked my phone. I scrolled through my messages and call history, but there were no missed alerts from him. *What a crock of shit? He could have at least told me he was leaving. What he did was so fucking rude and disrespectful.* I didn't even know how long ago he had left. I thought of an idea. Maybe he was on Facebook. A lot of people are on there first thing in the morning. I typed his name in the search bar and scrolled down past the other Dion Mitchells until I found him. I clicked his picture, and just thirty minutes ago he made a post saying, "On my way to enjoy this day off from work with my beautiful wife, Jasmine." *A wife? Oh hell no.*

I called his phone several times but got no answer. I was pissed off, to say the least. I looked at his page again and refreshed it. Bingo. He just posted where they were having breakfast so I hopped up out the bed and showered. I lathered up my skin and threw on an overcoat. I grabbed Jessica's car keys and left her a note saying there was an emergency. I hopped in her Toyota Camry and headed towards the Belga Café in DC. I couldn't find a close enough parking space, so I double parked because there was no way in hell I was walking damn near three blocks in these pumps to get back here. I pulled up and threw on the hazard lights. I swiftly walked into the restaurant and searched for Dion and his wife and once I spotted them, I trotted over to their table. They were laughing and giggling and just enjoying each other's company but as soon as I walked up on them, Dion's smile vanished and fear filled his eyes.

"Can we help you?" his wife asked with attitude. I looked at her and rolled my eyes at her.

"No, sweetheart, you can't, but he definitely can," I said, turning my head back to Dion. "So why didn't you tell me you were married?"

"Dion, who is this woman?" his wife asked.

"I d-don't know, Babe. I've never seen her before in my life."

"Oh really, Dion? Maybe this will refresh your memory," I said as I opened my overcoat and dropped it to the floor. I stood before them as naked as the day I was born. The only thing I had on were my pumps. I could hear people gasping and snapping pictures throughout the restaurant. I even got a couple of whistles thrown at me.

"Sweet baby Jesus," his wife said, gasping and covering her eyes.

"You still don't remember me?"

"No, I don't," he said, starting to sweat a little.

"Who the fuck is she?" his wife yelled across the table. This bamma shrugged his shoulders.

"Well, let me help you remember. This is the hickey you put on my titty last night. You put these two on my neck. And you put this one on my inner thigh," I said, pointing out each one. I turned around and pointed out the scratches he left on my back as well.

"I don't know you, lady. So please leave."

"So, you're still gonna play that game, huh? Maybe you'll remember me after this," I said. I turned his chair around to face me and dropped to my knees in front of him. I watched as his wife's eyes popped out of her head as I reached for his zipper to pull his dick out and he went off.

"That's enough, Desiree. Shit!" he yelled. I smiled from ear to ear as I stood up and walked back to where I was, then I leaned down to pick up my overcoat and put it back on, making sure the belt was tied.

"If you don't know her, then how the fuck do you know her name?" she asked as she rose to her feet and yelled. "You're cheating on me, Dion?"

"Jasmine, no. This woman is crazy."

"I may be a little crazy, but you still haven't answered your wife's question. If you don't know me, how do you know my name?" I said.

"Exactly," Jasmine asked in agreement. We both crossed our arms and stared at him as he sat there in silence with a dumb look on his face.

"You're a piece of shit, Dion," I said, walking away. I turned back and went back over to them. "By the way you, left your badge and name tag on my nightstand," I said pulling them out my pocket and throwing them on the table. I looked at his wife and she was on the verge of crying. "Look, I'm sorry, but I didn't know he was married. You're beautiful and you don't need a nigga like this, that don't know how to treat you," I said to her. I stepped closer and grabbed the back of her head as I pulled her in for a kiss. I tongued her down and again there were gasps and camera clicks going off. I released her and walked away. I looked back before exiting and she was throwing wine glasses and porcelain plates at him. Nobody came to his rescue. Upon walking back to the car, I saw that it was okay; didn't even have a ticket on it. I hopped in and drove back to Jessica's house smiling at what I had just done.

✳✳✳✳

I managed to get back to Jessica's house at a reasonable time and I ran into the house to put on some clothes and called an

Uber. I made it to Dr. Nicholson's office a little after 11. She had changed her office around, and it looked homelier now.

"I'm glad you reached out to me, Desiree. I have been so swamped I haven't had time to schedule any appointments. How are you doing?"

"Fair. A lot has been going on."

"Like what?" she asked, pulling out her notepad.

"Well, first of all, Mario put me out the house."

"And why on earth would he do that?"

"He caught me in bed with his cousin, Jay. He beat Jay to death, literally, and beat me near death," I said, wiping the tears that were forming in my eyes. I showed her the bandage that adorned my leg and she just shook her head in disappointment.

"Oh, wow, Desiree. Wait a minute; I thought he was locked up already?"

"He got out."

"Okay, so why didn't he go back?"

"I didn't turn him in, that's why, and I feel horrible. If I had never brought him to the house, this would have never happened," I said.

"Maybe you should have never done it all. Did you think about that?" she asked, looking at me through her glasses.

"So basically, what you're saying is that me almost dying is my fault?"

"I never said that."

"You implied it."

"Desiree, I didn't mean it like that."

"Then how did you mean it? You condone this shit?"

"Desiree, please. Calm down," she said, passing me a few tissues for my now wet face.

"I'm just so messed up right now, Dr. Nicholson. I just wanna die."

"Don't say things like that, Desiree. Let's switch the topic. What about Zaniyah? How is she doing?"

"I don't know. I haven't seen her in a while. I missed my court hearing and everything."

"Wow. I'm sorry to hear that. Were you in the hospital when it was scheduled?"

"No. I was high," I said, mumbling.

"Can you repeat that, please?"

"I said I was high."

She looked at me with saddened eyes and shook her head again. I just dropped my head into my hands and sobbed loudly. Seconds passed before I could feel her hand on my shoulder. She pulled my hands away from my head and lifted my head up. She leaned down and hugged me tightly. I hugged her back and I cried harder. We talked a little while longer and she told me to go to the addiction anonymous class that was being held that night. She said if I didn't like it, I didn't have to stay. I promised her that I would go and let her know how it went at my next session. After confirming my appointment for next week, I was on my way. I wandered down the street admiring the neighborhood. I looked around as I noticed how much the neighborhood had changed over the years. I felt like a damn tourist as I looked at all the businesses in awe. I looked across the street and saw a store called Charlie's that had a big sign in their window letting all the passersby that they were hiring. So, since my broke ass needed a job, I decided to go and check it out. I crossed the busy street and walked into the store.

"Hey welcome to Charlie's," a girl said from behind the counter. I looked in her direction and she was helping a customer pick out sex toys. *Wow*, was the only word that had come to mind. I wandered around and checked out the place. It was an interesting setup. It was huge, but it didn't seem like it would have been from the outside. I scanned the walls and took note of all the items. There were dildos of different colors, lengths, and girths. My eyes popped out of my head as I laid eyes on a 16-inch dildo hanging on the wall. I went over to it and pulled it from the wall. I was in amazement as I tried to get a tight grip around it but my little hand wasn't even close to it. I was caught up in playing with the rubber penis in my hand, that I hadn't noticed somebody was right beside me and staring. I looked at them and quickly walked away in embarrassment. I made my way around the rest of the store looking at lingerie, whips, chains, and all other good things to have a good time. Once the girl that greeted me finished ringing up the customers, she came to assist me. "Hi. My name is Gia. Did you need any help?" she asked.

Nymphopervtress 2: Degenerate

I turned to her and my mouth dropped open. I hadn't noticed at first how attractive she was. She was light brown skinned with platinum blond hair and brown eyes. She was a little shorter than I was, but she looked to be the same size as me. She had tattoos all over her body, along with several piercings. It usually turned me off, but it made me want to give her all of my undivided attention. She just stood there, smiling at me. I had to say something so I wouldn't come off kind of weird. "Yeah, I do. I wanted to inquire about the job opening. Is the manager available?" I asked, as professional as possible.

"Yeah, you can follow me to the office," she said, walking in front of me. "Hey, Louis, watch the front," she said to a guy she passed by. I was walking close to her, but then slowed my pace a little so I could get a glimpse of her nice, round, protruding ass. She had on some distressed jeans with a shirt that had the back cut up. She had more tattoos on her back. We walked through two doors, one that led to the stockroom and the other led to the office. We walked into the office and she told me to fill out an application. As I did so, she was monitoring the cameras and scrolling through her Instagram and Facebook pages. Luckily for me, her back was towards me; she couldn't see me stealing looks at her like a peeping tom. It took me ten minutes to fill in the application, and then I gave it back to her. She looked over it for a few minutes and was just nodding her head. I hated when managers did stuff like that, because I wasn't sure if that was a good nod or a bad nod. After a few minutes of silence, she began

Nymphopervtress 2: Degenerate

her questions. "So, I see you were working an office job recently. Why aren't you there anymore?"

I thought about that before answering. I didn't want to answer it wrong because it might mess up my chances working here with her. "Well, um, I was having some issues at home, and I had to stop working."

"Are you still having issues at home, uh, Desiree?"

I loved the way my name rolled off her tongue. It was mesmerizing. "No, I'm not," I answered. It's not like I was lying. Hell, right now, I didn't even have a home to go to.

"Well, we're looking for someone that can work the evening schedule. You would be coming in from 3 p.m. until ten Monday, Tuesday, and Wednesday. Our weekends start on Thursdays, so Thursday, Friday, and Saturday you would be closing the store at midnight. Do you have a problem working that schedule?"

"Not at all," I quickly responded.

"Great. You can come in tomorrow for training. Do you have any questions for me?"

"Yeah. What would I be doing?"

"Oh, shoot, I forgot," she said, laughing. "Well you would be working with me, of course, because I'm here every day. Louis, he's a transfer from another Charlie's, and he's a student, so he doesn't work every day anyway. You will be stocking merchandise, unloading trucks, merchandising, and point of sales. Overall, you will be doing a little of everything."

Nymphopervtress 2: Degenerate

"That's cool with me," I said. We both stood and shook hands. I walked out behind her again as we made our way back to the front. Louis saw me and told me to have a good day and I waved at both him and Gia before exiting the store. I was beaming with pride inside. This is the only good thing that has happened in my life since... I don't know when. Since I had a job now, I had to work on getting a place and getting Zaniyah back. The thoughts were getting ahead of themselves, so I slowed down my brain and focused on the fact that my stomach was growling uncontrollably. I checked the Uber app and saw that the closest car was one minute away. I needed more time than that. I decided to wait until I got my food before ordering an Uber. I saw the Chipotle sign and saw that the line was decent. I hurried inside and stood in the back of the line. I was surprised that the line was even this short at this hour and it was a weekday. I texted Jessica to see if she wanted anything. My phone vibrated in my hand and I checked my text. She sent me back what to put in a bowl for both her and Shannon. If Shannon asked me to get her something to eat, she must not be mad at me anymore. I knew this from past experience. Once I got to the register, I checked the Uber app again and it said the closest driver was four minutes away. I confirmed I wanted that car, and it was on its way. I paid for our food and went outside. The Uber app must have been having a glitch or something because as soon as I stepped outside, he was pulling up to the curb. I hopped in and headed home; well, to Jessica's house.

Nymphopervtress 2: Degenerate

I saw Shannon's car when I pulled up to the house. I slipped the driver a five-dollar tip and got out. I was headed up the walkway when I saw Jeremy coming out the house with two other dudes. He walked up on me and whispered, "Keep your mouth closed," and kept walking past. I turned and gave him an evil eye but he just smirked at me and kept walking. I watched as they got into an all-white SS Impala and drove off. I turned back around and headed into the house. I found Shannon and Jessica in the living room binge watching this TV show called "The Chi." I walked over and sat next to them on the sofa. I handed Jessica her bowl and she thanked me. I turned and handed Shannon hers and she thanked me as well. She also gave me a hug, and apologized for how she was acting towards me the other day. I accepted her apology and we all pulled each other into a tight group hug. I told them that I had got hired at Charlie's and they both congratulated me. After all the unfunny cracks about me working in a store surrounded by dicks, we focused our attention on the television show. It was fun having quality time with my girls. I just wish I could spend time with my favorite girl. I wasn't gonna rush it, though, because in due time, I was gonna have my baby back in my arms. I just hoped it wouldn't take forever like it did in those movies I watched.

Nymphopervtress 2: Degenerate

I walked into the cafeteria sized room and saw so many people. There were both men and women in attendance, all different ages and colors. Nobody was sitting around in a circle and kumbaying, like I had envisioned. It looked more like a social group. People were sipping coffee, eating donuts, and others were on their phones or conversing with others. Just from this view, this wasn't for me. Nobody even noticed me when I walked in, so I hoped they didn't notice me while I slipped out either. I was slowly backing out of the room and backed right into somebody.

"Hey, where are you going?" he asked. I turned around and a smiling face was welcoming me.

"I, uh, think I'm in the wrong room."

"That's what they all say," he responded with a laugh. "My name is Ben. What's your name?"

"Desiree," I said, staring deep into his eyes as we shook hands. I have never had an attraction to white guys but my panties were slowly getting moistened by him. He had sandy brown hair, blue eyes, scruffy facial hair and a medium build. There was no way he was an addict. Then again, I didn't look like one either, but everyone around me was so determined I was.

"Is your last name Davis?" he asked, checking a clipboard.

"Yes."

"Oh okay. Dr. Nicholson told me that you'd be coming here. So, let me give you the rundown. I'm the counselor for this group. We have been doing this class for going on seven years now, and we have had so many successful outcomes. I'm pretty

Nymphopervtress 2: Degenerate

sure that we will be able to help you as well. Do you have any questions?"

"Not at the moment."

"So, are you gonna stay, or are you gonna leave?"

"I think I might as well hang around since I'm here already. I just don't think I'm ready to talk about my, uh, issue. Especially with a bunch of strangers."

"That's completely understandable. This is anonymous group, so it's totally up to you if you wanna share your name and as far as your story goes, we are not here to judge. We are all here to support one another."

"Okay," I said. He got everyone's attention and informed them that the session was about to start. We all took our seats and fixed our eyes on the stage as he took to the podium.

"Good evening, everyone," he said into the microphone.

"Good evening, Mr. Matthews," they all said in unison.

"I'd like to welcome you all back again this week. I see we have some new faces in the room today. We welcome you all as well, and want to thank you all for taking the first step into getting over your addictions." It seemed as though his eyes were solely stuck on me. It made me uncomfortable when people made direct eye contact with me, so I focused my eyes elsewhere. There were low murmurs around the room as every attendee looked around to see who was new here. I caught a couple of glances and smiles in the process. "Who would like to take the floor first?" I looked around and nobody had their hand raised. They were too busy

Nymphopervtress 2: Degenerate

either looking around or looking down in their laps like children. I almost raised my hand into the air, but somebody else had beaten me to the punch. Whew. I dodged that bullet. I watched as the young girl, who looked to be no older than maybe twenty-three, walk up on the stage. Ben said a few words to her and then she walked up to the podium. I blocked out the surrounding whispers and gave her my focused my attention.

"Hi, everybody. I know this is supposed to be anonymous but I don't mind telling you my entire name. My name is Julie and I just turned twenty last week and I'm addicted to meth." *Twenty? Wow,* I thought. "I have been doing meth since I lost both of my parents, when I was only fourteen years old. I was sent to live with a foster family and they mistreated me all the time. They would slap me around if I didn't say stuff like 'please' and 'thank you', or if I didn't eat my food fast enough. I remember one time my foster mom, Ann, had choked me because I dropped a sock on the floor when I was putting the laundry in the washing machine. She always called me dumb and stupid and slow. My foster dad, whose name was Alan, wasn't any better. He was probably the worst of the two. He would make me dress in my foster mom's clothes when she wasn't home and make me pretend to be his wife instead of her. He said that I was much prettier and shaped better than her. I remember a time when she had gone to visit her mother one weekend and I begged her to take me, but of course she didn't. Instead, she left me behind with that monster she called a husband. The Wednesday before Ann had left, I had started my menstrual

Nymphopervtress 2: Degenerate

cycle and I had told her and she just gave me a box of tampons and told me to figure it out myself. The day she left was one I could never forget. Alan had been quiet around me all that day, but I didn't think anything of it. That night, he came into my room and took my innocence. I screamed for help, but nobody could hear me. Nobody had come to my rescue. After that night, my entire life changed. Anytime a boy looked at me or even stood too close to me at school, I would freak out and run away. I got to the point where I didn't want to live another day. I used to slit my wrists just so I could feel it was both pleasure and pain for me. Eventually it didn't work for me anymore, so then I took an entire bottle of Xanax and tried to kill myself. Obviously, that didn't work, because I'm standing here today," she said with a light chuckle. I felt for this young girl and my eyes began to well up with tears. I wiped my tears and listened on as she continued. "On top of all of this, I had gotten pregnant. I couldn't tell neither Ann nor Alan, so I just packed some things and ran away. I slept at bus stops, under bridges, in parks, inside boxes, basically wherever my body got tired and I found shelter. After living on the streets alone for about six months, I met this guy named Slim. He gave me a job as a prostitute after I lied and told him I was twenty-one. When he asked why a beautiful girl like me was homeless, I told him why. I made good money working the streets, but once I got a taste of meth, that's where all of my money would go. In the process of becoming a drug addict, I had lost my unborn child. That intensified my need to escape the world and it worked. Slim had

175   Nymphopervtress 2: Degenerate

gotten tired of my habit and kicked me out, telling me nobody wanted to pay top money for a methadone prostitute with half dead pussy. I was back on the streets after living in his house with other girls for two years. Afterward, I had run into one of my older teachers from middle school. She took me home with her and cared for me as if she was my birth mother. I was doing better and had even gone back to school. I was happy and so was she. In the past year, I had been hanging around the wrong crowd and started using meth again. She kicked me out the house and told me not to come back until I got myself together. Since I didn't, I now stay in a shelter and I come here once a week, but I do keep her informed about how everything is going. She told me I am always welcomed back when I'm 100% clean. I'm just trying to get better and go back home," she said before breaking down in tears. Ben rushed up onto the stage to her rescue. He walked her off the stage and out to the hallway. There were low murmurs and sniffling from me and the other patrons in the room.

We had an hour left in the two-hour group session and I kept thinking I should go and tell them my story, but I was afraid. I know it's not a place for others to judge, but that didn't matter to me. There were like three other people that had gone after Julie. One guy said he had been a crack head for the past twenty years and he was forty-six. After him, a lady came on to tell her story. She was into voyeuristic sex. I didn't know what that was but she explained to us that in layman's term, she liked watching people have sex. Whether it was porn, peep-shows, orgy parties, even her

Nymphopervtress 2: Degenerate

friends. I thought that was some wild shit, but as I thought back on my life, I wasn't that far behind her. The last person was a gay guy that said he was addicted to using inanimate objects for pleasure. He said he pretended that the objects were his stepfather that his mother had killed after she caught him raping her son. He said that he was upset and hurt badly after losing his stepfather, because he was the only person that saw him for who he really was, so now he tried replacing objects with the feeling that he used to receive from him. He said he had been like that since he had been ten years old. My heart went out to these young folks. They could get help and they could still change their lives around for the better, but what about me? I wasn't that much older than some of these people here. I was only twenty-four and I was diagnosed with hypersexuality, depression, and bipolar when I was eighteen. I had gotten better and then went right back to it as soon as something bad happened that I couldn't handle, and I was a drug addict.

Oh no.

I just admitted I had a drug problem. What the hell was I doing to myself? What kind of example was I setting for my child? I was becoming overwhelmed by my thoughts and emotions and I felt the sweat trickling down my forehead and down my face, falling into my lap. The room was closing in on me and I couldn't breathe. I started to panic. I could see people forming a circle around me. They were saying something, but I couldn't understand them because it seemed like they were so far away. I felt somebody place their hand on my shoulder and I jumped up out of the chair.

I made a dash for the door and ran out the building. The fresh night air felt good as soon as I burst through the doors and it hit my face. I ran to Jessica's car and hopped in. I cried and screamed as hard as I could. I wiped my eyes and started the car. As I looked in the rearview mirror, I could see Ben jogging towards me. I shifted the car into drive and sped away as fast as possible. I just made a fool of myself in there around all those strangers. Fuck what Dr. Nicholson said. I tried the anonymous group bullshit and I failed. It wasn't for me. I didn't need those people to help me find other ways to deal with my pain, but I did need to relieve some stress. I wish I hadn't fucked up shit with Dion; I could have had his penis knocking down my walls. I texted Jessica and told her I was gonna be home later. I decided to drive around the city until I could find my prey.

Chapter Sixteen

My Bestie's Boyfriend

I woke up in a cold sweat. I adjusted my eyes and looked around the dimly lit motel room. The shades were closed and there was music playing low on the nightstand. I was bundled up in the between the sheets as bare as the day I was born. I got up to stretch my limbs from the previous night's workout session. My eyes roamed the room looking for the guy that I had captured last night. I think his name was Paul. Or was it Jimmy. Maybe it was Eric. I laughed to myself. I couldn't believe that for the life of me I couldn't remember his damn name. I mean, his stroke game was okay, but it wasn't that A1 dick that I be seeing the people getting from porn stars like Shorty Mac or somebody. He was a basic nigga with a basic dick that could only afford this basic motel room. He wasn't even driving when I came across him; he was trying to hail a taxi. I told him I would give him a lift if he gave me one. So, this is how we ended up here. I guess he decided to dip out before I woke up, but it didn't matter to me; it ain't like I was gonna drop him off anywhere. He did his duty. Now I had to get back home so Jessica could get to work on time. I gathered my things and hopped in the car. I was driving down Georgia Ave

Nymphopervtress 2: Degenerate

when my cellular started ringing. I quickly glanced down to see who it was but I didn't recognize the number, so I silenced it. A few moments later, it rang again. I decided to answer it this time.

"Hello," as said as I answered the phone. I was a little agitated and I think the caller sensed that.

"Yeah, hi. This is Muriel Graham calling from Children and Family Services. May I speak with Mrs. Desiree Davis, please?"

"This is she."

"Hello, Mrs. Davis? How are you doing today?"

"I've had better days," I said sarcastically.

"Haven't we all? Well I'm calling in reference to your child custody case. I have been assigned to your case and I need to set up a meeting with you in your home."

"My home?"

"Yes. I have to make sure that you have a stable and safe home for the child. It's routine, that's all."

"Okay."

"So, how is tomorrow around 12?"

"Tomorrow?"

"Yes, Ma'am."

I thought about it. I might get away with Jessica's house passing as mine. I can see if it works. Or I can go to my own damn house. Mario would let me. For Zaniyah anyway. I gave her the address and we got off the phone. As soon as we hung up the phone, I called Mario to see if he was gonna pick up the phone. Surprisingly, he answered on the third ring.

"What do you want, Desiree?" he snapped into the phone.

"Hey, are you home right now?"

"Why?"

"I need a favor."

"Why the fuck would I help your thot ass, Bitch?"

"It's for Zaniyah."

He got quiet briefly. "I'm here," he said and hung up the phone.

I quickly took Jessica her car back and called an Uber. She asked where I was going, and I told her I had to handle some business before I started my first day of work. I got to our house in twenty minutes. It would have been shorter, but this crazy ass driver kept taking wrong turns. I think he was doing it on purpose because my head was in my phone the entire time. I hopped out of his 2015 Ford Explorer and headed up the walkway to the front steps of the house. I rated him two stars for his service and noted that he was going the wrong way the entire ride. Once I reached the front door, I reached out to knock on the door and it flew open. Mario was standing there looking as good as the first day we met. He was wearing those gray sweat shorts that I loved so much. His penis would just swing so freely inside of them. He stepped back and let me in the house.

"So, what's this all about, Desiree? What's wrong with my daughter?" he asked, walking into the living room.

"Nothing is wrong with her, Mario," I said, taking a seat on the sofa. "The case worker that was signed to our case has to do a home visit tomorrow."

"And? You don't live here anymore."

"Can you just pretend I still do just so she can come back home, please? You know you miss her," I said, looking at him with sad eyes. He looked back at me with a stare that I couldn't understand.

"Yeah I do miss her, but you know what else I miss?" he asked, walking over to me and standing in front of me.

"What?" I said, scooting back onto the sofa.

"That mouth," he said, sucking in his bottom lip.

"This is not the time, Mario."

"Oh, it most definitely is," he said, dropping his shorts to his ankles. His dick was standing straight out. He grabbed me by the shirt and pulled me to the edge of the chair. "Show Daddy how much you need his help."

"Mario, I don't wanna do this right now," I said, trying to move back again.

He grabbed me by the hair and slapped me. "I didn't ask you what you wanted to do, did I? I told you what you are gonna do. You wanna still be acting like a hoe after all I've done for you, then that's how I'm gonna treat you." That was all he said before shoving his dick in my mouth. After a while, I just gave in and took all of his manhood into my mouth, and down my throat. I didn't realize how much I missed pleasing him until globs of spit came

Nymphopervtress 2: Degenerate

from my mouth and covered his dick. He stood me up and undid the button on my pants. He pulled them all the way to the floor and turned me toward the sofa. He smacked my ass, giving me the signal to get on my knees. I leaned over the back of the chair and arched my back just how he liked and he rammed his slippery dick inside of my mildly wet vagina. He was sexing me so hard and making my pussy make fart noises. I screamed to the top of my lungs as he gripped my hips and dug his fingernails into my flesh. He held onto me tight, got deeper inside of me, and exploded. He didn't remove his manhood until every drop had come out. He pushed me away from him and pulled his shorts back up. He looked me dead in my eyes. "Get your shit, and bring your ass back home. We gonna do this little charade just until I get my daughter back, but just remember, you are no longer my wife. I'm gonna just treat you like some regular pussy since you wanna be community pussy."

I went into the bathroom to clean myself up and freshen up a little. I adjusted my clothes and looked at myself in the mirror. *Is this what I have become again? Nothing more than a hoe?* This fucking addiction was ruining my life. No matter how hard I tried, I couldn't get rid of this shit. I got myself together and went back to the living room. Mario was watching the basketball game; the usual. "I'm leaving now," I said to him.

"Don't forget your keys on the counter. And don't call me to help you move your shit either. Get those thieving bitches to help you, or that bitch ass nigga I caught you fucking," he said. He got quiet for a second then continued. "Oh yeah, I forgot. That nigga can't help you. He can't help anybody," he responded with a hearty laugh. Just the sight of him right now was making me sick to my stomach. Before I did something that I might regret later, I grabbed my car keys and the new house keys and left. I had to be to work soon and I needed to relieve the stress that had just built back up. I sat in my car and rolled a jay and laced it with a little coke. After I finished, I backed out the driveway and headed to Charlie's.

✳✳✳✳

The store has been hectic all day. I guess since it was Friday, the majority of people received a paycheck today. I had just clocked out for my break and it was a little after 7 o'clock. I'm a little blown, because we don't close the store until midnight, so I was unsure why I didn't take a break a little later. Oh well, I didn't make the rules. Before I headed to the employee lounge, I watched as Gia handled the crowd of people. Not one person complained about the line because she was moving so fast and she did it with such ease. My ass would've panicked if I had more than three people in line at one time. I guess it takes years of practice and patience, two things I lacked a lot of the time. I walked to the break room and grabbed my Subway sandwich out the fridge with my drink. I took two big bites out of the first piece and felt like I was in heaven. I hadn't eaten all damn day and it was relieving to have a chance to eat right now. I took out my phone to call Shannon and Jessica to see what those broads were doing. I had three missed calls from my mother. I listened to the voice messages she had left, talking about she needed money for Zaniyah. I rolled my eyes and texted her back telling her to figure it out herself. I had to worry about tomorrow and how it was gonna go. I hoped and prayed that I could get Zaniyah back, and in time, I wanted my family back. I watched as Gia quickly came into the room and grabbed a drink from the fridge before sitting down.

"Everything okay?" I asked, looking at her.

"Girl, yes. It's a madhouse out there," she said, gulping down her grape soda.

"Tell me about it."

"After I finished that line of people, I noticed there are a lot of freaky women in this area," she said, and we both laughed.

"I know, right?"

She checked her watch and said that it was already nearing 7:45. She told me that she was going back out there until my break was over at 8. I took the last fifteen minutes to call my friends. Shannon answered on the second ring and patched Jessica through on three-way.

"So how is your first day going, hooker?" Shannon asked. I could hear Jessica snickering on her end of the phone.

"It's cool. I think I might like it here. At least for now anyway," I said, finishing up my lunch.

"That's good. I'm so proud of you, Desi," Jessica said.

Nymphopervtress 2: Degenerate

"Me, too, Sis," Shannon agreed.

I'm glad they weren't sitting in front of me right now. They would probably tease me for tearing up and call me sensitive. "Thanks, y'all. Oh, and Jess, I won't be staying there anymore. I'll be moving my stuff out in the morning."

"Oh, you found a place already? That's great!"

"Actually, I'm moving back home with Mario." The line went quiet. "Did you hear me, Jess?"

"Yeah, I heard you, Desiree," she said, sounding agitated, a little.

"Why would you do that?" Shannon interjected.

"I think it's for the best."

"The best for whom?" Shannon yelled into the phone. "Didn't this nigga just beat the living shit out of you, and now you running back like some little ass puppy or something."

"I have to agree with Shannon. I don't think it's a good idea."

"I'm trying to get my daughter back, y'all, and if Mario is letting me back home I don't see the issue. Besides, he was mad and hurt. That's why he did that to me."

"Wow, Desiree. That is the dumbest fucking thing you have ever said. I'm done with this conversation," Shannon said, hanging up the phone. When her line clicked off, so did Jessica's but Jessica called me right back.

"Look, Desiree, just be careful, please, and you know if you and Zaniyah need to, y'all can come back to my house. It's always open for y'all."

"Thanks Jess. It really means a lot to me," I said. We hung up the phone and I went back to work. The thing I did notice about this job, I haven't dealt with a rude customer at all today. I guess that was a good sign so far.

The rest of the night had gone fine. It died down around like 10:30, so we just straightened the store up and restocked some of the merchandise. We made jokes about everything that happened that day at work. I loved the way Gia was. She was so down to earth and cool. She reminded me of Shannon and Jessica rolled into one. I could definitely hangout with this girl. At 11, she told me that I could leave after I counted my drawer and finished sweeping the floor. Shit, as bad as I wanted to leave and sleep, I hurried and did what I was told. I was headed out the door and to my car at 11:20. I was gonna head home to Mario, but I decided to just go to Jessica's house to get my things since she lived closer. When I got there, the house was quiet. All except for Jeremy's ass in the den. He saw me when I walked in and didn't even speak. I guess he was waiting for me to speak first, which was dead. I was in the room trying to get my stuff together as quietly as possible. I was so beat right now. I would probably just pack up everything and crash here one more night. As I was folding my clothes and putting them in my suitcase, I noticed the bag of coke in the bottom of the duffel. It had been a couple of days since I had a

187   Nymphopervtress 2: Degenerate

good hit and I hadn't even noticed. As soon as I opened the bag, the sweet scent hit my nose. My mouth began to water for the drug and I wanted it badly. I sat on the bed and dumped some of it on the back of my hand. I snorted up four lines with quickness. I could feel it take an instant effect. My vision became blurry and my hearing became distant. I pushed the duffel bag onto the floor and laid down. I removed my pants and threw them across the room. I was walking on cloud nine right now, but my high would soon be blown.

I could see a shadow appear on the wall. It looked to be a guy, I could tell by the shape of the shadow. They turned the light off with a hit of the switch. I turned onto my back as the figure climbed up on the bed. They pulled the covers back and pulled my panties off. They pushed two fingers inside of me and my back arched. I quickly clicked on the light beside the bed and saw that it was Jeremy. He put his finger to my lips, signaling me to be quiet. He moved his fingers in and out of me until I became moist. He climbed on top of me and pulled his dick out of his sweatpants. He entered me and I let out a hard moan. He was grabbing my breasts and squeezing my nipples as he fucked me. It was feeling great. His dick was the right length to hit the right spot. Hold on. *What the fuck was I doing?* I thought to myself. He was the fucking enemy. He was trying to steal from my best friend, and on top of that, this was Jessica's fucking boyfriend! I quickly snapped back to reality and began trying to fight him off of me. He slapped me two times and continued. I dug my nails into his face, but that still didn't stop

Nymphopervtress 2: Degenerate

him. He grabbed me around the throat with one hand and started squeezing my nipple harder. Any other time, with anybody else, this would have turned me on, but at this moment, I didn't want this. I tried to yell out but he threw his hand over my mouth. My arms were flying around trying to knock over something to startle him or something. The tips of my fingers touched the table lamp. I stretched my arm out as much as I could and smacked it off the stand, causing it to crash and shatter. He paused in mid-stroke, giving me the opportunity to try and escape. I managed to push him off and make it halfway off the bed. He grabbed at me and I pulled on the leg of the nightstand. I kicked and pulled, pulled and kicked until I was free. I landed on the floor and the bedroom door flew on with the light.

"What the fuck is going on in here?" Jessica yelled at the top of her lungs. She looked back and forth between me and Jeremy. Jeremy and I exchanged looks at each other then at Jessica. I looked guiltier than he did because I was damn near naked and he was still fully clothed.

"Baby, she tried to rape me," he said.

"What? No, the fuck I didn't. He's lying," I said, looking at her and hoping she would believe me.

"Baby, you gotta believe me. You know your girl's a hoe. Why would I do that to you, Jess? I love you," he said. *No, this motherfucker did not just try and play the love card.* I stood up to defend myself.

"Jess, please, I'm your best friend. Why on earth would I fuck your boyfriend? He came in here and stuck his dick in me, and he's planning to rob you," I said looking back at him. I thought his ass was gonna get scared, but he was quick on his feet.

"Are you fucking serious, Desiree? You're a freaking liar. I love this girl," he said, climbing off the bed and walking over to Jessica. He took her hands into his. "Baby, believe me. I would never want to hurt you. Your friend came onto me. I came in here to see if she needed help and she attacked me."

Jessica's face was soaked and wet as tears streamed from her eyes. She kissed this nigga and then looked at me. "Get the fuck out of my house. I knew I shouldn't have let you come here in the first place."

"Seriously, Jess? You gonna believe this nigga over your fucking best friend? This is ridiculous. You're gonna regret this, Jess," I said as I gathered my stuff. With tears in my eyes, I headed past Jessica and Jeremy.

"The only thing I regret is trusting you around Jeremy. I should've known better."

"It's okay, Baby. I'm just mad your girl tried to do that to you," Jeremy said as he held her. He smiled at me as I walked out the room and out the house. This wasn't the last time he was gonna see me. I can guarantee that. I put all my things in the trunk of my car and headed back home to Mario.

$$* * * *$$

I woke up the next day, later than expected, thanks to Mario's ass. When I got here last night, we had sex again and then fell asleep. It was 10 in the morning and that damn lady was due to be here at 12. I asked Mario for help, but instead he left out and said he would be back around 12 or 1. This shit was crazy. I called Jessica to see if she could help, but I forgot she was mad at me. I called Shannon, but she was at work. I thought about calling my mother, but she was the reason I was in this predicament in the first place. I wished my sister, Monet, was here, I know she would've helped me. But, lucky for her, she was away at college and didn't have to deal with the bullshit here. I had to simultaneously vacuum, clean off the tables, and wash dishes. This shit was insane. Mario had this place looking like a damn hurricane done been through here. After I finished downstairs, I went upstairs to make sure everything was intact in the bedrooms and clean the bathrooms. By the time I had finished, and sat down to catch my breath, the doorbell rang. I walked to the door and opened it up. There was a middle-aged woman with salt and pepper hair that introduced herself as Mrs. Muriel Graham. I shook her hand and stepped aside so she could come in. She said she had questions for me before she checked the house.

"How are you doing today, Mrs. Davis?" she asked pleasantly.

Nymphopervtress 2: Degenerate

"I'm doing well. Just relieved that someone has finally reached out to help me in my situation."

"Well, here I am but I have noted that you didn't attend court on your scheduled day. Is there some reason why?"

"Yeah, I, um, had my days mixed up. I have been super busy?"

"Too busy for your child, Mrs. Davis?" she asked, writing a note in her folder.

"I didn't say that," I shot back. "I have been busy running my household and working."

"So, you're saying that those things are more important than having your daughter home? Does your daughter ever spend time with you, Mrs. Davis?" I was stuck and I didn't even want to answer anymore of her questions. It seemed like everything I said she flipped it around to say something different. If I wasn't nervous before, I was definitely nervous now.

"I'm not saying anything that you're repeating. I love my daughter and I would do anything for her. We spend time together all the time. You need to stop trying to twist my damn words around," I said in my defense. She looked at me like I was stupid.

"Calm down, Mrs. Davis. Now, continuing with my questionnaire, where is your place of employment?"

"I work at Charlie's."

"And what type of business is that?"

"It's basically a sex shop," I replied.

She looked at me strangely, but wrote it down anyway. "My records show that you are married to a Mario Davis. Are you all still married?"

"Yes, Ma'am."

"And where is he now?" she asked, looking around.

Damn this lady was fucking nosey. Shit. "He's out right now. He said he will try to make it back in time before you leave."

"Great. May I see your kitchen please?" We got up from the sofa and headed into the kitchen. She checked all of the cabinets, the pantry, and the fridge. She informed me she was looking to see if there was food and make sure nothing was expired or anything. She also said she had to take pictures of everything and make sure there was nothing poisonous that Zaniyah could get into. In my head, I was like, *she's seven, and she knows right from wrong, so, what the hell could she possibly get into?* After we finished in the kitchen, I took her upstairs to the bedrooms. She checked Zaniyah's room and made sure stuff was clean and everything and she did the same in our room as well as the bathrooms. She was driving me crazy with all this damn walking and taking endless pictures, but I had to do what I had to do if I wanted my baby back home. The entire meeting was over within an hour. Just as we were heading back down the stairs, Mario came in.

"Hey, how are you doing?" Mario said as he and Mrs. Graham shook hands.

"Are you Mario Davis?" she asked.

"Yes I am."

Nymphopervtress 2: Degenerate

"Great. Do you mind coming with me and answering a few questions?"

"No problem." They went into the living room and sat in the same spots that she and I had occupied earlier.

"So where do you work, Mr. Davis?"

"I'm a businessman," he said nonchalantly. *Businessman? Nigga you're a goddamn drug dealer!* I wanted to yell that at the top of my lungs, but I didn't, because this wasn't the time or the place.

"That's wonderful. What type of business do you own?"

"I'm the head man in charge at a plant."

"Wow. That's fantastic. Well, I have already interviewed your wife. Do you all have any questions for me?"

"Yes. When can we get our daughter back?" I asked, butting in.

"That's actually up to the courts, but if you ask me, your home is fine and she should be home soon, but please do not quote me on that," she said, standing and heading to the door. "I will be in touch." With that she was gone.

"Thanks, Mario," I said to him as I shut the front door.

"I didn't do this for you. I did this for Zaniyah," he said, walking away.

"Mario, wait," I said, pulling him by the shirt. "Look, Baby, I'm sorry. I should have never slept with Jay. Everything is all my fault, but, Mario, I'm sick. You know this already. Please forgive me."

"Are you sorry because you did wrong? Or are you sorry because you got caught?"

I didn't even respond. I didn't know how to, because it was a little bit of both.

"You always blaming this fucking sickness like it's a fucking excuse. It's not, Desiree and you know it. You can control your fucking self, but you just choose not to. If we are ever gonna work through this shit, you're gonna have to do what the fuck you gotta do. If not, get me my fucking daughter back and step. At the end of the day, I love you, Desiree, but I don't fucking need you," he said before walking away again and heading upstairs.

I dared not to follow him. I felt so low. I felt as though I was the scum of the earth and like I wanted to die. Maybe I should do like that girl and try to kill myself, but what if I don't do it right? I wanna die for so many reasons. I lost my best friend in the world over a lie. I lost my child because of my disorder that I choose not to treat. I lost my mother because she caught me fucking another man. Then there was Mario. I have ultimately hurt him. I have been putting him and Zaniyah through so much because of this damn sexual addiction, but I didn't know what to do. I even lost myself. I wanted to have my cake and eat it too. It feels so good when you get what you're not supposed to have. It's the thrill of being caught up. At the end of the day, I was feeling overall worthless. I ran out to the car and grabbed my baggie out of the duffel bag. I ran back into the house and went down in the basement. I had to escape and I had to do it fast.

Chapter Seventeen

Congratulations

The week had gone faster than I wanted it to. Work was busy as usual and going well. As far as things back home, let's just say it was tolerable. Tonight, I have my group therapy, and I think I am ready to get up on that stage. I was looking forward to it. It was going on 10 in the morning, and I was on my way to the mall. I decided it would be nice to do a little stress shopping. I haven't done it in a while, and it was way past due. I wanted to be alone today, so I didn't invite my girls with me even though it may have been fun. I pulled into PG Plaza and observed the new renovations from the parking lot. They had a few new stores that I may have to check out. I went into Target first, to see what they had. I went straight for the home décor section in search of a new comforter for Zaniyah. After my mother stopped acting like an ass the other day, she let Zaniyah call me and she told me she was into some things called Shopkins. I searched up and down the aisle until I seen a pretty pink comforter set. I looked at the image of what it looked like, and it was adorable. I threw it into my shopping cart along with the matching sheet set and a giant

Shopkins pillow. She was gonna be so excited when she got home. I walked through the other aisles and threw towels, washcloths, and other shit I didn't need into the cart. I made my way over to the DVD section to see what they had on sale and I saw this guy holding the 50 Shades of Grey movies in his hand. I examined him closer and realized I knew him.

"Mark?" I said, more as a question than a statement.

"Oh my God. Is that you, Desiree? Desiree Logan?" he asked, walking over to me and giving me a hug. "Wow you look amazing," he replied.

"So, do you," I said, looking straight at his crotch to check out his print. I must say, it wasn't too bad. "How's your wife, um, what's her name again?"

"Morgan and we're not together anymore," he said, a little sad.

"Wow, I'm sorry," I replied with fake sincerity. I didn't really give a fuck about his wife. I wanted to know what that dick could do. Shit, he had four kids; he had to be doing something right.

"How about your husband?"

"Well, me and Mario are trying to hold things together."

"That's great. How long has it been since I last seen you? Like, six years?"

"That sounds about right. I see you checking out the 50 Shades movie. I didn't know you were into that kind of stuff."

"Well, I prefer old fashion but it's nice to check out new stuff," he said in a low whisper.

"That's true," I said as I watched him as he scanned my body with his eyes. I had on a sundress that hugged my curves just right. "Hey, you wanna go have some fun?"

"Yeah. I'm free tonight," he replied.

"I was talking about now, silly," I said as I pulled him away from the movie section. We walked to the family restroom and slipped in unnoticed. He quickly pulled the front of my dress down and exposed my breasts. I grabbed his head, bringing his lips to mine. His lips were so juicy. I always loved his lips when we were in high school. Now I was able to see just how succulent they were first hand. I unzipped his pants and massaged his dick. Once it was hard, he picked me up in his arms and fucked me against the bathroom wall. I had nowhere to run to as I lost control while he was hitting my spot. I threw my arms around his neck and held on to him as I came so hard. Seconds later, he followed. We cleaned up fairly quickly and left the bathroom at separate times. As I was making my way back to my cart, he ran up behind me and slipped his number in my hand. He told me to give him a call later if I wanted another round.

✳✳✳✳

I walked into the room and it was the same as last week. I grabbed a glazed donut and some juice before sitting down in the back. I observed the room and noticed a couple of faces that weren't here last week. Ben walked in and swiftly took the stage. He introduced himself to the newcomers and asked who wanted to go first. I looked around and saw that nobody's hand was raised. Before I chickened out again, my hand flew into the air. He motioned for me to come onto the stage and everyone applauded me. I guess that was for my bravery; who knows.

"Hi, everybody. My name is Desiree and I'm addicted to two things, actually. I'm addicted to cocaine and sex," I paused and looked around the room. Nobody seemed to be shocked or appalled at the words I had just spoken. *They weren't here to judge me*, I thought. I continued. "I was diagnosed with hypersexuality when I was eighteen or nineteen, and I have been trying to get over this for years. I thought it was over with once I got married, but it wasn't. My therapist told me that it can be triggered by many factors. Stress, anxiety, depression, anger, and others. It didn't start up again until a few months ago, when my husband cheated on me with another woman. They both came to our house and attacked me and raped me. They were high out of their fucking mind," I said with a slight laugh. "It was crazy. I had him arrested and then I thought about it. I wanted to get back at him. I wanted him to hurt, just like I was hurting, so I called up my ex, who is his cousin and the first person I had ever had sex with, and I slept with him. We had sex and he got me to try coke. My mother and my daughter walked in and caught us having sex in the living room, and she took her from me, so I started using more cocaine and having more sex. My husband came home when he got released from prison and caught me and Jay in bed and he fucked us up," I said, starting to cry.

"He killed him and I ended up in the hospital. He kicked me out of the house and everything, but now we're working through everything so we can get our daughter back, and that's all I want really. I just want to be happy again, but I can't, because the only way I know how to deal with pain and through everything is running to sex and drugs. I want out sometimes, and other times I don't. I'm just so confused," I broke down in tears and held my head down in shame. Ben, along with a few others from the group, came onto the stage and hugged me. They all told me that everything was going to be okay and that we were all gonna help each other beat these addictions. I welcomed all of the positive energy my way. I knew if they could believe in me, I could believe in myself just as much. I just didn't know when to give in. *When does one know the answer to such a question?* Once the meeting was all said and done, we were all packing up to leave. Ben insisted that I stay behind and help him clean up. I really didn't want to, but it wouldn't hurt to help since he was helping me out.

"How do you feel?" he asked me as we stacked the chairs on top of one another.

"As far as what?" I asked quizzically.

"For admitting you have a problem and conquering your fear of jumping in front of the group and speaking on your addiction."

Nymphopervtress 2: Degenerate

"Um, I feel good, I guess."

"That's good," he said. He walked over to me and placed a firm hand on my shoulder. "I'm glad you came."

I looked at his hand that sat upon my shoulder, and then I looked into his eyes. "I'm glad I came, too," I responded. He placed his hand on the back of my head and brought his face down to mine. "Whoa, whoa. What are you doing?"

"What? I'm doing what you want."

"What the fuck are you talking about, Ben?" I said, stepping away from him.

"I know you want me, Desiree," he said, stepping closer to me. Each time he stepped towards me, I stepped backwards. "And I want you as well."

"I don't want you, Ben. I am here to get better."

"Just a little bit. Please?" he said.

"No! I'm out of here," I said, turning to walk away. I made it to the door of the room before he pulled me back by my hair. He threw me onto the hard floor and pounced on top of me like a lion. I struggled to get from beneath him, but his weight overpowered my little frame. "Stop it! Stop it!" I cried. I kicked and punched at him. It didn't seem to do anything but anger him. I felt a stinging sensation on the left side of my face as he slapped me. My hands quickly flew to my face and I cried uncontrollably. He loosened his pants and pulled out his penis. He fumbled with it, trying to get the little picker hard. Once it was, for the most part, he pushed my dress up and pulled at my underwear until they were

Nymphopervtress 2: Degenerate

shredded. He didn't even give my pussy time to warm up or anything before he shoved his entire dick inside of me. It felt like my flesh had ripped, just as it did my first time. My cries became silent as I laid in the middle of the floor. With each passing moment, my soul was slowly oozing through my pores, and escaping my body. I couldn't do anything at this moment. I just laid there and took it as I thought about how I had finally reached rock bottom. From my first time with Jay, to the day I said "I do" to Mario, all the way up to now, but it's nobody's fault but my own. I brought this upon myself.

That's something Mario would've said to me, I thought.

It felt as if time had stood still and nothing in the world was moving except for Ben's strokes, and the tears staining my skin. It seems like he had been on top of me forever, violating my insides, and taking what doesn't belong to him. Was this his first time doing this? How many times has he done this before? What made him do this to me? Was it something I said? Was it something I had done? So many questions were running through my mind, but none were being answered. What seemed as long as eternity, the torture had finally ended. I watched as he adjusted his attire and clicked off the lights as he left out the room. I heard the door open to the outside, and then it shut. I heard a lock click and that was it. He was gone and I was still lying down on the floor. I was so cold as I felt the cold tile against my bare ass cheeks. I couldn't move. I didn't want to move, but I know I had to. I couldn't let this happen to me again. Do I have a sign tattooed across my forehead that read *rape me please* or something? I managed to rise to my feet. I grabbed my purse as I limped my way towards the door. I felt a sharp pain in my stomach. Then it was replaced with tightness. Felt as if someone was squeezing my intestines or something. I doubled over in pain as I leaned up against the wall. I made it to the front door and I unlocked it. As soon as I reached the outside of the building, the night air hit me. My face began to hurt again, but I couldn't hold my face. I was too busy using my hands to hold my stomach. People were looking at me crazy and I looked back at them with blurry eyes. The world was closing in on me. I dropped to the ground, and everything went black.

✳✳✳✳

Beep. Beep. Beep.

Those beeps had become all too normal to me. I knew exactly where I was as soon as my eyes flew open. I could see the nurse's station from where I was. I felt around for my buzzer and pressed the button. A pretty middle-aged woman with brown hair entered the room within seconds.

"Hi, Ma'am. I see you're finally awake. How do you feel?"

"I feel fine, I guess."

"That's good. Do you know where you are?"

"Yeah, in a hospital," I said in an as-a-matter-of-fact tone.

"Yeah, you are."

"How did I get here?" I asked, feeling my frustration starting.

"You got here by ambulance. You were found on the sidewalk. You managed to lose some blood, but we were able to stop it," she said, flipping through my charts. "And don't worry; we were able to save your son. Congratulations by the way," she responded, smiling.

Pause. "My what?"

"Your son. We did a sonogram for you after we did a blood test and found out you were pregnant, and like I said, don't worry, he is going to be okay. He is doing well and is already about five pounds. I know your husband will be excited."

"Oh, okay. That's great. Thanks," I said nervously. "How far along am I?"

"Looks to be about eight months. Anything else?" she asked sweetly.

"Yes, how do you know it's my husband's baby?" I asked angrily.

"Excuse me, Ma'am? I just thought because it says Mrs. on your chart. Sorry if I offended you."

"Don't be sorry; just don't go around assuming shit. I do have a husband. I also have sex with other people, too," I said, laughing maniacally.

"Like I said, I'm sorry, but not for you. I'm sorry for your husband."

Nymphopervtress 2: Degenerate

"To hell with your goddamn sympathy. You people don't care about me. You don't care about anybody. You just care about your goddamn self and my fucking husband. Fuck him, too," I said. I was crying and screaming and becoming more hysterical.

"I'm sorry you feel that way but, again, I'm sorry you have to go through with this. You're gonna need to inform your husband and any partners you may have."

"My husband? My partners? How many do you think there are?

"Well, if that's the case, I feel sorry for your husband for having a hoe for a wife."

"You little bitch," she said to me through clenched teeth. She closed the door and stormed out of my room. I guess she had to go calm down and remember that she had to stay in professional mode. Who the fuck cared?

I laughed as she left out the room, but now I was back to recollecting what she had just told me.

Wow, a son. I've always wanted a son.

My smile quickly faded as I thought back. *Whose baby could it possibly be, exactly? Was it Mario's? Possibly. Could it be Jay's? Maybe. Damn, did I use protection with Emmitt?* I couldn't remember right now. Thinking about this right now was causing me a massive headache.

"Ahhh," I yelled at the top of my lungs. The nurse came running back in the room.

Nymphopervtress 2: Degenerate

"Mrs. Davis, what's wrong?"

"I have a really bad headache. I need some medication, and I need it now!"

"Well, I'm sorry, Ma'am, but we cannot give you anything except Tylenol. Would you like that?"

"Tylenol? Fuck no! Give me some stronger shit than that. Bring me some damn Xanax or something. I want the good stuff."

"I'm sorry, but I cannot do that. You are pregnant and there's a chance it will hurt him."

"What did you just say to me?"

"You heard exactly what I said," she said, walking over to me. As she turned to walk away, I quickly grabbed her by the back of her head and pulled her hair. I managed to get her across my lap and I started choking her. She tried to get me to release my grip by digging her nails in my hands and arms, but I wouldn't let up. Another nurse was passing and saw all the commotion. She ran into my room, and to this bitch's rescue.

"Hey, what are you doing? Let her go! Security! Security!" she yelled loudly. Within minutes, three security guards bum rushed my room and handcuffed me to my bed. I scratched at them and tried to break out of the cuffs.

"Somebody calm this lady down," one of the security guards yelled.

The nurse that had come to the rescue ran out the room and quickly came back with a needle in her hand. She poked the needle into the tube that was hooked up to my IV. I relaxed a little

206   Nymphopervtress 2: Degenerate

and became calm. I'm not sure how long it had taken for the medicine to fully kick in, but once it did, I was out like a light.

✳✳✳✳

I woke up with extremely bright lights surrounding me. I didn't even give my body a chance to wake all the way up before I jumped up. *Where the hell am I?* I thought to myself. I was in a room surrounded by white walls. This time it wasn't a hospital. I rubbed my eyes so they could adjust properly. Oh my God. I'm in a fucking psych ward! I pushed onto the wall and it was soft like a pillow. I panicked. I ran over to the door and banged on it. The little window opened and I heard a man's voice speaking to me.

"What is it, Davis?" he said harshly.

"Wh-. Wh-. Where am I?" I asked.

"You're in a rehabilitation center, Ma'am," he replied. "Your husband told us to bring you here from the hospital."

"Why?"

"He said you had a drug addiction. So, hence why you're here," he said with a slight chuckle.

"Let me out of here, Goddamnit," I yelled.

"Sorry. No can do. Your husband signed you up for a 48-hour stay."

"You cannot make me stay here. I have a court hearing for my daughter tomorrow."

Nymphopervtress 2: Degenerate

"You're right, but unless he tells us to release you, or you complete the 48-hour program, you cannot leave the facility."

"This is fucking crazy," I yelled. "How long have I been here?"

"About two hours."

"Fuck!"

"Ma'am you have to calm down or we're gonna have to administer a shot to you."

"Fuck you," I yelled at him.

"Whatever," he said. He closed the little window. After a few moments, the door to the room opened, and in came two buff guys and a slim guy. The little guy opened a little case that looked like a Bible carrier.

"What the fuck are you gonna do with that big ass needle?" I said when I saw it.

"I warned you, Ma'am," he replied taking the needle from the case and walking over to me. I ran into a corner and crouched down like a cowardly dog. "Don't make this hard."

"I'm calm. I calm. You don't have to give me that," I said as I shook in fear. My cries fell on deaf ears as the two big guys pulled me from the corner. One held my hands while the other held onto my feet. The smaller guy pulled my pants down a little, exposing my left butt cheek. I felt a pain, followed by a sweet sensation. The released their grips on me and left me to lie there. I watched as they all looked at me before closing the door and walking back to wherever they were. I just lay there, motionless,

Nymphopervtress 2: Degenerate

feeling like I had no limbs. My entire body had gone numb from that one prick of a needle. I didn't have any fight in me right now, but just wait until this shit wore off. I know I was gonna get a phone call, and best believe Mario's ass was gonna have it, but for now, I was just gonna sit here and enjoy the scenery.

****

When they let me out of the padded cell hours later, I thought I was gonna be relieved, but boy was I wrong. I hadn't noticed earlier, but I was dressed in a gray two-piece set. I walked into the lounge area, thinking I was gonna see the sunshine outside. Turns out, a lot of sun wasn't allowed in here. The dark walls blocked out majority of the sunlight and only a smidge came through the small window. I looked around at the other people in the room. Some were playing cards. Some were watching television. The real weird ones were just standing in the middle of the floor, looking zombified. They had drool running down the side of their mouths and they were scratching their skin. *Gross,* I thought. I found a seat off in the corner, away from everybody. I walked over and observed the atmosphere. It was peaceful. Very tranquil. I felt like I was at peace; something I have never felt in my life before. I focused my attention on the television. They had some program on that was talking about how people should live a normal life.

Nymphopervtress 2: Degenerate

What kind of malarkey is this bullshit? I thought. *How can somebody tell another person how to live their life? What if they don't wanna be normal?* Hell, I loved my life. Well, as of lately I don't, but in the past I did. My eyes darted across the room when I saw an older lady walk in pushing a cart.

"Okay, people, its medication time. Line up in an orderly fashion to receive your prescriptions."

You would have thought the damn building was on fire the way all the patients jumped to their feet and scattered to get into the line ahead of the next person. It reminded me of when I went to work one day with Mario when he was still selling drugs on a street corner. The drug addicts would run to him, waving money in the air, as soon as they seen his car pull up. They practically threw their first of the month checks at him and disappeared for a couple days. Then they would come back and try to get credit until the next month. I looked at the line after it finished forming and noticed it was wrapped around the vicinity of the room. I just shook my head and laughed to myself. *Damn them, looking like they in line trying to buy drugs.* That's how the line looked at the Department of Social Services. I knew that all too well from when I was growing up. I watched as one of the male orderlies headed in my direction. He walked with a limp and he was bow legged. I couldn't help but to crack a smile at him, but he did not return the favor. He had a stoned face as he approached me.

"What's your deal, newbie?"

I looked around him and behind me, trying to figure out who he was talking to. "Excuse me, who are you talking to, Bruh?"

"I'm not your 'bruh,'" he said, using air quotes. "You are to address me as, Sir, or Mr. Simms."

"Simms?"

"Mr. Simms, newbie."

"Whatever," I said, laughing. "I don't have a deal, if you must know."

"You must. You didn't line up and get your meds like everyone else did. What, do you think you're something special or something?"

"No," I said, getting defensive and standing to my feet. I stood in his face and stared into his face.

"Oh, I know what it is. This isn't your drug of choice is it? I bet if it was PCP or marijuana or cocaine you would've been jumping for joy. You probably would've been the first one in the line."

"Shut the fuck up," I said. I reached my hand back and swung it at him, trying to slap the taste out of his mouth. He grabbed it in midair and pulled me close to him, so he could whisper in my ear.

"Look, you little bitch. You're no better than anybody here. You're a fucking drug addict, just like the rest of them. Don't play with me, because I will make your stay here a fucking nightmare that you're gonna wish you could wake up from," he said through clenched teeth.

Nymphopervtress 2: Degenerate

"Too bad I'm only here for 48 hours," I whispered to him.

"And I will make those 48 hours a living hell for you. Try me," he shot back. "Now get in the line." I stood there looking at him with evil eyes. If looks could kill, he would've been a dead motherfucker. "I said get in the line," he repeated. I flipped my middle finger at him and walked over to the line. I looked back at him and we briefly made eye contact. *You better hide,* he mouthed at me. I rolled my eyes and turned to face the back of the head of the person in front of me. I was the third person to get their meds.

"What is this crap for?" I asked the lady with an attitude.

"I don't know, sweetheart. It's the medication that's written beside your name."

"How do you know my name?"

"Wristband. That's how I identify you and everybody else in this facility."

"Great," I said sarcastically. I tossed the pill into my mouth and chased it with the small cup of water. The big horse pill felt just like those big ass prenatal vitamins that went down my throat. Speaking of those, I had to get some of those as soon as I got out. Well, after I take a visit to Mario first. "When can I have phone privileges?" I asked her.

"I can't answer that, dear. I only distribute medication. Nothing more, nothing less. I will see you later this evening with your prescription," she said. She packed the items back on her cart and left back through the gate. The guards locked the door back and stood there, blocking it from us. I walked over to them and asked them the same question I had just asked the medicine lady.

"So, when are we allowed to make phone calls?"

"We do them in alphabetical order. What's your last name?" one of them asked as he looked at a clipboard.

"Davis."

"First name?"

"Desiree."

He looked up from his clipboard and looked at me. His eyes roamed my face for a few seconds before he focused back on the clipboard.

"It says your phone privileges are from 1 p.m. to 1:30 p.m."

"That's it? All I get is thirty funky ass minutes?" I yelled.

"Ma'am, please calm down. It's not just you. That's for all the patients in the facility."

"Well what time is it now?" I asked, calming down a little.

"Its 12:55," he said, checking his watch. "I can escort you there now if you're ready."

"Well I'm ready now," I said, rolling my eyes and stood at the gate.

He blew air out of his mouth as he unlocked the gate for me and led me to the section where they housed the payphones. I actually laughed inside when I saw them. It was so weird seeing those things after they have been extinct as long as dinosaurs. I sat in one of the chairs and picked up the phone. The first person I was calling was Mario. The phone had rung four times before he picked up the phone.

"Yeah, who is this?" he said, answering the phone.

"Nigga, don't answer my motherfucking phone like that," I said, raising my voice into the mouthpiece.

"Who is this?" he asked, chuckling on the other end.

"Really, nigga? You don't know who this is, Mario?"

"Nope."

"It's your wife."

"Oh, yeah. I remember you. The drug addict that I caught fucking my cousin, right?"

"Yeah," I said in shame.

"Oh, hey, Baby. How are you doing in there?" he asked. His voice was dripping with sarcasm.

"Come and get me out of here, Mario. I have a court hearing tomorrow. You know that."

"You're right, I do know, and that's why you're in there. I needed you out of the way so that I could make sure they gave me my baby, and once they do, we're leaving town and never coming back. You will not ruin our child like you did yourself."

"You can't just take Zaniyah from me. She needs me and I need her."

"You don't need nobody but your fucking drugs. That's all you care about, right?"

"No, it's not," I said, starting to cry.

"Oh, right, I forgot. You need niggas, too. You don't give a fuck about me and Zaniyah. You never did. Did you?"

"Yes, I do, Mario. I love you and Zaniyah, and I love our new son," I said sadly.

"Our new son? Are you fucking kidding me?"

"No. I'm five months pregnant as we speak. They did a test when I was admitted into the hospital. Before they brought me here." He became silent. "Mario, are you there?"

"Yeah, I'm here."

"Well, what do you have to say?"

"How do I even know if there is a baby? You've been lying to me for God knows how long. It's probably not even mine. It's probably Jay's baby. Or is it another nigga? Or multiple niggas?"

"Neither," I lied. "It's yours, Mario," I said.

"You and that baby can go to hell."

"What? What do you mean?"

"I changed my mind. I'm not taking Zaniyah anywhere."

"You're not?"

"Nope. I'm gonna get your ass where it hurts the most."

"What are you gonna do?"

"Don't worry. You'll see." Click. He hung up the phone in my ear. I placed the phone on the cradle.

"Are you ready to go?" the orderly asked me, placing a caring hand on my shoulder.

"Not just yet," I replied. I picked the phone back up and dialed my mother's number.

"Hello? Logan residence," my mother said, answering the phone politely. If only people knew the real her they would be grossed out.

"Hey, Ma. It's Desiree. Can I, uh, speak to Zaniyah, please?" I could tell she was taken aback that it was me calling since I hadn't called in days. She hesitated for a minute or two before she called Zaniyah to the phone.

"Hello," Zaniyah said, answering the phone. Just hearing her sweet voice started my tears back up again.

"Hey, Sweetie," I said, trying not to let on that I was crying.

"Mommy!" she squealed into the phone. "Where are you, Mommy? I miss you."

"I miss you, too, Baby. Mommy's in the hospital right now."

"Are you okay?"

"Yes. Yes, I am. I have good news for you, though."

"What is it?"

"You're gonna have a new baby brother."

"For real? Oh, wow, that is cool," she said. "Grandma? Mommy said I'm gonna have a little brother." I could tell she was jumping around with excitement. Just hearing the joy in her voice changed my entire demeanor. Then my mother got back on the phone with her negativity having ass.

"Desiree, now you listen to me, you will not tell lies to this child anymore. You understand me?"

"Nobody's lying. It's true."

"Does Mario know?"

"Yes, he knows. Why wouldn't he?"

"Well, congratulations, I guess. It looks like you're gonna get to keep one child for now."

"For now? You've got it all wrong lady. I'm gonna have both of my children with me."

"Over my dead body."

"That can be arranged," I shot back.

"You're such a devil," she said to me.

"Well, I am my mother's daughter," I said. She hung up on me as well. It didn't faze me though. As long as my baby was happy about the news, I didn't give a fuck about whether my mother or Mario was happy. They both could stand in a line and take turns kissing my ass. "I'm ready now," I said to the orderly as I stood to my feet.

"Well, let's go," he said. He led me down the hall to the mess hall instead of back to the lounge where I had been earlier. "It's chow time, Davis," he said, walking me into the cafeteria. There were more people in here than I had originally seen earlier. *I guess everybody else was in their rooms,* I thought to myself.

I jumped into the line as quick as I could. I was starving so damn bad. It felt like I hadn't eaten a thing in days. Now that I thought about it, I wasn't sure the last time I had eaten. I reached the counter and they handed me a tray of food. I looked at it and got immediately turned off. There was a small portion of meat loaf, a piece of cornbread, some canned greens and some mashed potatoes that looked like they had been cooked a little too long. I would have thrown that shit in the garbage when I was walking over to the table, but my stomach was rumbling like a lion. I sat down at a table where a dark-haired chick was sitting at alone. I didn't want to disturb her so I sat at the other end by myself. As I tore into the monstrosity that they called food, I was looking out of my peripheral vision, and couldn't help but notice the girl looking at me. When I looked up from my food, and looked in her direction, she diverted her eyes to her tray of food. I rolled my eyes and focused back onto my food. A few minutes later she did it again.

"What the fuck is your problem, Slim?" I yelled down at her end of the table. The loud chatter that was just drowning out my thoughts a few seconds ago had ceased to exist. I looked around at everybody sitting in the cafeteria and all their gazes were fixed on me. I stood up and flipped all of them off with both of my middle fingers. I sat back down and continued to finish my food. The weird girl at the other side of the table didn't make eye contact with me anymore. She didn't even think to cough in my direction.

✳✳✳✳

Later that night, I couldn't sleep. I was sweating. I was shaking, and all the bones in my body were hurting. On top of all of this, my skin was itching so badly. It felt like there were a million bugs crawling all over my body. I just couldn't stop scratching.

Nymphopervtress 2: Degenerate

Every time I tried to move, or sit up, I would feel pain all over in my joints. "Help me! Help me!" I yelled at the top of my lungs. It seemed like it took forever for somebody to come to my rescue. *I'm glad I wasn't on fire or anything,* I thought. The light in my room came on and the orderly, Mr. Spencer, rushed into my room and to my bedside.

"What's the matter, Mrs. Davis?" he asked. As soon as he got up on me, I threw up everything that I had in my system. Lucky for him, he jumped out of the way in the nick of time.

"I think I'm sick," I said after I finished emptying my guts.

"No shit," he said, giggling a little. "Are you done regurgitating?"

"I think so," I said, sitting up and throwing my legs to the side of the bed.

"Okay. Well, let's get you into the shower and in a new change of clothes." I didn't even put up a fight with him. I just went along, because there was no way in hell I was going to lay here and smell throw up all damn night long. We walked down the quiet and dimly lit hallway to the shower room. He stopped in a hall closet and grabbed a clean uniform and a new toothbrush for me. He grabbed a towel and we continued on. Once we arrived to the shower room, I adjusted my shower water to my liking. Before I started to strip out of my clothes, I saw that he was still standing in here with me.

"Isn't there something else that you have to do?" I asked.

"It can wait. I actually have to monitor the patients when they take showers?"

"Why?" I asked bluntly.

"Just in case somebody tries to hurt themself in the shower."

"How can somebody hurt themselves in here? There's nothing here," I said, looking around the shower room.

"They could hang themselves with the rope on the soap bar. They could break glass on the mirror and stab themself or slit their wrists. We even had a patient one time that managed to pull the little square tile up from the floor. She tucked it into the seat of her panties. She sharpened it on the floor of her room once she got back in there."

"Let me guess, she killed herself?" I said, cutting him off.

"Nope. She slit her roommate's throat in her sleep."

"Why would she do such a thing?"

"She said the voices in her head told her to do it."

"Well, that is such an unfortunate event, but you don't have to worry about me. I'm not gonna do anything like that," I said as I stripped down to nothing and got into the shower.

"That's good to know. That means this will be an easy job for me," he said, grabbing a chair and sitting in it. I watched him as he watched me in the shower.

I let the steamy hot water run all over my sore body. The beads of water were so relaxing as the hit my breasts and my back. It like one of those little massagers was roaming around on my back. After drenching my body in water, I lathered up my rag and doused my body in soap. I closed my eyes and imagined Mr. Spencer washing my naked body. He must have been a mind reader, because after about ten minutes, I felt his hand on my back. He grabbed the back of my neck and gently squeezed it. I opened my eyes up to look his way. He was fully naked, exposing his thick white penis, which was already standing at attention. This was a big surprise to me. I thought all white guys had little peckers, thanks to pornos. I guess they were either wrong or they hadn't come across him yet. I pulled back the shower curtain so he could get in with me.

"What are you doing, Mr. Spencer?" I asked.

"I thought you could use some help. Besides, I'm a little dirty, too," he replied, licking his thin pink lips.

"Oh yeah? How dirty are you?"

"Filthy."

"Oh, that's not good."

"No, it's not," he replied.

"Let me help you take care of that," I said. I lathered the rag back up again with soap. I drug the washcloth all over his body, starting with his slightly hairy chest, and ending with his hairless back. I moved the shower head towards the wall before I dropped down to my knees. I took his penis into my small hand and massaged it with the rag. I used the soapy rag to cover his lower body with soap and I jerked it with my other hand. His head was thrown back in ecstasy as it rested on the shower wall. His eyes were closed as he enjoyed his wash up. I washed the soap out of the rag and then wiped the soap from his penis. I dropped back to my knees and grabbed a tight hold of it. I opened my mouth and put half of it in my mouth. I was trying to put the entire thing in my mouth, but I couldn't, because it was wider than I first thought. So, I just sucked half of it. After a few sucks, slurps, and slight deep throats, his precum trickled down my throat. I stood up and he picked me up. He carried me out the shower and he sat on the chair he was previously sitting in. I straddled his lap and took all of him in me. *Maybe I should tell him about my newly discovered condition,* I thought. That thought quickly faded. I didn't want this to stop. If I couldn't get drugs, I guess this was the next best thing. He came after a few moments, and I quickly came right after him. We both washed again and I brushed my teeth. We got dressed and we headed back to my room.

"That was good," Mr. Spencer whispered to me as he walked me back over to my bed. "How do you feel?"

"I feel a little better," I said, even though I was lying. "My pussy feels better and my skin isn't crawling anymore."

"That's good," he said. "Let me know if you need anything else. Just holler."

"I will."

He headed to the door, but came back to my bedside. "This is for you. Don't tell anybody," he said shoving something in my hand. I looked at it before he shut my light off. It was a tiny bag of coke. As my light went out, I sat up in my bed. I dumped the drug in the palm of my hand, and sniffed it up as best as I could. I laid back down as soon as I finished.

If you could see me in the darkness, you would see the biggest, dumbest, and cheesiest smile that you have ever seen in your life, plastered across my face.

Chapter Eighteen

Staking Out

"All rise. The honorable Judge Meyer will be presiding in this courtroom," the bailiff said as the judge entered the room. "You may all be seated," he replied after the judge had taken her seat.

"Good morning, everyone."

"Good morning," the courtroom attendees replied back.

"We are gonna be starting the hearings this morning with Logan v. Davis. Are both parties in attendance?" she asked looking up from her stack of paperwork.

"Present, your honor," Desiree's mother said as she stood up so she can be acknowledged. She looked over to Desiree's table.

"Where is your client, counsel?" she asked the public defender sitting at the table. He didn't know. He just shrugged his shoulders.

"Sorry, I'm late, your honor," Mario said rushing to the front of the courtroom and sitting at the designated table.

"Excuse me, Sir, but who are you?" she asked.

"I'm Zaniyah Davis' father, Mario Davis."

"Where is your wife, Mr. Davis?"

Nymphopervtress 2: Degenerate

"She's, um, sick today. She asked me to come in her place."

"Look, this isn't a job where you two can just swap work hours. This is an important and delicate matter. I do not have time for games. Now, where is she?"

"She's currently residing at Marshall Hall Mental Rehabilitation Clinic. She took it pretty bad from the verdict of the last hearing and had a complete meltdown. She became depressed and had several anxiety attacks," he lied.

"Well, sorry to hear that, Sir. Send my prayers to her."

"Will do, your honor," he replied as he took a seat next to the public defender.

"Counsel, do you have any opening statements you would like to present to the court?" she asked Ms. Logan's lawyer. He stood to his feet and approached the bench.

"Yes, your, honor, as a matter of fact I do. My client, Ms. Logan, feels as though it is in the best interest that the child in question, Zaniyah Davis remains in her care," he began.

"Explain."

"I was informed by my party that her daughter has suffered depression over the years and it was not caused by the severity of this case. She was diagnosed by a Dr. Nicholson back in 2008, and has been deemed a threat to herself and others around her because of her addictions."

"Addictions?" she asked as she wrote on her paperwork.

"Yes, your honor. Not only have the defendant, Mrs. Davis, been treated for depression, but also a hypersexuality disorder. And as of lately, an apparent drug addiction has developed as well. We agree that it will be safer to keep the child out of these dangerous situations."

"Objection," the public defender yelled as he jumped out of his seat.

"Sustained. There will be no objections during an opening statement."

"Yes, Ma'am, your honor," he said sadly as he sat back into his seat.

"Is there anything else you would like to share with the courtroom, counsel?" she asked, putting her focus back on Ms. Logan's attorney.

"No, that's all, your honor," he replied as he walked back to the table and took a seat.

"Mr. McCoy, you have the floor for your opening statement," she said to the public defender representing Desiree.

"Well, your honor, my counterpart, Mr. Young, has his facts correct about one thing, that's for sure. My client, Mrs. Davis was indeed diagnosed with hyper behavior years ago, but she has gotten better. I have the files from her therapist and psychiatrist with me if you need it."

"Bring them to me," she said. He went through his stack of files until he found the right papers. He handed them to the bailiff and he handed them off to the judge. She shuffled through the paperwork then looked back at Mr. McCoy. "Is that all?"

Nymphopervtress 2: Degenerate

"Not yet, your honor. Mrs. Davis may have had a possible depressive state recently, but what parent wouldn't? She is missing her child and the stress is causing her to act out in a manner that she has tried to control over the years, but, do not overlook the fact that she is currently receiving help from one of the best facilities in the state of Maryland. I believe that if we give the child back to her mom, everything will be smooth sailing from now on. That's all I have for right now," he said.

"You may have a seat, counsel. Let's get this case on the roll. Mr. Young, please call your first witness to the stand."

"For my first witness, I call to the stand, the mother, Ms. Denise Logan."

"Will the witness please stand to be sworn in by the bailiff, please?" Ms. Logan rose to her feet and made her way to the stand. The bailiff walked over to her with a Bible in hand.

"Raise your right hand, Ma'am. Do you swear to tell the truth, the whole truth, and nothing but the truth?"

"I do," she replied and sat down in the chair.

"Can you state your full name for the court, Ma'am?"

"Yes. My name is Denise Logan."

"And what is your relationship to the child, Zaniyah Davis?"

"I am her grandmother."

"How would you describe your relationship with your grandchild?"

Nymphopervtress 2: Degenerate

"Oh, wow, it's amazing. I love my grandbaby. She brings me so much joy," she replied with a smile.

"And what about your daughter, Ms. Logan?"

"Pssh. That child is a piece of work. She is a disgrace to this family and I refuse to let her have my granddaughter around her and her ungodly shenanigans."

"So, are you saying she is unfit?"

"Yes, Sir."

"Can you describe shenanigans that you have seen that may seem like she is an unfit parent?"

"She is always having sex with random men and doing drugs. She and that man over there are always getting into physical altercations around Zaniyah and that can get out of hand sometimes. At least two times, I can recall, that I had to call the cops on her husband because he was trying to kill her," she said, pointing and rolling her eyes at Mario. He just smiled and laughed behind a folder.

"And when you would call the police, what would they do? Do they take him to jail?"

"No, because her dumbass tells them it's a false report and nothing is wrong."

"Language, Ms. Logan," the judge said, banging her gavel on its stand.

"Sorry, your honor," she replied.

"No more questions, your honor."

"I'd like to cross examine the witness, your honor," Mr. McCoy said, standing up from his seat.

"You may precede, counsel," the judge replied. Mr. McCoy quickly made his way over to the witness stand.

"Now, Ms. Logan, tell me what do you do for a living?" he began.

"I'm a janitor at a school."

"Do you work during school hours?"

"I work overnight."

"I see. And who keeps Zaniyah at night if you're at work? Do you pay someone for child care services?"

"No, I don't. She stays with my boyfriend."

"Your boyfriend, huh? And can you state his name for the record, please?"

"Ronnie Buchanan," she replied with a smirk on her face.

"And is this Zaniyah's maternal grandfather?"

"Obviously not, if I just stated that he was my boyfriend."

"Oh, yeah, that's correct. How long have you two been together?"

"About a year, give or take two. Why?" she asked with slight agitation in her voice.

"I'll ask the questions if you don't mind, Ms. Logan," he said, adjusting his tie with a light chuckle. "Next question, from your recollection, can you inform the court about what happened the night that you took the child from her mother."

"Yes. Yes, I can. Well, I had Zaniyah with me that evening because her mother said that she had a date. When I went to her house, I saw that her car was in the driveway, so I used my key to go inside the house. When we arrived inside, and were walking past the living room, we saw her having sex with another man, and when she climbed off top of him, I saw the white residue that was all over her nose from the drugs. I told her I was taking Zaniyah with me and she was not coming back home."

"Okay. So, question for you. Was the guy her husband, Mr. Davis?"

"No, it was not. I'm not sure who this man was."

"And how sure are you that she had drug residue on her face?"

"I know cocaine when I see it," she yelled into the microphone.

"No more questions, your honor."

The court became chatty as the questioning continued. The witnesses and questions continued to go back and forth for over an hour. After that, the judge told everybody to be back in court tomorrow at 10 a.m. for the final verdict on who would maintain full custody of Zaniyah. Mario and Denise exchanged dirty looks at one another as they exited the courtroom, escorted out by their lawyers and a couple of police officers.

"I'm so glad you're home," Shannon said, hugging me.

"Thanks, Shan. At least you're happy to see me. Have you spoken to Jessica?"

"No, I haven't," Shannon replied, shaking her head. "She hasn't spoken to me in days. She said something about me siding with the enemy or some shit like that."

"Enemy?" I said with a very light chuckle. "She's calling me the enemy, really? She might wanna watch that. Her motherfucking nigga is the enemy. I overheard him on the phone one night talking about robbing her for everything she had."

"Oh, fuck, really?" I nodded my head 'yes.' "Did you tell her that, Desi?"

"Of course I told her, but she's so fucking dickmitized that she thought I was lying. She actually took his word over mine. Can you believe that shit, Shan?" She never responded, verbally. She just shrugged her shoulders and shook her head in dismay again.

"Well, I don't know what to say, honestly. If she believed him over you, that shit is sad. Y'all have been going strong since forever."

"Exactly."

"That's why I don't fuck with niggas, man," Shannon said with a smirk on her face. I couldn't help but to burst out in laughter. "I'm serious, Desiree," she said, joining me in laughter.

We chilled out with the laughing after a while. "In all seriousness, though, we have to help her."

"But she doesn't wanna be bothered with either one of us."

Nymphopervtress 2: Degenerate

"So, the fuck what, Shannon. That's our girl, and no matter what, we're supposed to be here for one another and protect each other."

"You got a point. So, what are we gonna do?"

"We're gonna stake out the place tonight and see if anything seems out of the ordinary."

"But what if he doesn't make his move tonight?"

"Then we'll go back tomorrow night. Or the next night. We're gonna go every night until something pops off."

"That sounds like a lot of gas," she said.

"Oh, girl, please," I said, laughing. I slipped a twenty-dollar bill into her hand and put my stuff in her bedroom. She followed me in there to show me where to put my things. "You sure your folks are okay with me staying here?"

"Girl, yeah. They insisted on it once I told them all that Mario was putting you through at your house."

"You didn't tell them about the drugs, did you?" I asked in a whisper.

"Nope," she replied quickly.

"Okay, good. By the way, there's one thing I didn't tell you about the hospital?"

"Don't tell me the guy that raped you came there."

"No."

"Was it Mario?"

"Girl, no. Chill out," I said, laughing and sitting her on the edge of her bed. "I'm pregnant."

Nymphopervtress 2: Degenerate

"Again?"

"Uh, yeah, again."

"Oh my God," she said, pulling me into a hug. I busted out in tears as I cried on her shoulder. "What's the matter?" she asked, leaning me up. "Those better be tears of joy, Desiree."

"No. It's just that I don't know who the father is."

"Oh, I see. Well how far along are you?"

"Five months."

"You're five months pregnant and didn't know it? Is the baby okay?"

"No, I didn't know, Shannon, and yes, the baby is fine. The nurse said he's doing well."

"He? I'm gonna have a little nephew?" she asked, excitedly placing her hands on my stomach.

"Yep. I'm having a boy."

"You're not even showing that much, though. You just look like you're bloated," she said, pressing lightly on my stomach.

"I'm not surprised. I'm kind of glad I'm not. I don't like carrying all that weight around."

"Well, I'm glad I will never have to deal with that struggle." She looked at her wristwatch. "Well, it's nine o'clock at night. What do you wanna do?"

"Can we eat, please?"

"Sure. What do you and little man have a taste for?"

"Doesn't matter. Whatever y'all have in the kitchen we will eat."

Nymphopervtress 2: Degenerate

"Follow me," she said and we went into the kitchen.

****

I have probably been at this kitchen table eating for about an hour now. I ate chicken, leftover spaghetti, a few pieces of Texas toast, an apple, a banana, a pudding cup, a fruit cup, and some Doritos. I wasn't even close to being full yet, but I know I had to ease up before I ate everything Shannon and her parents had to eat.

"Damn, are you almost done?" Shannon asked, looking up from her cell phone. She caught me stuffing my mouth with Doritos. I smiled. She smiled and shook her head at me.

"Yeah, I'm almost done, Boo. Just let me finish these chips in my mouth. Then we can go."

"Go where?" she asked.

"We're going over to Jessica's house. Remember? We just talked about this a little while ago."

"Yeah, I remember, but I also remember that you just told me that you were seven months pregnant with my nephew."

"So, what's your point?"

"My point is that you don't need to be in no dangerous situation like that."

"Girl, bye. You better get out of my face with that mess," I said, standing up.

"I don't wanna hear any of that. You might need to sit this one out," she said, running to my side to assist me.

"Look, Shannon, I get that you're trying to look out for our best interest, but I have to do this. I have to prove to her that I was telling the truth the entire time about that no-good lowdown dog."

"Aight, man," she replied, sucking her teeth. "You ready to go now?"

"Just let me grab my gun out my suitcase first."

"Of course," she said. "I'm gonna go and grab my dad's gun out of his office."

"He lets you use his gun?"

"Hell no, girl. He would kill me if he found out I took it. That's why we're not gonna say anything about it. Okay?"

"Okay."

"Good, now go get your gun, and whatever else you need, and meet me in the garage."

"Cool."

We went separate ways as she headed down the hall and I headed upstairs to her room. I grabbed my gun and an extra clip just in case I needed it. I saw a pack of graham crackers on Shannon's stand and decided to grab those as well. *Shit, I might get hungry,* I thought to myself. I went back down the stairs and went into the garage. Shannon was already sitting in the car, scrolling through the playlist on her iPhone. I hopped in and adjusted my seat.

"You ready for this?" she asked me.

Nymphopervtress 2: Degenerate

"I've been ready," I replied. We both buckled up as she backed out of the driveway. We were on our way to Jessica's house.

****

We had been sitting across the street from Jessica's house for about three hours and there was still nothing stirring. I was beginning to get drowsy, but Shannon wasn't. She was too busy occupying herself with her phone. Between her playing Candy Crush Saga and scrolling through Facebook and Instagram, she was texting her girlfriend. I kept glancing at her every time she texted her back. They must have been in the middle of an argument or something. I could tell by the way she was texting and how fast the messages were going back and forth between them. I just sat in the passenger seat laughing.

"I have to pee, Shannon," I said as I started squirming in my seat.

"So, what you want me to do? Want me to drive down the block to Royal Farms?"

"I do, but what if Jeremy comes while we're gone?"

"Desiree, be for real. Nothing has happened since we've been here, and I doubt if anything will happen within the next ten minutes."

"You never know," I said, squeezing my legs together.

"So, what do you want me to do? You wanna squat outside the car and piss? I have some napkins in my glove compartment."

Nymphopervtress 2: Degenerate

"Eww, fuck no. That's trifling."

"Shit, I do it all the time. I can't always get to a bathroom and I be damned if I ruin my bladder because I'm too proud to pee outside like a wild animal."

"Well, I am too proud and I refuse to use the bathroom outside like an animal in the wild. Let's just hurry there and hurry back."

"You got it," she said as she started the car back up. As she drove past the house, I hoped that nothing would happen while we were gone.

As soon as Shannon pulled into the parking spot at Royal Farms, I jumped out before she even threw the car into park. I ran inside as quickly as I could. I could feel trickles of piss wetting the inside of my panties. That is not the kind of wetness I cared to deal with right now. I reached the bathroom and ran into the stall. I struggled to get the button loose on my jeans but when it did open, and I dropped my pants to my ankles, that piss came out like a river. "Ohhh," I said out loud. I was feeling so much better now that I had released all of the urine that was irritating my bladder. I wiped myself and went to wash my hands. As I looked at myself in the mirror, I saw that I looked worn out. I didn't have that perfect glowing skin like I did when I was pregnant with Zaniyah. Instead, I looked like an overworked and underappreciated house wife. My face had gotten a little fatter and the bags under my eyes were bigger than they used to be. I threw some water on my face to see if that would wash away some of the dreariness that lingered, but it didn't. I dried my hands under the eco-friendly hand dryer then exited the bathroom. I saw Shannon's greedy ass in her favorite aisle of any store; the snack aisle.

"What are you getting now?" I asked when I approached her. She turned around and smiled at me. She had the goofiest grin on her face that gave away the fact that she was completely stoned. "Forget I asked," I told her.

"You know I just burned one waiting for you to come out of that bathroom, right?"

"I see."

"Yeah, and now I got the damn munchies."

"Well, hurry up and get what you're gonna get so we can get back."

"Okay, okay," she said. She scrambled and just started pulling different bags of chips and snack cakes off the shelves. I walked behind her cracking up. After they totaled up her items, and bagged them, we rushed out to the car. I opted to drive so she could enjoy feeding her high. She didn't even argue with me about it as she hopped her happy go lucky ass in the passenger seat. I drove quickly back to Jessica's house. That fifteen-minute drive felt more like seven minutes. Either way, we were now sitting across the street in the same spot we had previously been sitting in.

"Do you think he's gonna show?" I asked Shannon.

"It's hard to say," she replied as she scarfed handfuls of Cheetos into her mouth. "I think if he was gonna show up he would have been here by now. Just look at what time it is," she said, pointing to the clock on her radio. It's almost 2 a.m. and nothing has happened. I say we try again tomorrow night."

I looked up at the house again. I didn't want to leave, just in case Jeremy and his little punk ass friends decided to come. I wanted to help Jessica, I really did, but I was getting exhausted and I was tired of just sitting around, and gorging myself with snacks. I needed sleep. "I guess we can roll out, but, are you sure we're coming back here tomorrow night?"

"Yes," she said.

I started the car up again and headed back to her house.

After we got back to Shannon's house, I checked my phone. I didn't have any calls from Mario, but I did have a missed call from both my manager and the judge handling Zaniyah's court case. I messaged my manager and told her I would be into work on Friday and she texted me back a thumbs up. I listened to the message that the judge had left. She informed me to be in court tomorrow morning at 10 a.m.

"So, what are your plans for tomorrow?" Shannon asked me as she hopped on her bed.

"Going to court," I replied.

"Court? For Zaniyah?"

"Yeah," I replied hesitantly.

"Well, don't worry about it, Sis. Everything will be okay," she reassured me.

"I sure hope so," I said. I stripped down to my shirt and panties and hopped into Shannon's bed.

Nymphopervtress 2: Degenerate

"Good night, Desiree."

"Good night, Shannon."

The next morning had come and I tried to drag my feet as much as possible. I was not ready to face this judge again. Not just yet. I arrived at court a little over an hour earlier than scheduled. Shannon had called out of work so she could be here with me for moral support.

"You didn't really have to come with me. You know that, right?"

"Yeah, I know. I wanted to come," she said, hugging me. It was always nice when I had somebody in my corner that had my back and always looked out for me and my well-being.

"I really appreciate you coming today, Shannon."

"I'm just happy to be here. Side note, I didn't wanna go into work today anyway," she whispered.

"Girl, why you playing hooky from work?" I asked with my hands on my hips.

"Because, I need a fucking break. They act like they're gonna die if they give us at least one day off a week. I'm freaking tired. Besides, I didn't wanna have to deal with Alana today at work."

"Y'all two still beefing?"

"She's beefing with her damn self. She got mad because she went through my phone yesterday and saw that I was texting another female."

"She should be mad," I said, smacking her arm.

Nymphopervtress 2: Degenerate

"Forget that. I never even met the girl I was texting. I met her on Instagram and we've been having very intense conversations." I rolled my eyes at Shannon and went to sit down on the bench that was positioned in the middle of the hallway.

We were sitting there, chit chatting a little and scrolling through social media. I had seen my mother come into the sitting area where we were about twenty minutes after we had gotten there. She looked at me and quickly turned her head away when she saw me look her way. *I don't care if you don't wanna look at me,* I thought to myself. *My day was still gonna go on whether she gave me attention or not.* Shannon noticed the shade that my mother had thrown our way. She burst out into loud, uncontrollable laughter. I could literally see the steam seeping through my mother's head. I cracked a smile inside my shirt so she wouldn't see. Eventually, my laughter became a little loud and obnoxious as well. I guess she had gotten fed up with our ignorance because she grabbed her purse and got up to move to another bench down the hall.

Just about fifteen minutes before we were to head inside the courtroom, Dr. Nicholson had shown up. She came to give me more moral support and to speak on my behalf. She informed me that they had summoned her to come and get onto the witness stand as well. While she was talking to me, I looked behind her and saw Mario walking towards the courtroom. *What the fuck is he doing here?* He made eye contact with me. At first, he looked surprised to see me here today, but the reactions flipped really quickly. Now I was the one surprised to see him here. *What kind of games was he trying to play?*

Chapter Nineteen

Case Closed

Mario and I were exchanging looks as we sat at the same table. I don't even know why the hell he was here. I know he loved Zaniyah but be for real, he was fronting. Then I turned my attention away from him and looked towards my mother. She was grilling me and staring me down like she wanted to fight, and if she did, I was gonna be all in for it. I was getting fed up with her and all of this nonsense she was putting my family through.

The judge came out of her chambers and we all rose to our feet. She stopped and whispered something to the bailiff before heading to her seat. As soon as she sat down, so did the rest of us in attendance. We made brief eye contact before she looked down at her paperwork. I couldn't really make out what her facial expression was. I brushed it off and went back to giving her my undivided attention.

"Good morning, everyone," she stated. "Let's get this ball rolling. Bailiff, call the first case please."

"Case number 4227685, Logan vs. Davis. All parties are already in attendance, your honor."

Nymphopervtress 2: Degenerate

"Thank you, Bailiff," she replied. Then she looked over to us and began to speak. "We will start with the plaintiff. Mr. Young, you may have the floor."

"Thank you, your honor," my mother's lawyer said. He came from behind the table and walked up to the stand, before turning to face the audience in the courtroom. "Well, your honor, it has been brought to my attention that the defendant, Mrs. Davis, has reached out to her mother recently. She called and she became very hostile and spoke vulgarly to my client." I sat there with my mouth gapped open. I looked at my mother and she had a blank stare on her face, but it was as phony as that dry ass ponytail piece on the back of her head. I could see in her eyes that she wanted to crack a smile but she wouldn't, not in front of the judge anyway. I looked back at her lawyer as he continued. "I do believe that in the last hearing, I informed you, and everyone here, that my client was in an in and outpatient facility for people with mental disorders. As I dug deeper into her background, I have come across the fact that she has a really bad attitude. She lashes out and become violent towards herself and others."

"Do you have proof of these accusations?" the judge asked. Hell, I wanted to know, too. I knew I didn't have anger issues, but I didn't play with motherfuckers either.

"Yes, I do your honor. I have this file as well as a video of her." He handed both the folder and the tape over to the bailiff. The judge scanned over the documents that were now placed in her possession. "If you look at the paper, your honor, you will see that those are official documents from her therapist. Dr. Nicholson has been Mrs. Davis' therapist for a little over eight years. And that video, here, will show you all how violently she can actually get." He pressed play on the remote and a surveillance camera video popped up on the screen. I remembered that day. That was the day I beat up those two bitches up at the grocery store. I shifted my eyes to the judge and she just looked on in disappointment. If the jury falls for this, I'm gonna be dead inside with my baby. I might as well fuck around and kill myself. After the video played, Mr. Young smirked at me and Mario.

"Will you call your first witness to the stand, please? Unless you have more to share about your recent discoveries."

"Oh no, it's perfectly fine. For my first witness, I would like to call Mario Davis to the stand." I looked over to him and he grinned at me as he stood to his feet. I wasn't sure how I should feel about him being here. Let alone speaking on the witness stand. He stood before the bailiff and smiled cheerfully at all of us.

"Mr. Davis, do you swear to tell the truth, the whole truth, and nothing but the truth?"

"I do," he replied.

"You may have a seat."

"Now, Mr. Davis," Young began, "how would you describe your relationship with your wife?"

"Well, I mean, it's just like any other marriage, ya know?"

Nymphopervtress 2: Degenerate

"When you say it's just like any other marriage, are you implying that most wives are drug users and have an extremely crazy disorder that they cannot seem to control?"

"No, that's not it at all. We have problems just like any other couple, but at the end of the day, our love for one another and our child is what keeps our family strong." If I could cry at this very moment, I can bet your sweet ass I would be crying. He has never spoken that highly of me before, and I liked it.

"So, Mr. Davis, you do not deny the fact that your wife was, or is currently, using drugs? Is it only cocaine or is it more? Maybe a little meth? How about heroin? Are you even aware of her drug habit, Mr. Davis?"

"Yes, I am aware of it. I have taken matters into my own hands and had her admitted into Marshall Hall Mental Rehabilitation Clinic. They had her on a 48-hour watch while she attended there."

"And do you mind telling the court how those two days magically stopped this woman from wanting to do more drugs once she was released?" he replied, pointing directly at me as I sat at the table.

"I have no problem sharing that with the court. The staff informed me that my wife did great. Just like anybody else with an addiction that goes there, she had her episodes and withdrawals. In the end, her love for our child changed her mind set and got her back on track, and now I believe she will be back to normal,"

Mario said, glancing at me. I was astounded and just stared blankly back at him.

"Next question, what's your relationship with my client, Ms. Logan?"

Mario took a deep breath and a sip of water before answering the question. "I feel as though our relationship could possibly be a little better. I love my mother-in-law, but she be losing her canon sometimes."

"Can you specify, Sir?" Mr. Young added.

"She goes ballistic if she goes days without her medication. She is not only rude and disrespectful, but she is like that to both children and adults alike. I have seen her become violent and everything."

"Can you recall an incident, Mr. Davis?"

"Not at this time, but I will inform you when we have time to talk privately."

"No problem, Sir. I'm finished with my questioning, Your Honor."

"Would you like to cross examine, Mr. McCoy?"

"No thanks, Your Honor," McCoy responded.

"You may have a seat back at the table, Sir," the judge said to Mario. He got up and gratefully sat back into his original seat. "Mr. McCoy, would you please call your first witness?"

"No problem, Your Honor." He turned to the court for drama and theatrical purposes. "I would like to call my witness, Dr. Nicholson to the stand, please?"

Nymphopervtress 2: Degenerate

"Ma'am? Can you approach the bench, please?" The judge said, motioning Dr. Nicholson to come from the back of the courtroom to the front.

"Good morning, Your Honor," she said as she took the witness stand.

"Raise your right hand, Ma'am. Do you swear to tell the truth, the whole truth, and nothing but the truth?"

"Yes," she replied and sat down in the seat.

"How are you doing this morning, Dr. Nicholson?" Mr. McCoy asked her nicely.

"I'm doing well, Sir."

"That's great. Before we start, do you mind telling us a little about yourself?"

"As far as what?"

"As far as your line of work."

"Uh, sure," she said before inhaling deeply and then exhaling. "Well, I have been a therapist for about fifteen years now. I am also a counselor and a volunteer at several rehabilitation facilities."

"Is that all?"

"Yes," she replied, raising her eyebrows. "That's all."

"And how is your relationship with Mrs. Davis?"

"We have a standard client-doctor relationship. I have been treating her since she was about seventeen or eighteen years old, if I'm not mistaken."

"Uh huh, I see. In your sessions, what do you all talk about?"

"I cannot disclose that information," she said, speaking closer into the mic.

"Your Honor?"

"Sustained. Restate your question."

"I'll rephrase then. Do you all ever talk about her day-to-day life? About her family? Specifically, her daughter?"

"Yes, she does. That's a normal tactic I use with all of my clients."

"So, I see. Has she ever informed you about her drug use?"

"Yes, she has."

"And what did you tell her?"

"I told her I would help her get through it."

"How so?"

"I signed her up for group therapy with people whom have various addictions as well."

"Has your client ever come to you about hurting herself?"

"No, Sir."

"How about her daughter?"

"Oh, God, no. She loves that little girl. She would never hurt her."

"But she is hurting her. She is hurting her by choosing drugs and sex over her own child."

Dr. Nicholson became quiet and the people started a low murmur.

"That's all the questions I have," McCoy said as he took his seat back next to me.

"What the fuck are you doing up there?" I whispered to him.

"It's okay. I got this."

"What the fuck do you possibly have? You're making me look bad."

"Pipe down, people," the judge said as she banged her gavel a few times. "Mr. Young do you have any questions for Dr. Nicholson?"

"Not at the moment, Your Honor," he said from the table.

"Well, we're gonna take an hour recess. Court will resume at 12:30." She hit her gavel one more time before getting off the stand and heading back to her chambers.

Just as I saw my mother walking away from her table, I slipped between her and her lawyer and landed a left-right combo to the back of her head. She dropped all of her papers and her purse on the floor as she turned around and swung. Her right fist connected to my chin, and my left came back like fire as I connected to her chin. Before you knew it, we were pulling each other's' hair weaves and falling all over the place. I heard a whistle and I could see the bailiff and another officer rushing over to the commotion. I see Shannon out the corner of my eye running over to us, with Dr. Nicholson right on her heels. They were trying to pull me off of my mother but I had her hair in a tight grip. I was holding on to that cheap shit as if my life depended on it. Dr.

Nymphopervtress 2: Degenerate

Nicholson managed to free my mother's hair from my grasp and push her away. The judge came over and screamed at the top of her lungs.

"Have all of you people lost your freaking minds! This is a courtroom, not a wrestling ring. You all had better get it together before that child becomes a ward of the state. If you think I'm playing, try me." She glared at all of us sternly before heading back through the door she had come from. I adjusted my clothes as I looked at my mother. She just laughed and left from out of the courtroom peacefully with her lawyer as if nothing had just transpired between us. Everybody that caught the show was now grabbing their things and heading out of the courtroom. I looked over and Mario was gone. I had to go find him. I quickly left the courtroom in search of him.

✳✳✳✳

"Hey, what the hell do you think you're doing, Mario?" I said through clenched teeth. I found him standing at the end of the hall talking on the phone.

"Yo, let me call you back, Bro," he said into the phone. He ended the call and slid the phone into his pocket. "I'm here trying to get my daughter back."

"I'm supposed to do that. I said I just needed your help with the home visit, nigga," I said, pointing to myself.

Nymphopervtress 2: Degenerate

"You must be outta your fucking mind if you think he judge is gonna just hand her over to you. You don't even have a stable place to stay, Desiree."

"Motherfucker! I stay with you in our house."

"I've been meaning to talk to you about that," he said, cracking a smile. "Desiree, you have to realize that you're an addict and a sexual deviant who exposed our child. She could have been hurt or anything behind your actions."

"How so?"

"What if Zaniyah had gotten her hands on that bullshit? Then our fucking daughter would've had cocaine in her system. Did you ever think about that? If she had, CPS would've taken her with quickness and there would probably not be a hearing."

"Well, she isn't hurt by my actions," I responded, rolling my eyes.

"So, what the fuck you call this?" he asked

"I need help, Mario."

"Oh please, that's a crock of shit. Your ass don't need any help. You were a hoe when I met you and it seems like you're gonna always be like this, and if you are, then I don't need you in my life. Neither does Zaniyah. So once this case is one, just leave me and my daughter the fuck alone."

"You think I'm gonna just let you take my child all willy nilly and shit?"

"Nope. I'm gonna get her back though in due time. Just watch." He walked away with that GQ walk that I loved so much.

Today, his funky ass walk was not turning me on. I checked the time and saw that I had twenty minutes left before the recess was to be over. I sat down and Shannon came and sat down next to me. As soon as she sat down, I threw my head onto her shoulder and started wailing like a baby.

"What's the matter, Desiree?" she asked, throwing her arms around me and holding me in a tight embrace.

"He's trying to take my baby from me," I said through my hard tears.

"Who? Who's trying to take Zaniyah?"

"Mario. He's not here to make sure we get her back. He's making sure they don't give her back to me."

"Desiree, look at me," she said, sitting me up. "They are not gonna do that. As soon as they take a look at that nigga's rap sheet, they're gonna rethink that decision."

"No, they're not. Even though I'm trying to get help, they're still not gonna give her to me. Especially because I keep having relapses. Plus, I can't shake this cocaine addiction. I need that to deal with everything that's been going on." I broke down more and cried into my hands.

"It's gonna be okay, Desiree. It's almost time for us to go back in," she said, helping me up. She took me by the hand and hurried me into the ladies restroom. She cleaned my face up with some paper towels and water. She went into my purse and grabbed my makeup bag. She threw a little makeup on my face and turned me around to face the mirror. I actually looked better than I did

Nymphopervtress 2: Degenerate

before I had come into court this morning. She rushed me back out and into the hallway. Court was to resume in two minutes.

✳✳✳✳

"I hope everybody was able to get themselves together and leave all of that nonsense outside of my courtroom," Judge Meyer said as she sat back down in her chair. I think she was referencing that to everybody, but she had her eyes fixed on me. I gently nodded my head in agreement. "Mr. McCoy, you have the floor."

"Thank you, Your Honor. I would like to call my client, Mrs. Davis to the stand," he said. I sat there for a moment. It's not that I didn't want to go up there. I couldn't move. My feet felt like they were pinned to the ground from my nervousness. He came over to me and whispered in my ear. "It'll be okay, Mrs. Davis. It's just a few questions, okay?" I vigorously nodded my head and got up from my seat. He led me over to the witness stand and the bailiff swore me in.

"Mrs. Davis, do you swear to tell the truth, the whole truth, and nothing but the truth?"

"I do," I responded quickly.

"How are you doing today?" my lawyer asked me.

"I'm good, I guess. I've seen better days."

"Yes, I can understand that. Can you give the court an insight look on your day-to-day routine with your child and husband?"

"Sure. Well, I get up and I get Zaniyah's clothes and everything out for school during the week. She gets dressed, I help her brush her teeth, tie her shoes, and check her backpack to make sure everything is there. Then I walk her outside to her bus once it arrives. I go back into the house and I make breakfast for my husband. Once we have breakfast together, and he leaves for work, I'm doing everything from laundry to grocery shopping."

"What about the weekends? Do you all spend time together on the weekend?"

"My daughter and I do. My husband is always working so it gives me and her lot of time to bond," I said, smiling.

"Where do you work, Mrs. Davis?"

"I currently work at a place called Charlie's. It's an adult store," I said in a low tone. I could hear the judgmental murmurs floating around.

"Quiet in my courtroom," the Judge snapped. The crowd quickly became silent and Mr. McCoy continued.

"I see. How would you describe your relationship with your daughter?"

"Zaniyah is the greatest gift I have ever received in my life. She's smart, funny, and always full of questions. She makes my days better as they pass. I couldn't imagine my life without her."

"I take it that your life has been turned upside down these past few months since she's been gone, huh? How has that interfered with your life?"

255   Nymphopervtress 2: Degenerate

"It has taken a toll on me. I happened to have had a relapse."

"What kind of relapse, Mrs. Davis?"

"I started having sex with other people to deal with my pain and depression."

"How many people others do you think? Two? Three?"

"I'm not sure. I lost count after eight," I said, hanging my head down in shame. I could feel the tears welling up in my eyes.

"I understand. Is that all? Have you only had sexual intercourse with others outside of your marriage?" I nodded my head 'yes'. "Well, I have to stop you there, Mrs. Davis. You have also taken an interest in drugs. Am I right?" I shook my head 'yes' again and hung my head again. "And what was the cause of that?"

"Sex wasn't helping me like it used to in the past. I needed something else and I chose cocaine."

"So, in your own words, are you telling me, the Judge, and everyone in attendance, that you never wanted any of this and the only reasons you are doing these things are because you're in pain?"

"Yes, Sir," I said into the mic.

"Your Honor, my client is simply a victim in this case. She is just trying to deal with the fact that she doesn't have her child home. I believe that she will be perfectly fine. She's receiving help and going to therapy as scheduled, and none of it was required by the state. She took these matters into her own two hands, and realized she was doing wrong. Now she wants to make everything right and get her life back on track." He ended his statement and then my mother's funny looking ass lawyer jumped to his feet.

"I would like to cross examine the witness if I may." She waved her hand and gave him his spotlight in the middle of the room. "Mrs. Davis, how long have you had these sexual cravings? Are they consistent or are they seasonal?"

"They used to be constant in the past. Lately, I have been having those more frequently."

"And isn't there prescribed medications that you can take in order to stop these situations?"

"Yes, there are."

"So, why not take the medications? Why would you put yourself in harm's way like that by having sexual interactions with strangers? Do you care that this may affect your child? Or how about your marriage. Do you care about your husband?"

"Yes and no."

"Yes and no what, Mrs. Davis?"

"Yes, I care how this affects my child. I try to control it but I can't a lot of times. And as far as my husband, no, I don't care. He tried to rape me with some drug addict girl, and that's where it all started. Him and his shenanigans could have hurt my baby," I said rubbing my belly.

"And is this your husband's child?"

"Yes," I lied.

"Bitch! You dirty ass don't know who the father is," Mario said, standing up and yelling at me.

"Yes, I do," I yelled back.

"Shut your mouth, Desiree," my mother said, standing to her feet as well. "That child does not deserve to be with you either. You're poisonous and dangerous to both of those babies. You are a whore and you do not deserve to be nobody's mother!"

"Exactly! I should've never married your ass. The saying is right that you cannot turn a hoe into a housewife."

The Judge began to forcefully bang her gavel on the base. I was under attack by the people that were supposed to love me. A mother that hasn't been a mother lately was yelling and screaming at me, telling me she should've aborted me when she had the chance to. My husband, the man I gave my entire life to, was also attacking me. He kept hurling hateful and disrespectful slurs at me as he continued to say that he should have never married a whore like me. He even had the nerve to say that Zaniyah probably wasn't even his. I buried my head into my lap and covered my ears. I was trying my best to block out all the yelling. I was screaming myself as tears flowed freely down my face. I felt someone tugging on my arm. I looked up to see Jessica and Shannon standing behind her. *Where did she even come from?* At this moment I didn't care. I let her take me by the hand and I got down from the stand. The bailiff escorted the three of us to the area where the Judge goes. We could hear officers rushing into the courtroom, and people screaming. I caught a slight glimpse of a couple officers handcuffing people, just as the bailiff shut the door behind us.

"Thanks for coming to my rescue, Jess," I said after I cleaned up my face.

"That's what friends are for," she said.

"Friends? You mean we're cool again?"

"We're gonna always be cool, Sis. I was just tripping. I missed you."

"I missed you, too," I said, running and hugging her. We hugged each other tightly and Shannon came and joined in.

"Now that we're all back and in our right minds, I think we need to get out of this damn chaotic courtroom," Shannon said.

"I second that motion," Jessica said in agreement.

"I can't just leave. I have to see what they're gonna do about Zaniyah. I need to know if-"

Just then the judge came in and slammed the door shut behind her. She took off her gown and hung it on a hook. I looked on and admired her frame. She was actually a decent size for an older lady. When she took her glasses off, she didn't even look to be no more than forty.

"Look, Mrs. Davis, I'm so sorry you had to go through all of that. I am granting you custody of your child immediately. Your husband and mother, on the other hand, will be spending the weekend in jail for harassment; that is one requirement though. You will have to take a drug test every week and if at any time it comes back dirty, your daughter will be taken from you and she will become a ward of the state. You are to continue therapy and your group therapy until the court sees fit. Do you understand?"

Nymphopervtress 2: Degenerate

My friends snickered and giggled behind me like some middle school kids.

"Yes, Ma'am I do. Are you serious? I get to bring my baby home with me?"

"After a representative from Child and Family Services get to your mother's house and get your daughter and all of her belongings, they will be bringing her to you. Is your address still the same on file?"

"No," Shannon said cutting in. "She will be staying with me from now on."

"As long as it's safe and spacious enough for you to have the child there, I see nothing wrong with that," she replied, smiling.

Out of reflex, I threw my arms around her and hugged her. She patted my back and told me that everything was gonna be okay. Moments later, the bailiff came in and said that the courtroom had been cleared out and it was safe for us to leave. The Judge told me she will be checking in on us, as well as the representative from CPS. We got our things and we left. I felt like a brand-new person as I headed out the doors of the court building smiling from ear to ear. I had my best friend back, and pretty soon, my daughter will be back as well.

✳✳✳✳

"This was such a blissful day," I said to my girls. We were over Jessica's house chilling and watching TV, as we sipped some wine. I picked up the third bottle of wine that we had just recently opened and poured myself another glass. I was feeling lovely. I haven't had a day this great in months.

"Yeah, it is. I'm so glad we were able to make amends. It's gonna be nice to have you and Zaniyah back around."

"You got that right," Shannon said. She threw her glass of wine back like it was a shot of liquor or something. Straight chugged it. "This is some good wine, Jessica. Where did you get it from?"

"Girl, I got that from Costco," she said, bursting into laughter.

"Wherever you got it from, be sure to get a lot more next time," I said through slurred syllables. "So what movie are we gonna watch now?" I asked as I watch the last of the end credits disappear from the screen.

"How about we watch that movie called "Hereditary?" Shannon replied.

"I seen that and it was creepy as fuck," Jessica said.

"How was it creepy?" I asked, laughing.

"It just is."

"Ohhh, let's watch it then," I replied.

"Y'all go ahead. I'm getting ready to go to bed."

"Already? It's still early as shit," Shannon said. She looked at her watch. "It's only midnight."

"Only? Bitch bye. I don't know if it's from the alcohol or just being around you two bitches, but I am beyond tired."

Nymphopervtress 2: Degenerate

"I hear you," I said. Our laughter stopped as we heard multiple car doors close outside the house. We tiptoed over to the window and saw three people dressed in all black, wearing ski masks, walking towards the house. Lucky for us, the lights were already out so the people couldn't see us.

"Who the fuck is that?" Jessica asked in a whisper.

"It's Jeremy. I told you he was trying to rob you, Jessica."

"I'm sorry, Desiree. I should've believed you," she cried.

"Don't worry about that right now, because it's neither the place nor time. It doesn't matter who's to blame or who needs to apologize. Right now, we have to make sure that motherfucker and his friends know they messed with the wrong bitches. Follow me." They followed me closely behind as we headed into the kitchen. I handed each of them a knife and we ran up the stairs to her son's room. I got his Louisville Slugger from behind his door once I shut the door behind us. We all pressed our ears against the door to listen. We could hear them shuffling and flipping over furniture downstairs. We heard a loud thud and then footsteps coming up the stairs.

"Split up and search everywhere. Get whatever you can. I'm not sure how long she's gonna be gone, so we gotta move fast. Her car is outside, so that means she rode somewhere with one of her thot ass friends," we heard a voice say. That was definitely Jeremy's voice; I knew his voice from anywhere. We could hear a set of footsteps heading our way. We stopped leaning on the door and scattered around the room. I stood behind the door with the

Nymphopervtress 2: Degenerate

bat in my hand. Shannon stood off into a dark corner where she would see the person coming in first. And Jessica, she was hiding in the closet. The door eased open and a figure, maybe probably the same height as I was, entered into the dark room. They turned on a flashlight and flashed it around the room. I leaned closer against the wall so he wouldn't see me in case he closed the door. I heard Shannon gasp loudly, and the guy jumped. He turned around and his light fell right onto Shannon.

"Yo, Jeremy," he yelled. "I found something in here." He walked over towards Shannon. Jessica slightly pushed open the closet door as I walked up on the dude. I got into a baseball stance, prepared to knock this nigga's head clean off his shoulders. I gripped the bat tightly and with all my might, I swung. He fell into the dresser and yelped out in pain. Shannon ran over to assist as she stabbed him in the arm. Seconds passed by, and Jessica made her way over as well. She stabbed him in the shoulder of the same arm that Shannon had just stabbed him in.

"Ay, what the fuck is going on in here?" Jeremy yelled as he burst into the room and turning on the light. The room flooded with the bright fluorescent light. Jeremy looked at Jessica and saw the knife in her hand. He charged at her and knocked her onto the bed and then onto the floor. I ran over with the bat in hand. I tried to bring it down on Jeremy's back, but somebody stopped me in midair. I looked back and it was the other guy. Shannon ran to my rescue and stabbed him multiple times in his midsection until he fell to the floor. Once he did, the bat was under

Nymphopervtress 2: Degenerate

my control again. I cracked right in the side of his face. He flew off top of Jessica and she got up. She snatched the bat from me and started beating the breaks off of him. Shannon and I watched for a few moments before we stopped her. When we looked at Jeremy's face again, it was covered in dark and bright red blood. His nose looked all distorted and some more.

"Are you okay, Jess?" I asked after she calmed down a little.

"Oh, I'm good. As long as y'all got my back, I know that's a fact." She walked over and stood over top of Jeremy's limp body. "You messed with the wrong bitches, Jeremy. How does it feel?" he didn't respond to her. He just laid there with swollen eyes that were damn near closing. We left the bodies in the room and headed downstairs. We all poured another glass of wine and called the police. By the time we had finished drinking our second glass, the police were knocking at the door. I went to open the door and was in shock.

"Hi, Desiree," Dion said.

"Hello, Officer. Thank you for responding in time to our call," I said as I stepped to the side. He walked into the house followed by two other officers. One of the officers walked over to Jessica and Shannon and talked to them while Dion continued to stand near me.

"Hello, ladies. I'm Officer James Lloyd. What seems to be the problem?"

"These three jackasses just broke into my sister's goddamn house," Shannon said.

"Ma'am, please refrain from using that kind of language. And this is your house?"

"Yes, Officer it is," Jessica replied.

"Was anything taken from the home?"

"Not that I know of, but those niggas are still upstairs."

"Do you mind showing me and my partner?"

"Nope. Come on," Jessica said. She and Shannon led the two officers upstairs to Raheem's room. Now I was left with Dion's ass.

"Don't you think you need to be going to follow your partners, Officer Mitchell?" I snapped walking away. He stopped me from walking away by grabbing me by the arm.

"Desiree, please. I miss you. I have been going crazy all this time because I haven't heard from you."

"How the fuck can you miss me when you got a whole wife at home? Besides, I'm pregnant now," I said, snatching my arm from his grasp.

"So I see. But, my wife left me, Desiree."

"Oh, ho, ho, so that's why you all of a sudden miss me, huh?" I said, breaking out into laughter. "It's because your wife took her pussy away from you. That's funny."

"This shit isn't funny. It's serious, goddamnit. I haven't had sex in months because of that stunt you pulled."

　　　　　　　　Nymphopervtress 2: Degenerate

"Don't give me that bull crap, Dion. You deserved to get embarrassed. How could you possibly think I was gonna be okay when I found out you were married? Nigga you were sleeping with me, in my bed, while your life partner was probably at home hugging a pillow so she could go to sleep. You're fucking unbelievable."

"You have some nerve," he said, stepping closer to me and backing me up against the front door. I inhaled the sweet aroma of his Dolce & Gabbana cologne. It was intoxicating and making my pussy awaken. "I did some snooping of my own on you, Desiree Logan. Or do you prefer to be called Desiree Davis? I found out that you had an entire husband as well, and a child. So, who are you to pass judgment on someone about telling lies?"

"Don't you try and pull that with me, Dion."

"Don't give me that, Desiree. We both lied and we can put that behind us now. You know you miss me and that you want me just as bad as I want you," he said. He grabbed my hand and placed it on his crotch. His dick was bulging and trying to bust through his slacks. He lifted my head up so I can look into his dark brown eyes. His lips touched mine and my panties became instantly soaked with my juices. We could hear everybody coming back down the stairs and we had to break our kiss. He moved over a little and pulled out his notepad as if he had just been taking my statement and whatnot.

"We've apprehended the perpetrators, Officer Mitchell," Officer Lloyd replied as he escorted Jeremy and one of the other

Nymphopervtress 2: Degenerate

guys through the living room. Jeremy looked at me with a sinister look and I just rolled my eyes at him.

"We do have to get an ambulance here for the other guy. He lost a tremendous amount of blood and he can't walk that well. He was going in and out of consciousness."

"Doesn't matter. He can still go and we can take them all to the hospital once we get out of here. We can handcuff them to the beds and do our questioning there. Once they're all patched up, we can take all of their asses to county."

"Will do, Officer," he said. He left Jeremy with the other officer, who escorted both of them out the door. Moments later, Officer Lloyd was practically dragging the other guy down the stairs with his arms locked behind his back. He walked him right out the house and said his goodbyes to all of us. Shannon and Jessica went upstairs to clean up Raheem's room and I told them I would be up in a second.

"Is that all, Dion?" I said, focusing my attention back on him.

"No, it's not, Desiree. Can I please see you tonight?"

"What for exactly?" I asked, folding my arms across my chest.

"We can make up," he replied, walking back up on me.

"Maybe. Just call me later."

"Are you gonna answer the phone?"

"Maybe," I said, pushing him out the door. I didn't let him get another word out as I slammed and locked the door in his face. I ran upstairs to help my girls clean up the mess.

"Look at this mess," I replied. There were blood stains in the light carpet and on Raheem's little bed. There was a big hole in the wall behind the dresser and toys were all over the place.

"I know, right?" Shannon said, tossing me a sponge. I went over and knelt down with them to scrub the carpet.

"How could I have been so fucking blind and stupid?" Jessica asked as she dropped her sponge and leaned up against the bed. We dropped our sponges as well and rushed to her side. "How could I have not seen this coming?"

"There was no way you were gonna know, Sis," I replied, laying her head on my shoulder. "He was just slick and sneaky with it. I just had happened to overhear him that night in the kitchen talking about it."

"I'm sorry again, Desi," she said, looking at me.

"It's okay, Hun. You were just blinded by love, that's all."

"Yeah, you were," Shannon hopped in. "but, it was nice to retaliate on their asses and make their plan backfire." We all broke out into laughter at her comment.

"That is an upset of things, but now, I have to go shopping for a new carpet and comforter set for Raheem."

"Well, let's finish this up and get to it. That is, if you're up to it. We can always wait until tomorrow."

"I think I would rather wait until tomorrow. We can hit the mall in the morning."

"Cool with us," Shannon said.

We gathered up our things and hugged Jessica goodnight. We got in the car and I checked my phone. Dion had called me multiple times and sent me text messages. One of them had an address attached to it. Ironically, it was about twenty minutes from Shannon's house. I asked her if she could drop me off and she gladly offered.

✳✳✳✳

We arrived at the address Dion had given me. I hugged Shannon and told her I would be catching an Uber home in the morning if Dion couldn't bring me. She told me to be careful and to let her know if I needed her. I told her okay and hopped out of her car. I watched as she pulled off and her taillights disappear into the night. I focused back to the house in front of me. It was a regular house, I guess. He had a white picket fence that all women dreamed about, and a freshly mowed lawn. I walked through the opening of the fence and admired his house. It was a brick house and looked to be about three levels. *They must have kids,* I thought. I walked up on the porch and contemplated ringing the doorbell or just knocking. Before I could come to a final decision, the door opened and Dion was standing there, wearing nothing but some gray lounge pants. I looked down at his dick and it was for sure swinging freely. My heart started racing and my mouth started to water as I thought about slurping and sucking all over that big ole thing. He stepped to the side and invited me in.

"I'm glad you decided to come over, Desiree. Would you like a drink? I have soda, water, wi-"

"Look cut the shit, Dion. We all know I'm not here for a casual visit. Let's just have sex and get it over with," I said bluntly.

"Is that all you came here for? Just to have sex?"

"Yeah, and we need to hurry up because I have shit to do in the morning."

"Desiree, I'm not just a piece of meat," he said.

"Look, I'm leaving then. I didn't come here for a fucking conversation," I said, heading back out the door.

"Okay, stop. Let's just go upstairs so I can make love to you."

"Nigga, you can't be serious right now. Nobody in this room loves the other person. Let's just fuck and get back to our lives like we never knew each other."

"Is that how you want it?"

"Yep."

"Fine. Let's go upstairs then."

"Right behind you."

He led me upstairs to his bedroom. The entire room was red and black. The bed was huge and was covered in satin pillows. I stripped out of my clothes and hopped on the bed. He watched as I made myself comfortable as if this were my own home. He

Nymphopervtress 2: Degenerate

stripped out of his clothes and joined me. His dick was already erect and standing at full attention, but I still wanted to cover it in my saliva. I pushed him back on the bed and made a trail of kisses from his neck down to his manhood. I put my hands behind my back, and started licking the tip of his penis. I heard him moan softly and I looked up at him. His eyes were staring back at me. I opened my mouth wider and began to suck his penis. I started out slow then quickly picked up the pace. He moaned loud and grabbed the back of my head, forcing his dick deeper down my throat. I was slightly gagging and my eyes were welling up with tears, but I didn't let that stop me from completing the task at hand. The slurping noises came soon after, causing him to move around a lot. He looked like he was having convulsions. When I tasted a little bit of his precum, I swallowed it and went back to lie beside him.

He quickly got on top of me and started kissing me. I was resistant at first, but then I thought, oh well. I grabbed his head and kissed him deeply. I kissed him like he belonged to me. At this moment, he kind of did, so I thought I'd take advantage of it. He moved from my lips down to planting sweet kisses on my neck to my breasts. He took the right one into his mouth and cupped the left one with his hand. I moaned softly and grabbed his head again. I placed my hand on top of his head, instructing him to go ahead and head down south. He got the message quickly and dived right in.

He licked and sucked my clit, making my pussy tingle. He used his fingers to open my pussy a little more, allowing himself more lead way to put his tongue in deeper. I pushed his head in as much as I could and wrapped my legs around his head, damn near smothering him. This went on for about fifteen minutes, then my legs finally broke away from one another, and a river of my juices covered his lips and chin. He wiped his face and pushed up on his hands. He reached over into the nightstand drawer and pulled out a condom. Before he could open it, I stopped him.

"You're not gonna need that," I said seductively.

"You sure? I don't wanna hurt the baby."

"Yeah, I'm sure and it's okay. I want us to feel all of each other," I replied.

"That's cool with me," he said. He happily tossed the condom onto the floor and kissed me again. He eased his dick inside me and my back arched from the impact. He laid gently on my stomach so that he wouldn't hurt the baby. I could feel my walls tightening up on his dick as he rammed it in and out vigorously. After a while, he had come all inside of me, and in return, I released my juices all over him, soaking the bed underneath me. When his last drop finally landed inside me, he removed himself and laid down beside me.

"Wow. That was great. I have never been in pussy so wet in my life."

"I'm sure you have. I'm pretty sure you have kids, right?"

"Yeah, we have three kids, but, while she was pregnant, my wife never let me have sex with her. She was so fucking evil to me throughout the entire nine months. It was madness."

"Well, now you don't have to worry about anything because she's gone."

"And what about you?"

"What about me?"

"Are you gonna leave me, too?"

"I don't know right now. We'll just see how everything plays out."

"I don't want you to leave me, Desiree. I need you," he said desperately.

"I think we should talk about this another time. Like, when we're both fully clothed."

"That's cool. Wanna go another round?" he asked, grinning.

"It's getting really late," I responded looking at the time on the clock beside me. "Maybe we can have sex for breakfast."

"That's my favorite kind of breakfast," he responded.

"Mine, too." I snuggled under the comforter and got comfortable. He came up behind me and held me. Soon, we were both drifting off to La La Land.

Chapter Twenty

Emergency Birth

"Rise and shine," I heard Dion say. I squinted my eyes just enough to see that he was fully clothed and wearing his police officer uniform.

"What the fuck, Dion? Why are you up and dressed already?"

"It's almost 8 o'clock and I have to be down at the station at 9. I was gonna drop you off wherever you had to go so you won't be here all day alone."

"Maybe I want to. It's too damn early to be up, Dion."

"Check this out, I will just leave the spare house key on the nightstand for you. That way you can lock up whenever you leave and come back whenever you want, and I can leave you a couple of dollars for a cab."

"Just CashApp me the money so I can take an Uber home."

"Whatever makes you happy, I will do," he said. I looked at him strangely and let out a nervous laugh.

"Thanks," I replied. That's the only thing I could muster up for a response.

Nymphopervtress 2: Degenerate

"I'll see you later."

"See ya." As soon as I heard the door slam, and the sound of his car unlocking, I laid back and nestled back into the bed. I was not ready to deal with the world just yet today. I just needed to be home by 4 o'clock. The representative from Child and Family Services had left a message yesterday, but I still wasn't sure how I missed the call. I guess she must have called while we were over Jessica's house enjoying ourselves after court. I think I had this shit in the bag as far as this piss test thing. I would be trying my best to not disappoint my child. I yawned and stretched wildly. I was getting sleepy again so I shut my eyes and went back to sleep. The sweet thoughts of my child running into my arms in about eight hours made me smile.

I'm not sure how long I had slept for, but I felt great when I woke up again. It was almost 11 in the morning. I checked my phone. I had a couple of messages from my friends and Dion. I checked in with my girls and told them I was good and that I would see them shortly when it was almost time for Zaniyah to come home. I opened Dion's message thread and smiled. He sent me a kissing emoji and told me how beautiful I was. It reminded me of how my heart used to flutter whenever Mario told me that. I was so caught up in my phone that I didn't notice I had company.

"What the fuck?" a female voice said. I dropped my phone and saw that it was Dion's wife, or ex-wife, whoever the fuck she was.

"Hey, girl. Jasmine, right?" I said, smiling as I got off the bed wearing nothing at all. I extended my hand her way and she just looked at it.

"What the hell are you doing here you trifling little bitch?"

"Ouch," I said, placing my hand on my chest as if I was in shock. "Why do you have to be so mean?"

"What are you doing here?" she repeated through clenched teeth.

"Dion invited me over for a rendezvous. I hope you don't mind."

Her eyes were filling with tears of hurt and anger. Her eyes roamed my body but grew increasingly large as they fell on my stomach. "Are you pregnant?" she asked.

"Uh, yeah, I do believe so. I only say that because I haven't eaten this morning so there is only one other way I could be big like this," I replied sarcastically.

"Is that Dion's baby?"

"Yeah it is," I lied.

"I can't believe this shit," she yelled and my ignorant ass just stood there smiling and giggling. "How could he do this to me? To our children?"

"I don't know, Sis, but if I were you, I would beat his ass."

"Nobody asked you, Bitch."

"Whatever. You can see yourself out whenever you're ready," I said, making my way back to the bed. I laid down and stared at her.

"What do you think you're doing, Hoe?"

"I'm going back to sleep, if you let me. Sheesh. People are so damn rude and disrespectful these days," I replied. I closed my eyes and tried to block out her heavy and uneasy breathing.

I could hear as she rushed across the floor towards me but I couldn't move out of the way in time as she grabbed me by the throat and started choking me. I reached up and punched her a couple of times but it did not work to my advantage. She was pushing down on my neck, making it harder for me to breathe. The thought of me not being able to see Zaniyah or my unborn child gave me all the strength that I had needed. I managed to grab her around her throat and apply the same amount of pressure she was giving me. The only thing that had eventually given me the upper hand over Jasmine was the fact that she released her hold on my neck, but mine had gotten tighter. She was grabbing at my hands, trying to break free, but I bit down hard on her hand and she dropped them back down. Once I got her on the floor, I started pounding her in the face with my fists. After she stopped moving and fighting back, I stopped throwing blows to her face. I got off top of her and went into the bathroom because thanks to this bitch, I was all sweaty and shit. While I had my back turned, this punk bitch rushed me and grabbed me from behind by my hair. She slammed my head into the mirror, causing the glass to break and several pieces dropped into the sink. I wrapped one into my hand and waited until I had a chance to retaliate. She released the hold on my hair and I took that as my cue as I turned and tried to

Nymphopervtress 2: Degenerate

cut her face, but, instead, she had her hand up in the way and I sliced that motherfucker like a slice of bread. She screamed out in pain and I ran out the bathroom. She ran behind me and jumped on my back, and I fell stomach first onto the floor. She turned me over and I kicked her in her stomach and as soon as she bent over, I kicked her in the face and she flew back onto the floor. She was lying on the floor holding both her stomach and her nose. Blood was gushing from her nostrils. I stood up and went to put my clothes on as she laid there. I guess she decided to give up. Pregnant or not, no bitch was ever gonna punk me and think she sweet. I had already put on my pants and shoes and now I just had to put my shirt on. My stomach was hurting badly, which felt kind of weird. On top of that, I felt like I had to pee really, really, bad. I hurriedly went into the bathroom to pee before I accidently pissed myself. When I pulled my pants down, I saw a great amount of blood. It wasn't like before, though. It was thicker and darker and the pains were far more painful than the last time. Instead of calling an Uber, I dialed 911 and told them to send an ambulance immediately. I finished using the bathroom and went over to Dion's wife. I kicked that bitch in the head one last time and told her to never try something so damn suicidal again in her life. I grabbed my bag and my phone and walked at a steady pace down the stairs. Once I reached the bottom of the step, the paramedics were walking to the door with a stretcher.

"Ma'am, were you the one that called for an ambulance?"

"Yes, Sir. I'm pregnant and I think I'm in labor. I believe my water may have broken," I lied.

"Well, let's get you to the hospital and get that baby out into this world," he responded cheerfully.

"Thanks," I said, returning a smile to him as he helped me to get up on the stretcher.

"Is there someone you need to call to meet you at the hospital?"

"Yes, my husband," I replied. I dialed Mario's number and the phone call went straight voicemail. *Oh shit, I forgot he was locked up*, I thought to myself. Oh well then, I tried. I laid back on the bed and let the contractions have their way with me. I decided to call Shannon and I told her I was on my way to the hospital. After she piped down from thinking Dion did something to me, I told her that it wasn't him and that I thought the baby was coming early. I told her to let the caseworker know where I was and for them to bring Zaniyah up to the hospital later on once she got there. She promised me that they would and she told me good luck and have a safe delivery. Unfortunately for me, I didn't have Mario to be in the delivery room with me this time to coach me. It saddened me and I cried on the inside. If it weren't for me and my ways, he would be here by my side like a husband is supposed to be.

Nymphopervtress 2: Degenerate

Once I arrived at the hospital, they rushed me through the hospital's emergency entrance and into a room. They quickly hooked me up to an IV and monitor. The nurses saw that my contractions were getting closer than before. They were now two minutes apart. The doctor came about ten minutes later and told me he had to check my cervix. I placed my feet in the stirrups and waited patiently for him to begin playing with my vagina. He informed me that the baby was turned around and he couldn't get him to get in a better position. So, instead of me doing a traditional vaginal birth, I had to have an emergency C-section. Now my black ass was nervous. One of the nurses left the room and came back. She prepped this extremely long needle with a clear liquid and turned towards me.

"Oh no, you don't have to do that. Just try again. I'm sure he'll turn around," I said frantically.

"We don't have time for that. We have to get this baby out now," she said under her face mask.

She came closer towards me and tried to push me onto my side, but I fought against her. Instead of her giving up, she had her nurse goons both turned me over onto my side so she could put the needle in my back. After she stuck me with the needle, the pain in my stomach subsided and my entire lower body had become numb. I actually had to look down and make sure my body was still there. The nurse that stuck me turned me back over onto my back and they put a curtain up so I wouldn't see anything.

"Put the curtain down goddamnit," I yelled.

Nymphopervtress 2: Degenerate

"Sorry, Ma'am. It's hospital procedure," the doctor said to me.

What a crock of shit, I thought to myself. Not only did I have to get a C-section, but I was gonna miss watching them pull my son from my body. Tears ran out my eyes because I was getting pissed and it seemed like the process was taking forever. Just as I was about to say something else, I heard loud cries from the other side of the sheet. *That's my little boy* I said to myself. I saw as they carried him over to the table and weighed him and cleaned him up. They wrapped him tightly in a hospital blanket and laid him in the crib across from me. He was lying there so peaceful and motionless. I looked back at the doctor and the nurses. I saw some thread and scissors on the table, so I guess that meant they were about to sew me back up and have me looking like the guy from The Texas Chainsaw Massacre movies. After they told me the dos and don'ts of having stitches, they gave me my baby and had finally left us alone. I held him close to me and acted as if nothing else in this world mattered at the moment.

"You're a handsome little boy," I said to him as he held his eyes closed from the bright light. Or was he keeping them closed because of me? People always said that babies can sense when a person is not a good person. Did this little human think that I was mad for him already? Could he sense the whoreness of me seeping through my pores? Could he inhale my toxic ways into his nostrils as he breathed in my arms? Maybe he could or maybe he couldn't. I wouldn't be able to tell right now, probably never. But, for the moment, I was gonna enjoy this private time with him. I reached for my phone on the table beside me. I took a couple of quick photos to post on my Instagram and Facebook pages. Since I didn't really think about a name for him, I asked my followers to help me pick out the perfect name for my little prince. He started to squirm in my arms so I sat the phone down and held him close again. His eyes eased open and I could see them clearly. They were the same brown color as Mario's. I took a peek at his hair under his little hat. His hair was curly just like Zaniyah's was when she was born. It was soft as a bed of feathers.

Knock. Knock.

I looked to the door to see who my unexpected visitor was. My eyes widened with excitement and joy as I laid eyes on Zaniyah. She stood at the door next to a slim dark-skinned lady whom I guess was the representative from Child Protective Services. She looked at me as if I were a celebrity, the way her eyes smiled at me. She looked up to the lady and the lady just nodded her head. I guess she was confirming that she could come over. She ran over to me and threw her arms around me, hitting my freshly stitched wound. I cringed a little but I didn't let her notice it. I just sucked it up and smiled through the pain.

"I'm so happy to see you, Mommy," she said, squeezing me tighter.

"I'm happy to see you, too, Zaniyah. Look who's here," I said to her as I brought the baby over to the other side.

"Is that my baby?" she asked energetically.

"Oh, no, no, Stink. It's your baby brother."

"He's so cute. What's his name?"

"I'm not sure. I haven't picked out a name for him yet."

"Oooh, can I pick it out?" she asked, jumping up and down.

"I don't see why not." She paced the floor like she was in deep thought. I just smiled. I looked over at the lady who was still standing by the door. I motioned for her to come in. she came to my bedside.

"Congratulations on the new baby," she said.

"Thank you, uh, Ms.?"

"Oh, sorry. My name is Ms. Alicia Montgomery. I was assigned to Zaniyah's case."

"What happened to the other lady?"

"Not sure. I didn't ask questions when your daughter's case came across my desk."

"Oh okay. So what now?" I asked trying to get this meet and greet over with so I can spend some time with both of my children.

"Well, I have already been to your best friend's house that you will be staying at. Everything checked out just fine and she helped me set up Zaniyah's room with her. I was supposed to actually leave her at the house, but she begged me to bring her. I couldn't say no to that beautiful little baby," she said, smiling at Zaniyah.

"Thank you," I said, grabbing her by the hand.

"No problem. Well, once you're released, you're gonna have to inform the judge that you have gone into the hospital and just gave birth. She may or may not grant you six-week probation while you heal up, that's up to her. I will be doing visitation checks twice a month and then once a month after a year. Do you have any questions for me?"

"Not at the moment."

"Well, if you think of anything, here is my card. It has both my office number and my personal cell phone number in case you need to call me after hours. I will leave you to your children."

"Goodbye, Ms. Montgomery," I said as she walked out the room. She turned and waved and kept on moving. Zaniyah ran back over to the bed smiling from ear to ear as she looked like she just solved a case.

"Mommy, I know what we should name my baby brother."

"What name did you come up with, Sweetie?"

"We should name him Zakai."

"I love that name. Where did you get it from?"

"This boy in my class. We're the only ones who names start with the letter Z. And since that's my baby brother, his name should start just like mine," she proudly smiled.

"Okay, so we shall call him Zakai. What about a middle name?"

"His name should be Mario like our daddy."

My smile faded away from my face. She thought that this was Mario's baby. Maybe it was. Only time would tell.

"What's wrong, Mommy," she asked, looking sad.

"I think daddy would love for Zakai's middle name to be Mario."

"Yayy," she said, jumping up and down again.

I looked back down at the precious little bundle of joy lying in my arms. "Zakai Mario Davis. Welcome to the world, baby boy." I kissed his head and put his hat back on.

"Can I hold my new baby brother, Mommy?" Zaniyah asked. I nodded my head and patted the bed beside me. I scooted over and she sat up just how I was. I handed the baby over to her and she held him so motherly. I grabbed my phone and took some pictures of me and my babies. I let Zaniyah pick the one she liked best and I posted it on social media with the caption 'welcome, baby Zakai Mario Davis.' I felt proud to have my babies with me, but the day was coming to an end for a while. I felt the medicine starting to make me feel a little woozy. I buzzed the nurse into the room. I asked her to put the baby in his crib and bring it closer to me. She volunteered to take him to the nursery with the other newborns but I kindly declined. I heard so many stories about babies getting either kidnapped or switched at hospitals. I would not be in that predicament with my son. So, she pulled the crib over close enough so I can get to him if he started to cry and so I wouldn't reach out too far and accidently rip my stitches. Zaniyah took her shoes off and got under the blanket with me. I put her in between me and Zakai, with our backs facing the window. I kissed her head and stroked her hair until I fell asleep.

****

I had awakened from my sleep because Zaniyah accidentally backed into me and hit my stomach. The pain meds must have worn off while I was sleep. I opened my eyes up to admire my sleeping beauty. She was sleeping so peaceful and pure. She looked just like an angel. I looked over into the crib at Zakai. The blankets were balled up in the space where he was sleeping. *I guess Zaniyah must have thought he was cold and decided to cover him up,* I thought to myself. I sat up and leaned over a little more, carefully reaching over Zaniyah so I wouldn't wake her. I moved the covers and the crib was empty. Zakai was gone! I began to panic. I got out the bed against the doctor's orders and walked around to the other side of the bed. I snatched the blankets out of the clear crib and threw them all over the floor. It was true that my son was definitely gone. I reached for the buzzard to call for the nurse. I pressed the button repeatedly but nobody ever came. Then I noticed why. I lifted the buzzard off the bed and noticed that the cord had been cut in half. *What the fuck?* I heard the toilet flush and I turned around.

"What the fuck are you doing here?" I asked Jasmine. She had emerged from the bathroom carrying Zakai in the baby blanket.

"Well, well, well, you did a good job, Desiree. Your little boy is beautiful. Or should I say, my little boy," she said, giggling.

286   Nymphopervtress 2: Degenerate

"Why the hell do you have my baby, Jasmine?"

"Your baby, huh? See, that's where you're wrong, Sweetheart. I distinctively asked you was this my husband's baby and you told me it was, and since he and I are married, what's his is mines and what's mines is his. You should know all about vows since you're married and all, too."

"That's not Dion's baby, Jasmine. That's my husband's baby. I lied to you this morning about that being your husband's baby."

"Now, I don't even know if I can believe you, Desiree. You told me that you were pregnant with my husband's baby and now you're not. When I called him this afternoon after I woke up from you knocking me unconscious, he told me that he didn't know you were pregnant until recently. So, now I'm thinking that when you came into the restaurant a couple months ago you were lying about that one-night stand. Exactly how long have you and my husband been fucking around? Hmmm?"

I stood there glaring at her as anger overpowered the pain from my C-section. "Look, Jasmine, your husband and I had sex twice. That was a few months ago and last night. I swear to you. Just give me the baby and I will leave your husband alone."

"I don't believe you," she said. She unwrapped the blanket from around Zakai and hung him upside down by his feet.

"Holy shit! What the fuck are you doing?" I screamed at her.

Nymphopervtress 2: Degenerate

"I don't think you deserve this precious little baby. You done had sex with my husband, your husband, and God knows who else? Are you even sure that this is your husband's child?"

"Yes, I'm sure. Just like I'm sure you need to give me my baby."

"What are you gonna do if I don't?"

"Mommy, who is that lady and why is she holding my baby brother like that?" Zaniyah asked as she rubbed her eyes and hopped off the bed.

"She's a very bad lady, Sweetie."

"Hey? Put my brother down lady," Zaniyah yelled at Jasmine.

"Aww, she's so cute, Desiree, but that little thing better not come near me or I'm gonna kick her across the floor." I pulled Zaniyah close to me and whispered in her ear. Moments later, she ran out of the room.

"You will not touch my daughter and I'd be damned if you hurt my son."

"Are you sure about that, Desiree?" This bitch started transferring Zakai back and forth between her hands. He woke up and began crying at the top of his little lungs.

"Jasmine, please. Sit him up like he's supposed to. You're gonna kill my son."

"Why should I care if your son lives or dies? It's not like he belongs to me."

"I'm warning you, Jasmine. If you hurt Zakai, you will regret it. I will kill you."

"I don't think you're in a position to make any types of threats like that to anybody. It's skanks like you that make it hard for married woman like me to live happily and peacefully. Y'all always gotta come around with your hot pussies and throw them up in our husbands' faces."

"I'm married, too, Jasmine, so I know where you're coming from."

"Bullshit! You know nothing of where I'm coming from. You're a home wrecker. Your home was a mess and then you went around being messy at another woman's home. How do you sleep at night knowing that you are ruining somebody's marriage? Do you ever think about the consequences of your actions?"

Before I could answer, Zaniyah came back into the room. She was followed by two officers, one of them surprisingly being Dion, and a couple people from the nurses' staff.

"Jasmine, what the hell are you doing?" Dion asked her.

"Well, now it's a party," she said, smiling. "I just came here to see you and your girlfriend's new baby boy. Congratulations."

"Desiree, I know you didn't tell her that that was my baby did you?"

"Yeah I did."

"Is that really my son?"

"No, it's not. I just told her that to piss her off when she came to the house this morning."

"Yeah, I went to our house this morning, and what did I find? This little home wrecking floozy laying butt ass naked in our bed. How could you do this to me, Dion? Did you think about the fucking kids while you were lying up with this bitch all those nights?"

"No, Baby, I didn't and I'm sorry."

"Yeah, you're sorry alright. You're just a sorry motherfucker, Dion. You always have been and you always will be."

"I know, Jasmine, but, I need you to hand the baby over to his mother right now. I have to take you in to the station."

"Me? What for?"

"Child endangerment."

"Are you seriously gonna arrest me? Your own fucking wife? I got your ass." She lifted Zakai up into the air, while he was still crying uncontrollably, and held him over her head.

"Put my fucking son down, you crazy bitch!" I yelled at the top of my lungs.

"You want me to put him down, Bitch?"

"You heard what the fuck I said!"

"Sure. I'll put the little fucker down," she said. She put her arms high up in the air and dropped Zakai from her hands. Me, Dion, and one of the other officers quickly ran over in an attempt to catch him before he hit the floor. The first officer was too far away, Dion hit the baby with the tips of his fingers, but I was the one that caught him. I caught him in my hands as he was just about to hit the floor. I got up on my feet and staggered over to where Zaniyah was.

"Hold your brother, Zaniyah and go sit on the bed."

"Where are you going, Mommy?" she asked in her innocent little voice.

"Mommy's got some trash to take out," I said as I charged toward Jasmine and knocked her into the wall. She punched me three times in my stomach, but I didn't let that distract me from whooping this bitch's ass. I grabbed her by her hair and swung her head into the wall. I punched her two times in the face and then threw her across the floor. Once I did, Dion placed his knee in his wife's back and slapped the cuffs on her wrists. He read Jasmine her Miranda Rights, as they escorted her out of the room. I looked down at my hospital gown and it was covered in dark blood. I fell to the floor and the nurses rushed to my aid. I had blacked out just as they placed me on the stretcher. My beautiful daughter and my handsome baby boy were the last things I seen as my eyes had shut.

✳✳✳✳

I woke up with a breathing tube in my nose and a bunch of beeping surrounding me. I looked around and I saw the board up on the wall saying that I was currently in the Intensive Care Unit of the hospital. I hit the button to call the nurse and within seconds a nurse came rushing into the room.

"Yes, Mrs. Davis? How can I help you?"

"Hi, I'm just wondering where my kids are?"

"Oh, your sister, I believe her name is Shannon, she came and got your daughter. Your son is in the nursery. You had put her down as your emergency contact so we called her once you passed out last night."

"How's he doing?"

"He's doing well. Nothing harmed him at all. He was just hungry and cranky."

"Thank you."

"No problem. Did you need anything else?"

"Just a pitcher of ice water please."

"Coming right up," she said with a smile. She left out and came back quickly with the water and cute little cubes of ice. I slurped up the cold drink to drench my parched throat. It was quite refreshing. I sat up in the bed as best as I could and reached for the phone. I quickly dialed Shannon's number and waited for her to pick up the phone.

"Hello?" she said when she picked up the phone.

"Hey, girl," I said, as cheerfully as I possibly could.

"Oh shit, hey, Sis. How do you feel?"

"Girl, I'm good. I'm just feeling the aftermath of the pain right now because the medicine is starting to wear off.

"That must suck ass," she said, laughing into the phone. I couldn't help but laugh right along with her. It felt good to laugh for a change.

"It really does. What is Zaniyah doing?"

"She's taking a nap. She went to sleep with the blanket I had bought for the baby. She said that's her brother's blanket and she want to hold it for him until he comes home."

"She's a mess," I said, chuckling again.

"Yeah she is but I love my little niecey pooh."

"I know you do. Did you get a chance to see Zakai?"

"Yeah, I seen your little nugget baby. He's really cute. He looks just like Mario."

I'm glad, I thought to myself. "I know, right?"

"Have you spoken to him? Does he know that the baby is here?"

"I called him, but he didn't pick up. I don't know what's going on with him honestly. Have you talked to Jessica?"

"Yep. She wants us to come visit you but I told her I wasn't sure if you were gonna be up to it."

"Girl, please. Y'all better bring y'all asses up here to see me. And make sure y'all bring Zaniyah and Raheem."

"No shit, Sherlock. I will see if she wants to come later. If not, we will come down first thing in the morning. You just get some rest."

"I definitely will. I'm about to lay back down now. I will call you later or you guys can call up to the hospital. I think we can get phone calls up until eleven. I'm not sure, but I think that's the right time."

"Cool. Love you, Sis."

"Love you, too. Take care of my baby until I get home."

Nymphopervtress 2: Degenerate

"Most definitely."

"Thank you so much, Shannon?"

"For what?"

"Being such a great friend."

"Man, stop all that gay shit. You know I'm gonna always be here for you no matter. You already know that."

"Yeah, I know. I'll talk to you later."

"Later, Babe."

We hung up the phone and I laid back down. I buzzed the nurse back into the room and asked her what time it was. She informed me that it was 3 o'clock in the afternoon. I wanted to go back to sleep again, so I asked her to pull the curtains closed and turn the lights down in the room. She did and told me not to be startled by the various nurses and doctors that were gonna be coming in and out of my room, checking my vitals and my stomach that they had to stitch back up. She also told me that they would probably be bringing me my dinner plate around like six or seven. That was enough for me to get a nice amount of sleep for now. And that's just what I did when she walked her peppy little butt out of the room and closed my door.

As I lay in my bed, I replayed back the last seven years of my life. I had been through all that shit with Jay, just to end up with his cousin, Mario. Then I find out that this nigga is fucking bisexual, even though he denies it still to this day. Then I had Zaniyah and got married to the person that I wanted to spend the rest of my life with; at least that's what I thought anyway. Then

Nymphopervtress 2: Degenerate

over the years, Mario and I have been going back and forth and being at each other's throats for everything. From the way I wore my hair, all the way to whose turn it was to pay which bills. Now, I gave birth to a beautiful baby boy, and my entire life has been spiraling out of control because of Mario and my addiction, and now my fucking skin started to itch and feel like something was crawling on me as soon as I thought about cocaine. This shit was beyond me. I didn't want any part of this life. If I could turn back the hands of time, and pick the times I wanted to keep, it would probably be the births of my children and the day I said 'I do." Everything else, like all that disorder and addiction shit, they could miss me with that shit. I didn't want it but, in all honesty, I needed it. I needed it to get through my stressful and depressing days. I needed to clear my mind and get some real sleep. I made my mind go blank and think about a happy place. I thought about my childhood. I thought about the last thing that happened to me as a kid, and just my luck, it was traumatizing, just like everything else in my life.

I remember lying in the bed with my mother and her boyfriend, Ronnie. I was probably about five, maybe six years old at the time. Surprisingly, I was a little on the thick side for my age. I had snuck into my mother's bed and slept between them after watching a scary movie that night. Ronnie felt me climbing into the bed and turned over. He put his finger to his lips, telling me to be quiet, and not to make a sound. He pulled the covers back, allowing me to get under the covers with them. He pulled me close

Nymphopervtress 2: Degenerate

to him and told me to lie next to 'Daddy.' Before I could doze off to sleep, I felt his hand on my small thigh. I pushed it away but he told me this is how he was gonna protect me from the monsters, so I allowed it. He slipped two fingers into my Disney princess undies and rubbed on my private parts. I gasped loudly, loud enough for my mother to hear me, but she didn't. She was too drunk to hear me and be aware of what was going on right next to her in her own bed. I pushed his hand out of my panties and got out from under the covers. He pulled on my Little Mermaid nightgown and made me lay back down. He placed one of his large hands onto my small frame so I wouldn't move. He pulled my little underwear to the side and licked up and down on my private area. My mother told me that nobody is supposed to be touching me down there, but here he was. I was frozen and didn't know what to do. He tried to push a finger inside of me and I yelped in pain. My mother stirred a little, but didn't wake up. I was hoping she would, but she didn't. So, I just laid there. Laid there and just let him fondle me until he decided to stop. Once he did, I climbed out of the bed and went back into the room. I ran out of my room and came into my mother's room looking for safety and to be protected from the monster, but, I found out that the real monster was lying beside my mother and still to this day is. I went into my room and curled up into a ball and cried myself to sleep. Those tears from my memories caused me to cry right now. But I never opened my eyes. I thought about all those nights Zaniyah had stayed at my mother's house and wondered if Ronnie had done that to my baby. Or

Nymphopervtress 2: Degenerate

maybe worse. I didn't wanna think about that. Maybe he has changed over the years. People change all the time, don't they? Zaniyah didn't seem like anything was wrong and I know she would have told me or Shannon or Jessica if something had happened. One thing I can say is that my child always told me everything no matter how big or small it was. I hope that if this situation were to ever arise, I hoped that she would still be the same and tell me if anything happens.

✳✳✳✳

I was watching TV and eating what I think might have been meatloaf. The nurse had given me some more pills for my pain, but instead of me swallowing them I crushed them up with my plastic spork and snorted it up my nose. It didn't give me the same rush as the cocaine, but it was surely close enough. There was a knock at my door and a handsome doctor walked in and greeted himself.

"How are you doing today, Mrs. Davis," he said, flashing me a 100-watt smile.

"I'm doing a little better, I guess. I could be better, ya know?"

"Yeah, I hear you. I just came to check on you and get some blood work done."

"Do we have to?" I asked like a little child that didn't want to get their yearly vaccines.

Nymphopervtress 2: Degenerate

"Yes I have to do it."

"I guess so," I said. He tapped my arm until he found a strong and steady vein. Once he did, he cleaned the spot with one of the packs of alcohol pads. He slowly stuck the needle in my arm and I inhaled deeply. After it got in as far as it was supposed to, he let the blood flow into the tubes until they reached the designated line that it needed to be at. Once all my blood was drained that the doctor needed, he put a bandage on the area to cover it up.

"Do you feel better?"

"Not after you done stuck me with that gigantic horse tranquilizer needle."

He burst into laughter at my corny joke. "That's the first time I've ever heard that reference for a needle. It's pretty cool."

"I have an idea that could make us both feel better," I said as I took his hand into mine and he allowed me to place his hand on my chest.

"Did you want me to check your heart rate while I was here?" he asked stupidly. *Was this guy serious?*

"No, I wanted to feel you hand on my titty," I simply said bluntly.

"Oh, no, sorry. I'm a married man," he said with a smile.

"So? I'm a married woman."

"Maybe I should rephrase that. I am a *happily* married man, *Mrs. Davis*," he said, putting emphasis on his words.

"I won't tell if you won't tell," I said, reaching for his dick that was practically popping out of his slacks. He jumped from my touch and knocked the tray of blood samples down onto the floor. He picked them up quickly and left the room. *Oh well,* I thought. I tried. I went back to eating my dried up mystery meat and continued to watch TV. Now, my show Criminal Minds had come on and I was excited. I turned the volume up as far as it could and tuned out everything behind me. My focus was on Spencer Reid's fine self. I loved that haircut that he wore. As I ate my dinner, I wished that I really had some hot sauce for this bullshit.

There was another knock at my door and I told the visitor to come in. And low and behold, here was my mother and Mario. It was a little unexpected but it wasn't suspicious seeing these two conniving shitholes together.

"Well, well, well, look at what the cat drug in. I thought you fuckers were still locked up," I said when they walked into the room a little more.

"Shut the fuck up, Bitch," Mario said to me.

"I told you to quit disrespecting me, Desiree," my mother said, chiming in.

"Whatever. What do y'all want? I'm in the middle of my dinner."

"I wanted to see my grandbaby and he wanted to see his son."

I burst into laughter. "No, seriously. What the hell are y'all doing here for real?"

"That's why we're here. Plus, I wanna make sure he's actually mine."

"I already told you that he was yours, Mario."

"Yeah, well, you also told me that you loved me, too."

"Nigga, whatever, and why all of a sudden are you interested in seeing my son? I thought you didn't want anything to do with me?" I said, looking in my mother's direction.

"I don't want anything to do with you and I don't give two shits about you. I care about those children. Zaniyah and whatever his name is are my main concern, not you."

"His name is Zakai, for your information, Mother."

"Zakai? Where the fuck did you get that name from? Is that the name of one of those niggas you been fucking?" Mario asked, walking over to me with his hands balled up into fists.

"Chill the fuck out, Nigga. First of all, Zaniyah gave him that name. Second of all, I was too busy fucking Jay to be fucking somebody named Zakai," I replied with a sarcastic smile.

"Oh, you think you cute, huh? You think this shit is funny?" he asked through clenched teeth.

"Maybe."

"Bitch, I will break your motherfucking face."

"Do it, I dare you. I will call the police in here and they will be courting your black ass back to jail, Nigga."

"I wish you two would kill all that fucking noise. Can you two act civilized for one time in your damn lives? Desiree? Please buzz the nurse so they can bring Zakai in, please?"

"Wow, please? Somebody acting like they have some common courtesy." I buzzed the button and the nurse popped her head into the room. I asked her to bring Zakai into the room and she came back in the room ten minutes later, pushing my baby on the cart, in his little clear crib.

"Oh, wow, he's beautiful. He looks just like Mario."

"Let me see that little bastard," Mario said as he held his hands out for Zakai.

"Watch your fucking mouth. Don't you dare talk about my son like that."

"Oh, shut up," he said. My mother passed Zakai over to Mario and he sat down on the bed as he rocked him. "He does look like me."

"I told you he was yours, but your ass don't listen."

"I'm sorry," he replied.

"Come again? Was that an apology from Mario Davis?"

"Don't push it. I'm still taking Zaniyah from you because of your ways."

"And I'm gonna help him," my mother chimed in.

"Whatever. Just give me my baby, and get the hell out of here." Mario handed the baby over to me and he and my mother left the room. Before he shut the door behind him, he snarled at me and I rolled my eyes at him in return. When they left, I buzzed the nurse back in.

"Is there something I can get for you, Mrs. Davis?"

"Yes. Those two people that were just here make sure they can never come back as long as I'm here."

"I will let security know. Is there anything else?"

"Not right now, and thank you."

"No problem," she replied and back out the door she went.

****

My day of discharging had finally come and I couldn't be more excited to leave this damn place. On top of the mystery food they gave me, I damn near froze to death these past few days. What made the situation worse was the fact that I had multiple blankets, and a heated blanket, and my ass was still cold. I hope I wasn't catching a cold or anything. As the nurse came in with the wheelchair for me and Zakai, I was packing up his bag with the Pampers and formula that they told me I could help myself to, while he was in his little photo shoot. It was so exciting and I couldn't wait to see his pictures.

"Are you all set, Mrs. Davis?" the peppy nurse asked.

"Just about. Are they almost done with Zakai?"

"They should be momentarily. Would you like me to go and check for you?"

"No, it's fine, but do you mind helping me, please? My wound is starting to hurt."

"No problem. Just have a seat in the wheelchair for me and I will run and get you some meds right quick."

"Thank you," I replied. She sat me down comfortably in the wheelchair and ran to get me some pain meds. Not even a minute had passed before she was power-walking back into the room carrying a cup of water in one hand and a pill cup in the other. Right behind her was Jessica and Shannon.

"Hey, Sis, you ready to go?" Jessica asked.

"More than ever," I responded.

"Gees, your hair looks a freaking mess," Shannon said, tugging on my weave.

"Bitch, chill out," I said, smacking her hand away.

"Don't worry about her, Desi. You know I'm gonna hook you up tomorrow."

"I know, but why do we have to wait until tomorrow? I need this beady shit done like yesterday."

"Because I know you're tired and probably want some rest."

"Girl, bye. I have been resting since I been here. I just want to go home and drink some wine and hit a jay," I said. *I wanna hit a little cocaine, too, if I can find some that somebody could bring to me,* I thought.

"Actually, I don't recommend you doing that, Mrs. Davis," the peppy nurse chimed in. "The discharge forms distinctively forbid any recreational drugs during your recovery stages. I recommend waiting at least about six weeks, after your check-up, to make sure everything is okay and healing properly. It's all in this paperwork." She handed me a stack of papers and told me to sign her copy.

Nymphopervtress 2: Degenerate

"I will follow these directions to a tee." I'm definitely lying through my teeth. As soon as I got in the car, I was gonna roll a jay with my sisters.

"Great. Well, you all take care, Mrs. Davis, and they will be bringing your son in momentarily."

"Thanks." She left out the room and went back to wherever she goes when she leaves each room.

"Where is Zakai, anyway?" Jessica asked.

"Getting his pictures taken."

"Aww, I can't wait to see them," she responded.

"If you don't shut your goofy ass up, Jess," Shannon said. We all burst out into laughter.

"Hey, y'all, where is Zaniyah?"

"Oh, she's with your mother," Shannon said.

"What?"

"Yeah, your mother said that you said that it was okay for her to stay the night over there tonight."

"I said no such thing. Her ass is lying. Hand me my bag. I need my cell phone." Jessica handed my bag to me. Then, I rolled myself to the bathroom.

"Where are you going?" she asked.

"I have to pee badly."

"Do you need help?"

"Naw, I got it, Sis."

"Okay. We'll just wait here for Zakai to get back then we can leave."

"Cool." I rolled into the bathroom and made sure I shut the door all the way and locked it. I dug around in the bottom of my bag until I felt a small baggie. I quickly pulled it out along with the discharge papers that I had stuffed inside. As fast as I could, I dumped the coke out onto the paper and sniffed it as best as I could. I had to be high and calm before I dialed my mother's number. I pulled out my cell phone and scrolled down to her name and hit the send button.

"Hey, Desiree, honey. How are you feeling?" my mother said cheerfully. What the fuck?

"Okay, who the hell are you and what have you done with my mother?" I said as serious as a heart attack.

"Oh, ho, ho, Desiree, you slay me."

"I slay you? Seriously? Where the fuck is Zaniyah?"

"Oh, she's right here. You wanna talk to her?"

"Duh. Why the hell else would I call? You know I don't wanna talk to you."

"Hold on," she said, literally ignoring what I had just said.

"Hi, Mommy," Zaniyah said happily into the receiver.

"Hi, Stink. Are you okay?"

"Yes. I'm watching SpongeBob on TV."

"That's nice. Are you excited to see your brother tomorrow?"

"Yes, I can't wait. I got him a blanket in my room so he can sleep with me."

"I'm sure he's gonna love it."

Nymphopervtress 2: Degenerate

"Okay, Mommy, SpongeBob back on. I will call you later. I love you."

"I love you, too, Sweetie." I could hear her running away from the phone and my mother got back on the phone.

"Desiree, are you still there?" she said.

"Yes, I'm still here, and I want you to know that you better bring my child home tomorrow. Don't try any funny shit."

"Girl, bye. We will see you tomorrow," she said, hanging up the phone. I fake flushed the toilet and ran the sink water. I waited for a few minutes to pass before I excited the bathroom. I rolled back into the room and Jessica and Shannon were holding my son and making googly eyes at him.

"Ready to go?" Shannon asked as she passed the baby to me.

"Yep. Get me out of this place."

"Will do," Jessica responded. She and Shannon grabbed me and Zakai's bags and we headed out of the hospital.

✳✳✳✳

It was 6 o'clock at night and Shannon, Jessica, and I were getting high as a kite. We had Shannon's living room lit up like Jamaica for the past couple of hours. I didn't give a damn what the doctor's orders were right now, this weed was taking all the pain from me.

"So, have you heard from Mario today?" Shannon asked me.

"Nope and I don't want to."

"Well, if you must know, his ass got locked up again. But, this time, he's gonna be gone for a while most definitely."

"Oh, Lord. What the fuck did he do now?"

"Something about him getting pulled over and he had a pound of weed in the car. The officer tried to arrest him and they saying Mario assaulted the officer."

"Welp, I know his ass mad as fuck," Jessica said, bursting into laughter. I joined her in laughter, but deep down I was sad. I think he was gonna come around eventually, now I will never know. On the bright side, I didn't have to worry about him trying to steal Zaniyah from me, at least not for a while. I pulled out my phone and texted Emmitt to see if I could score some coke for the night. He instantly texted me back and told me he could come to me and be there by 8. I told him that that would be cool but I rather meet him. So, we agreed to meet at the Ihop on Central Avenue.

"What's on your mind?" Shannon asked me.

"Nothing," I said, giggling. "I'm just a little high, that's all."

"I hear that," Jessica said, passing the blunt to me. I took a deep toke of it before exhaling deeply. I took another quick puff and passed it to Shannon.

"So, now what's your plan?" Shannon asked me.

"Well, I guess I'm gonna stay here until I'm healed and then me and the kids will go back to our house. I hope Gia lets me get my job back."

"I'm sure she will," Jessica assured me. "What about your mandatory recovery classes that the judge told you that you had to go to?"

"I'm gonna go. I actually have a class tonight," I lied.

"You sure you wanna go tonight? You're supposed to be resting," Shannon said.

"Yeah, I'll be fine. Do you guys think you can keep an eye on Zakai for me?"

"Sure," they both said in unison. I excused myself and went into my room to get a little cash. Fuck, I said to myself. I didn't have enough to even get a small baggie. I peeped into the living room and Shannon and Jessica was still out there chit chatting. So, I took it upon myself to sneak into Shannon's room and borrow a couple of dollars. I went into her sock drawer and found a stack of twenty-dollar bills. I wasn't sure how many I took, I just grabbed as many as I could without it being too noticeable. I tiptoed back into the room and changed into some sweats and a t-shirt. By the time 7:30 hit, I was on my way to meet Emmitt at the Ihop.

I arrived at the restaurant's parking lot at 8:05. I saw Emmitt hop out of a dark green Denali. He walked over to my car and hopped in the passenger seat.

"Hey, stranger," I said.

"You the stranger, Boo. Where you been?"

"Hospital."

"Everything okay?"

"Yeah, everything is fine. I just had a baby."

"Congratulations. I didn't even know you were pregnant."

"Neither did I," I chuckled.

"It's not mine is it?"

"No," I said, laughing, but he wasn't. *This bamma was dead serious. It hadn't even dawned on me that Emmitt could have been Zakai's father.* It didn't matter now, though, because he's already born now and he looks just like Mario's black ass.

"Cool, cool. You wanna go somewhere and hit this together or you on your solo shit tonight?"

"We can do it together if you want. How much is it gonna be?"

"$40."

"Cool," I said. I handed him the forty dollars and he passed me the baggie. He told me to follow him as he hopped out and went back to his truck. I followed behind him for twenty minutes, reading signs for Landover. Eventually, we pulled up to a small store of some sort. I exited my car the same time he exited his truck.

"What is this place?" I asked.

"It's an office."

"What kind of office?"

"For my construction team."

"Oh, okay," I replied. I didn't want to keep asking questions because he might get annoyed with it eventually. We went into a room that I presumed was the break room. I only figured that because of the tiny microwave and coffee maker.

"So, how long have you been out of the hospital, Desiree?" Emmitt asked as he prepped the cocaine on the metal lunch table.

"I just got out earlier this morning. I was there for about four days. I had to get an emergency C-section."

"Is the baby alright?"

"Yeah, he's fine."

"That's good, that's good," he said. He handed me a rolled up twenty-dollar bill and traded spots with me. I snorted up two of the four lines and he finished it off.

"This shit always makes me feel like I'm walking on the moon," I said to him. Knowing me, I knew I had a goofy ass grin on my face right now.

"It always makes me horny," he said, rubbing on my arm.

"I'm not sure if we could do anything, Emmitt. I just had a baby the other day and my wound hasn't even healed a little yet. And, on top of everything, my pussy is as bloody as the girl was on the movie Carrie."

"And, what's your point? A little blood has never hurt anybody," he said. He untied the string on my sweats and when he did, my phone started to ring. I grabbed it and looked at the caller ID and saw that it was Shannon calling. I ignored it and texted her back, telling her I was in my group therapy session. Emmitt went back to what he was doing and pulled my pants down to my ankles. As he was making his way back up, he was kissing on my calf muscles and my knees and my thighs. He started rubbing my pussy through the bloody pad that was inside my overly large Granny panties. He pulled them down as well, and stuck two fingers inside me. I almost gagged and threw up as I imagined how his fingers looked right now. My phone started ringing again and this time it was Jessica calling. I ignored her call as well and sent her the same text I had sent Shannon only moments ago. I focused my attention back on Emmitt and his nasty ass task at hand. He sat me up on the metal table and dropped his pants to the floor. He didn't even bother putting a condom on before he stuck his dick in my bloody coochie.

"Damn, this shit feels bomb," he said as he gave me stroke after stroke. I so badly wanted to throw up all over him. The smell from my vagina reeked of fish and a dead body. I know he smelled it, but he probably didn't care. Or maybe the coke was so strong it might have dulled his smelling sense. If I had, I wish it had dulled mine. The smell was making me dizzy and making my stomach turn. I looked into his face, and saw that it was distorting, a sign that he was getting ready to cum. For the third time in a row, we were interrupted once again by my cell phone. This time it was Zaniyah's phone number that had popped up on my screen. This one I had to take, especially because Zaniyah never calls me this time of night when she's at my mother's house. She probably just wanted to come home to be with Zakai.

Nymphopervtress 2: Degenerate

"Hello," I said trying not to moan and pant on the phone with my child.

"Mommy?" Zaniyah said crying and sniffling.

"What's the matter, Zaniyah?" I asked holding the phone closer to my ear and blocking out Emmitt's low moans.

"I-I-I need to go to the hospital, Mommy. I'm bleeding from my private parts."

"Oh, Baby, it's okay. It's probably just your period. Remember we talked about you becoming a big girl and- "

"It's not that, Mommy."

"Then what is it?" I asked frantically and fully kicking into Mommy Mode. She became silent on the phone and all I could hear were her low cries and sniffling. "Zaniyah! What's wrong?"

"Grandma."

"Grandma what, Baby? What did Grandma do?"

"Mr. Ronnie pushed Grandma down the steps when she stabbed him."

What the hell? "Why did Grandma try to stab Mr. Ronnie?"

"He put his private part in my private part, and now I'm bleeding and I can't stop it."

"Where is he, Zaniyah?" I asked as my eyes filled with tears.

"He's looking for me. When he was on top of me, Grandma stabbed him and he got off top of me. I ran off while he chased behind her and pushed her down the stairs. He went to the bathroom and put Band-Aids on after that."

Nymphopervtress 2: Degenerate

"Where are you now?" I asked crying.

"I'm hiding in the basement behind the washer and dryer."

"You put your phone on vibrate and don't make a sound, Zaniyah. Mommy is on her way."

"Hurry, Mommy, please. I'm scared." I hung up the phone with her and pushed Emmitt out of me.

"Yo, what the fuck, Desiree? I didn't get all of my cum out yet."

"Fuck you and your cum, Emmitt. My child needs me." I ran to the counter and snatched some paper towels off the roll and folded them nicely into my panties on top of my pad. I fixed my clothes, grabbed my keys, my cocaine, and ran out of the building. I had to get to my mother's house and I mean fast.

Chapter Twenty-One

Family Over Everything

Iwas driving like a bat out of hell as I dipped in and out of traffic heading to my mother's house. I ran through at least three traffic lights and the cameras flashed. Fuck them cameras and those tickets, I thought. My child was more important right now and nothing was gonna stop me from getting to her before Ronnie had a chance to. I came to a screeching halt outside my mother's house and I popped my trunk and got my baseball bat out. *Oh, shit* I thought. The pains were coming back which meant the effects of the weed and the cocaine were quickly starting to wear off. I crept onto the porch and I could hear Ronnie yelling Zaniyah's name throughout the house. I could see vaguely through the sheer curtains that my mother had up on the windows on each side of the front door. I saw my mother lying helplessly at the bottom of the steps. I saw him walking his ugly ass slowly down the steps and decided to go around the back way instead, that way I could possibly sneak in unnoticed. I moved as quickly as my pain would allow me to get to the basement door. I found the spare key that I had made and put under a brick when I used to live here. I always used it when I snuck in and out the house. I was surprised my mother or Ronnie's ass had never found it. I opened the basement door and it was pitch black in the room. I turned my volume off just in case somebody decided to call me at the wrong time. I gently closed the door, succeeding at not being too loud.

"Zaniyah. Zaniyah," I whispered. "It's, Mommy." She turned the light on her screen so I could find her. I went over to her just as the basement light flicked on and the door at the top of the stairs opened. I looked in my baby's brown eyes and saw fear and pain. I hugged her and we shed a couple of tears. I looked at the spot she was crouching down in and saw blood spots. My heart dropped into my stomach as I thought how I failed my child. This was my entire fault. My child's innocence was taken because of me. Instead of me following my first thought, and coming to get her, I chose the latter and decided to go and smoke. Once again, drugs had cost me my child. Only this time, I couldn't fix it. There was no going back from this and my child would be permanently scarred with this memory for the rest of her life. Just like me.

"Zaniyah," I could hear Ronnie saying as he came down the dilapidated staircase. I pushed Zaniyah back a little more, just to be sure that he didn't see her. I peeped through the crack that sat between the washer and dryer. I could see him as clear as day. He was wearing a dingy ass wife beater that looked like it had rust on it; not sure how that's even possible. Then, I saw that he wasn't wearing pants, just a pair of boxers and some Crocs. This motherfucker was real live looking for my baby with his dick on hard. "Zaniyah, are you down here?" He looked on the other side

Nymphopervtress 2: Degenerate

of the basement and as I was trying to shift my body so I wouldn't be in pain, I had bumped the washer. He heard it and swiftly walked back over to where we were. I emerged from behind the washer and he jumped back. He looked as if he was startled for a second and his scared face turned into one of a clown's. "Oh, hey, Desiree? Have you seen, Zaniyah? I really need her to help me," he said, grabbing his dick and smiling broadly.

"What the fuck is wrong with you, Ronnie? Did you really think I was gonna let you hurt my child and scar her like you did me?"

"You? I'm afraid you're mistaken, Desiree. I did nothing to you and you know that."

"Liar. You touched on me and my mother didn't believe me and you were gonna do Zaniyah just like that."

"Actually, I enjoyed Zaniyah very much. Her sweet little body felt so good. I should have seen what that cute little mouth of hers did before I stuck my dick inside her, ya know. If she's anything like you, I know her head is gonna be fire. I heard stories about you from your friend, Jessica's father. He said he loved when you stayed over. If you needed a daddy, you should have just come to me, Desiree. I would have loved to have been there for you like he was."

"Fuck you. I'm gonna kill your black ass," I said, walking toward him.

"Ha, ha, ha, ha," he laughed. "Would you actually believe me if I told you I believed you for a second? After I kill you, I'm gonna find that little hoe in training and train her right. By the time she turns twelve, she will be overly experienced. You watch and see," he said, continuing to smile.

"No, you won't. You will never touch my daughter again," I said I swung the bat with all my might and he backed out of my reach each time. He ended up backing into a work table and I used that to my advantage and managed to hit him in his left shoulder. I hit him hard enough for him to lean over but not hard enough to fall to the ground so I could beat the shit out of him. He snapped back up like the Matrix and came towards me. I swung the bat again but this time he grabbed it and snatched it out of my hand. He threw it across the room and walked towards me again, as his shadow towered over me as I backed away. He backhanded me and I flew onto the floor.

"You wanna be a hero, huh? Well, heroes can die, too," he said. He used his big size thirteen foot to step on my stomach. I screamed out in agonizing pain. I could feel the stitches tear as he put more pressure onto my wound and the cool air hitting it; causing more excruciating pain. I tried to push him off me but I was becoming weaker each second that more blood drained from my body.

"Stop hurting my, Mommy," Zaniyah yelled as she came from behind the washer and dryer, running over to my rescue. As Ronnie continued to apply his foot deeper into my wound, Zaniyah ran up behind him and sunk her teeth into his flesh. I watched as she was biting down to the white meat on his leg.

Nymphopervtress 2: Degenerate

"Aarrghh," he yelled out in pain. He looked down at Zaniyah who had him in a grip as if she were a pit bull or something. He removed his foot from my stomach and tried to shake her off his other leg. I tried to get up from the floor, but it didn't work. My vision was blurry and I could only make out the images in front of me a little bit. I did however see when he grabbed Zaniyah by her ponytails and tossed her across the room, causing her to knock over some boxes that were stacked on top of one another. He threw the boxes out of the way until he found Zaniyah. I looked over and saw my baby holding her arm, it was a good possibility that it had just gotten broken.

"Don't touch me," Zaniyah yelled. She was trying to fight him off with her one good arm and her feet but she was too little to protect herself. I tried not to think of the pain and try to get up again. I made it to where they were by sliding across the floor on my side. He pulled off Zaniyah's pants using only one hand. He held her down by pushing down on her small legs. She was just screaming at the top of her lungs. I picked up a brick that was in a stack right beside them. I positioned myself right behind him, with a tight grip on the brick, and knocked him upside his head with it. He fell over and hit the cement floor and laid there without moving a muscle.

"Zaniyah? Are you okay, Baby?"

"Yes, Mommy. Are you okay?"

"As long as you're okay I will be, too. Come over here, Zaniyah," I said.

"I can't move, Mommy because I'm scared."

"It's okay. He's not even moving, see?" She nodded her head.

"I don't know, Mommy."

"Just hop over here, it will be okay."

"I'll try," she said. She stood to her feet and pulled her pants up. She didn't even jump over him, instead she decided to tiptoe. Surprisingly, she got to me safely. We threw our arms around each other and hugged. That hug was short lived as he popped up like The Undertaker from wrestling and grabbed Zaniyah once again. He pushed her out the way and wrapped his hands around my throat. I kicked and screamed, but they fell on deaf ears. As I was slowly slipping out of consciousness, I could see my mother coming down the steps holding a cast iron skillet ready to knock Ronnie's head off. She was walking slowly behind him and I'm just lying there watching my life flash before my eyes, wishing she would hurry up. Just as I almost threw out the thought of her helping, that skillet came crashing down onto his skull. He fell onto the floor and laid there motionless.

"Are you okay, Desiree?" my mother asked, helping me up off the floor. I took her hand and stood to my feet.

"I'm okay. Zaniyah are you okay?"

"Yes, but my body just hurts."

"You'll be okay, Sweetheart," my mother assured her.

"You saved me, Ma. Why?"

Nymphopervtress 2: Degenerate

"You may be all those things I said, but you're still my child."

"I guess," I said, rolling my eyes at her. I thanked my mother for helping and protecting Zaniyah as I helped her off the floor when I heard the sirens blaring coming down the street.

"I love you, Desiree," she said, looking at me with pleading eyes.

"No, you don't. You're just saying that because you think I'm gonna keep Zaniyah away from you after this incident. Right?"

"Yeah, you're right."

"And you thought correct. I wish the fuck I would allow you to see my child after this bullshit."

"But, I protected her. I didn't know he was looking at her in that way, Desiree. I swear to-"

"No, that's bullshit and you know it! Don't you dare say that you swear to God that you didn't know that he was having impure thoughts about my daughter. I told you about what he had done to me when I was around her age and you didn't believe me. You didn't even sugarcoat shit and you called me a liar straight to my face. Do you realize how the fuck that made me feel?"

"No, I don't, and I am so sorry."

"You're right about that."

"Right about what, Desiree?"

"Being sorry. You are a sorry excuse for a mother and I wish you were never my mother to begin with. Come on, Zaniyah,"

I said. I was leading her away from my mother but my mother grabbed my wrist and stopped me.

"I just saved your life, goddamnit! Shouldn't that count for something?" she said through tears.

"Thanks for saving my life, but no it doesn't count for anything. If you would have gotten rid of that bastard back then, I would be gracious because you would have saved me when I needed you the most. I don't need you now and neither does Zaniyah or Zakai. So, stay away from them."

Zaniyah and I headed up the steps and out the door to the ambulance and the police. We gave the police officer partial statements and they said that they would get the rest of it once we got checked out at the hospital. I informed the paramedics that my mother would probably need to go to the hospital as well, but I asked that she get her own and be taken to another hospital. I was dead ass about not seeing her again or having her around my children. In my mind, now I understand why I am the way I am. It's all her fault. It's all Ronnie's fault. If he had never told me that sex was a way to get comfort and not be scared of anything, I would have never been going through what I have been going through. Because of him, I was having all of these partners, picturing them as the father or father figure that I was missing in my life. Now he was gone and I hoped like hell that I could finally get through this, and Zaniyah, my sweet little girl. She had her most prized possession taken away from her and she did not deserve that. Now I had to figure out how to deal with that situation. All I could do was pray that she didn't turn out like I did. Especially all that damn medication that Dr. Nicholson prescribed to me. I needed to take meds that were supposed to calm down my want for sex, and the nightmares, and my depression and anxiety. I didn't want my daughter to go through with that, especially not at this tender age. However, therapy was definitely necessary. If my mother had paid attention to me and how my behavior changed over the years, she could have gotten me some help and maybe I would have turned out different. Right now, I didn't have time to think about all of the what ifs and whatnots. I had to get my daughter and me seen at the hospital. We laid down on the two stretchers and held hands the entire way to the hospital.

✳✳✳✳

Once we got to Prince George's Hospital, and I told them what was going on and the events that had taken place, they separated us. They took me to surgery and took Zaniyah straight to the Rape Crisis and recovery Center. I told them that I wanted to be with her and that she needed her mother by her side, but they didn't want to hear that shit. They said she would be fine until I finished up in surgery. They said that it was critical that I get sewn back up as quickly as possible in order to avoid possible infections. I texted my friends and told them to get to the hospital as soon as they could so I could tell them what had happened. They took me to the surgery room and immediately gave me a mask with anesthesia so I could get numb faster. My mind wasn't even on the fact that my organs or whatever could get infected. All I cared about was getting to my daughter and giving her a shoulder to lean on in her time of need. I was out within a matter of minutes.

"Hi? How are you? My name is Ms. Jeanette. What's your name?" the lady asked Zaniyah.

"My name is Zaniyah Alesia Davis."

"Oh, wow, I like that name."

"Thank you."

"Can you tell me how old you are?"

"Eight."

"Wow, you're a big eight. You're the tallest one in your class I bet," she said, smiling.

"Maybe, I don't know. I try not to look at the other kids that I don't really know."

"I understand. Do you think you can tell me what happened tonight?"

Zaniyah nodded her head. "Well, I was watching TV in my room at my Grandma's house while she was downstairs having some drinks. Her boyfriend, Mr. Ronnie, came into my room and touched me."

"Touched you where?"

"All the places Mommy said that nobody should be touching me at."

"Do you mind showing me, Zaniyah?" she asked, passing her a Baby Alive doll that wasn't wearing anything but undergarments. She pointed to her chest, her vagina and her lips.

"He told me not to tell anybody and that it was gonna be our little secret. He said that if I told anybody they wouldn't believe me and that they were gonna call me a liar. I didn't want to be called a liar. He laid down on top of me and kissed me and told me I was a big girl."

"What happened next, Zaniyah?" Ms. Jeanette asked as she wrote down in her notes.

"He, um, pulled my clothes down and told me that this is what big girls do. He touched on my private part with his hand and then he used his mouth. I seen him pull out his private part and he told me don't move or scream or he was going to kill me. I was crying when he put his thingy in me. My Grandma saw him on me and she grabbed a knife and stabbed him to save me. When he got up, he was angry and he pushed my Grandma down the stairs."

"Where is your Grandma now?" Zaniyah shrugged her shoulders.

Knock. Knock.

Both Zaniyah and Ms. Jeanette looked over to the door where the other volunteer of the Rape Crisis and Recovery Center was standing.

"Ms. Jeanette?"

"Yes, Ms. Rita?"

Nymphopervtress 2: Degenerate

"I got in contact with a representative from Child Protective Services and she already seems to know the child, so she said she will be coming here shortly. Other than that, the rape kit is in the room and waiting for you to begin."

"We will be right in. Zaniyah, I need you to be a big girl for me, okay?"

Zaniyah looked at her wearily and skeptical with her big brown eyes.

"Oh, no, no, no, no, Honey, not that kind of big girl. I need you to help me make sure that that big old mean man doesn't hurt you or anybody else again, okay?" Zaniyah nodded her head again and followed the lady into the room where she had to get her entire body examined.

✳✳✳✳

Downstairs in room 4406-B, Desiree was just coming down off the anesthesia that was given to her before her surgery had begun. She was surrounded by her best friends and her newborn son.

"How do you feel, Sis?" Shannon asked me.

"I feel like my insides just got ripped out by a goddamn alligator or something."

"It looks like it, too," Jessica said, peeping at my scar under my hospital gown.

"I wish you two would stop hogging my son," I said to Jessica and Shannon.

"Don't be stingy," Shannon said.

"Whatever," I said, taking Zakai from her. He had his eyes open all the way today and it warmed my heart to be able to look into them.

"Hey, where's your mother?" Jessica asked.

"Don't know nor do I care. I told her to stay away from me and my children and that we didn't need her."

"That's a shame," Jessica said, shaking her head.

"What is?" I snapped.

"Everything you had told us about your mother and her boyfriend, and now Zaniyah. All this shit is crazy and a bunch of madness."

"You got that right," I agreed. There was a knock at my hospital door.

"Are you expecting somebody?" Jessica asked.

"Like who, Jess?" I asked sarcastically and she shrugged her shoulders. "Come in," I yelled through the door and in walks Alicia Montgomery, the representative from Child and Family Services that was assigned to Zaniyah's case. Behind her there were two police officers wearing blank and grim faces. I looked at her and she darted her eyes to the floor.

"Good evening, Mrs. Davis," she said sadly.

"Hi, Ms. Montgomery, what's going on? I asked as I rocked Zakai back to sleep.

"I have some bad news, Mrs. Davis. I would like to speak to you in private."

"Naw, fuck all that. Whatever you have to say to her you can say while we in the room," Shannon said, jumping to her feet. Jessica and I both quickly grabbed both of Shannon's wrists so she wouldn't go after the lady. The officers saw her behavior and placed their hands on their guns.

"There is no need for all of that," I said to the officers and they put their hands back down to their sides. "Look, Ms. Montgomery, what she meant was there is no need to have a private conversation. We're all family here."

She looked back and forth between us and the officers before continuing. "It's a couple of things actually. First off, you failed your drug test and tested positive for cocaine, again."

"Seriously, Desiree?" Shannon said, getting up off the bed again and staring at me.

"It was just one time and it was only a little bit."

"That doesn't matter, Desiree," Jessica chimed in. "You're not supposed to be doing it, period."

"I know. I couldn't help it. I'm just going through so much and I needed help to get through all this stress and shit."

"That's what we're for, Desi," Shannon yelled at me. I buried my head in my hands and cried and before you knew it, my girls had stopped cursing me out and bashing me. Now they were consoling me and telling me that everything was gonna be fine.

"Back to what I was saying," Ms. Montgomery butted in, "there is something else that I left out."

"What else could you possibly have to say?" Shannon asked.

"Because of your recent drug tests and the fact that they were both dirty, we have to take Zaniyah with us."

"No, no, no, no, no, please don't. You can't take her from me."

"And we're taking Zakai as well."

"No! I will not give him to you," I said as I held him tighter in my arms and buried myself into the bed.

"Officers," she said. The officers rushed over and pushed Shannon and Jessica out of the way because they were trying to block them from getting the baby from me. One of officers squeezed my arm tightly, turning my brown skin red, but I didn't let go. But, somehow, someway, the other officer managed to snatch Zakai out of my arms while the other restrained me. I grabbed onto the officer when he tried to move, pulling me off the bed into the floor.

I crawled across the floor towards Ms. Montgomery as she held me baby boy in her arms. I grabbed her by her ankles and pleaded with her to give me my babies back and give me another chance. She just kept telling me she couldn't. While I was down on the floor groveling, I saw Zaniyah appear standing with another officer, with tears streaming down her face. I stood to my feet and ran to my baby girl. We hugged and held onto one another until the cops separated us. I held her hand, but when that one strong pull came, her small hand slipped out of mine. I screamed at the top of my lungs as I watched as the officers and the social worker walk down the hall carrying Zakai and literally dragging Zaniyah away. My friends came out into the hall with their own tears flowing down their faces, trying to pull me up from the floor. As I sat on the cold, tiled hospital floor, I realized everything that I had lost in just a short amount of time. I done lost my husband, my home, my mother, and now my children. It was time to give up and throw in the towel. "Somebody just kill me!" I screamed at the top of my lungs. "I just wanna die."

Epilogue

So many years have come and gone since the last time I had physically seen my children. If my memory serves me right, my little, Zaniyah, should be turning about twelve or thirteen and Zakai should be about four or five. I was glad that the people found them a foster family that would keep them together and let them stay in contact with me. They call me sometimes and send me school pictures, but it's not the same. Zaniyah be excited to talk to me most of the time, and the other times she is just here and there. And Zakai, he barely even knows me so we don't be having much to talk about and when we do talk, he's always getting off the phone too quickly for me.

Shannon and Jessica are still hanging around as much as they can. Jessica has gone off and gotten married to a terrific guy that adores her and her son, Raheem. It's like a breath of fresh air for her to finally have met someone that worships the ground she walks on. I'm happy for her. Shannon is mostly still the same. She was still dealing with her crazy and insecure girlfriend. All they still ever do is fuss and fight, but Shannon said that's how they express how much they love one another. I guess so.

My mother and Mario don't even speak to me anymore. Mario's ass is still locked up for another year or two for assaulting that officer. Stupidest thing he could have ever done in his life. My mother had completely washed her hands of me and my poisonous antics, as she calls them. When she found out that I had lost the kids to the system, she turned her back on me and treated me like trash on the street.

As for me, well, I was never the same after my kids had gotten snatched from me. I couldn't even live a normal life, or a semi-normal life for that matter. I had checked myself into a psychiatric hospital where I could be with my own kind and not be judged by the outside world. I didn't know how to handle life anymore without my medications or anything. I even had me a little boo up here that snuck in and gave me quickies during the late-night shift. The best upside of being in this place was that I was able to kick my cocaine addiction 100%.

Knock. Knock.

I heard somebody at the door and told them to come in. I thought it was my prescription lady, but it was the doctor from the infirmary downstairs. I had just seen her scrawny ass last week so I don't know what she was doing here. I was praying she wasn't telling me I had to get more blood work done. That crap hurts!

"Hi, Desiree, I just came to tell you that your blood work results came back."

"And? So? What are you gonna tell me I'm pregnant?" I said, laughing.

"No, it's not that. I'm sorry," she said, handing me a piece of paper.

"Sorry for what?" I asked, snatching the paper out of her hand.

"Sorry to tell you that you have HIV."

The smile quickly faded away from my face as I pondered on what she had just told me. A lump jumped into my throat, causing me to become speechless. A single tear fell from my eye, then more followed behind.

"I'm so, so, sorry," she said, reaching out and hugging me sincerely.

About The Author

American author Rachelle Jarred is entranced by the magic of written words. She's had an unflinching love for writing since she was seven, and now lives her dream of being a published author and a poet. Writing is more than just her career; it's her way of life. Rachelle prides herself on exploring multiple fiction genres. With sizzling hot erotica, blood-cuddling horror, and scintillating suspense, she has enticing packages for every book lover. She is looking forward to diving into children's stories in the near future.

She was born and raised in Washington, D.C., and currently works full-time as the CEO of BluGem Publishing where her books are published. Between her writing career and her life as a mother of two, Rachelle enjoys spending time with her loved ones and always makes time to help new authors find their way in the writing industry. She currently resides in Prince George's County, Maryland.